M. J. FARRELL

is the pseudonym for Molly Keane. She was born in Co. Kildare, Ireland, in 1904 into 'a rather serious Hunting and Fishing and Church-going family' who gave her little education at the hands of governesses. Her father originally came from a Somerset family and her mother, a poetess, was the author of 'The Songs of the Glens of Antrim'. Molly Keane's interests when young were 'hunting and horses and having a good time': she began writing only as a means of supplementing her dress allowance, and chose the pseudonym M. J. Farrell 'to hide my literary side from my sporting friends'. She wrote her first novel, *The Knight of the Cheerful Countenance*, at the age of seventeen.

Molly Keane published ten novels between 1928 and 1952: *Young Entry* (1928), *Taking Chances* (1929), *Mad Puppetstown* (1931), *Conversation Piece* (1932), *Devoted Ladies* (1934), *Full House* (1935), *The Rising Tide* (1937), *Two Days in Aragon* (1941), *Loving Without Tears* (1951) and *Treasure Hunt* (1952). She was also a successful playwright, of whom James Agate said 'I would back this impish writer to hold her own against Noel Coward himself.' Her plays, with John Perry, always directed by John Gielgud, include *Spring Meeting* (1938), *Ducks and Drakes* (1942), *Treasure Hunt* (1949) and *Dazzling Prospect* (1961).

The tragic death of her husband at the age of thirty-six stopped her writing for many years. It was not until 1981 that another novel—*Good Behaviour*—was published, this time under her real name. Molly Keane has two daughters and lives in Co. Waterford. Her latest novel, *Time After Time*, was published in 1983 and her cookery book, *Nursery Cooking*, was published in 1985.

Virago publishes *Devoted Ladies*, *The Rising Tide*, *Two Days in Aragon*, *Mad Puppetstown* and *Full House*. *Taking Chances* and *Young Entry* are forthcoming.

M. J. FARRELL

FULL HOUSE

With a New Afterword by
CAROLINE BLACKWOOD

PENGUIN BOOKS – VIRAGO PRESS

PENGUIN BOOKS
Viking Penguin Inc., 40 West 23rd Street,
New York, New York 10010, U.S.A.
Penguin Books Ltd, Harmondsworth,
Middlesex, England
Penguin Books Australia Ltd, Ringwood,
Victoria, Australia
Penguin Books Canada Limited, 2801 John Street,
Markham, Ontario, Canada L3R 1B4
Penguin Books (N.Z.) Ltd, 182–190 Wairau Road,
Auckland 10, New Zealand

First published in Great Britain by Collins 1935
First published in the United States of America by
Little, Brown and Company 1935
This edition first published in Great Britain by Virago Press Ltd. 1986
Published in Penguin Books 1987

Printed in Great Britain
by Cox and Wyman, Reading, Berkshire.
set in Baskerville

I

" Oh, thank you so much, Miss Parker. Those are lovely. Or do you think you might pick them just a shade longer. Oh, I see you've picked the rose-coloureds. It was the flame I wanted. The flame at the back of the border, and then the smoke. Not the rose. Or the yellow."

Miss Parker, the little bearded governess, gazed sadly at her basket of tulips. All her life long she could trust herself to do the wrong thing. Now she had done it again. Just one little once again mounting up the mistakes and misfortunes of a stupid little thing. But she means well.

" Oh, Lady Bird, I am ever so sorry," she now breathed distressfully. " Whatever can I do about it now ? "

It was sufficiently tiresome of Miss Parker to have gathered dozens and dozens of the wrong tulips, thus entirely defeating Lady Bird's colour scheme for the drawing-room, without adding to her short-comings that appalling " ever so " . . . . " whatever can I do ? " . . . . The question ran once more through Lady Bird's mind. Was she or was she not justified in keeping Miss Parker on as a governess for Mark ? A Swiss girl would probably be cheaper, and certainly sew better, although she might not

work so diligently in the garden nor be so attentive
to the dogs when they were sick. There again she
had nearly killed Susan by administering a most
excessive purge, and had dragged up unknown
quantities of treasures in the rock garden. But Mark
liked her. He would gaze on her tenderly and sometimes pat her face. However, Miss Parker dis-
couraged this sort of play in public because it must
draw attention to her beard, a subject on which she
was agonisingly sensitive.

The sun shone alike upon Lady Bird and Miss
Parker within the shelter of the kitchen garden.
The late fruit blossom was trained, rosy and trim,
against the walls, the early cabbages throve, the
peas and the beans throve, also the spring onions,
the lettuces and every other class and kind of
vegetable that was grown there. The subdued
regularity of their squares and lines and patches
was solid and pleasing and as it should be. The
flowers were good too. A calendar for 1934 depicting,
in gross and in detail, a long pair of borders with
a sundial and three fantail pigeons in the middle
distance could scarcely have bettered the rich and
orderly profusion of Lady Bird's early summer
display of flowers. Except that the calendar
would somehow have contrived to reproduce a
hedge of yew, preferably cut into zoological
shapes.

" Well," said Lady Bird, squeezing her rolex
garden scissors sharply together, to cut out a dead
piece of rose wood ; " it can't be helped now, can

it ? But do be careful another time. When I ask you for Flame don't pick Rose. Can't you see how different they are ? Where is Markie ? "

" Sheena found a wren's nest for him with eggs in it, and he's gone to look at it. Wasn't it funny, Lady Bird ? I was reading to him only yesterday in *Birdies for our Tinies* about the wee wrens, and he was so excited."

" I wish you would teach him the difference between a Black-backed gull and a Herring gull. Now, Miss Parker, you might take those tulips into the house. The yellow ones will do for Sheena's room and the red ones can go in the blue vase in the library. I hadn't meant to do flowers in either of those rooms till to-morrow but there it is. Then perhaps you'd take Chunky and Cheerio for a little bit of a walk, and tell Mrs. Brand the end of the chocolate cake is to go up for the school-room tea, and if Mrs. Blundell has arrived, tell her I'm out here and give her a pair of scissors so that she can do some work. Would you ? Thank you so much."

Oh, lucky, lucky Lady Bird, thought Miss Parker as she stepped out briskly with her bunches of tulips —such smooth, bright flowers. Lucky Lady Bird, still so beautiful, so unbelievably young for all those forty-eight years, set down in many books for all to see ; so blessed with riches and with lovely children. Sheena and Mark, and that other who was coming back to-day. But Miss Parker had never seen that other. She had only heard very strange things about him. Whisperings from the servants and more than whisperings. All very peculiar and strange and sad. These nervous breakdowns Miss Parker knew about. They had called it a nervous breakdown when poor Aunt Alice turned on the gas. But one knew what Aunt Alice was. She was as mad as a hatter, and that was all about it. But this must be different. This youth they all spoke of with a sort of hushed worship, withholding any word of pity, was a beloved creature beside itself, who would return both to itself and to them. Who was returning. Who came back to-day.

As she hurried down from the kitchen garden Miss Parker was aware of a sense of waiting, of constant expectancy, that had been on the house and place and every person in it since morning. But especially, most especially, on the place.

The pathway down from the kitchen garden to the house was steep in places, for the garden was on the side of a hill and the wild hills came down nearly to the sea on this side of Westcommon. Between the hills and the sea this house called Silverue had been built. Groves of birch trees came chasing down the feet of the hills nearest the sea. Chasing because birches are forever in flight, maidenly and unsteady as maidens are. Springs burst up among them, wetting the rocks and soaking the dark mosses. These groves were quiet and drenching and full of the sea mists. A perfect buttress of a fuchsia hedge, almost, in parts quite, a tunnel divided them from the climbing path. Polite and formal distances of lawn held them farther apart from the house.

Miss Parker stepped out from the last heavy tunnel of the dark fuchsias, across a turn of the avenue and over the lawn towards the house. The lawn was soaking in the sunlight. It had received so much that now it seemed to be giving out a warmth and light from itself. There was an ample, generous air upon the bland turf, an hallucination of reposeful bosoms about its totally flat expanses. Miss Parker walked across it satisfied.

And now the house. It was dark and flat and just too high in the middle like some early Georgian houses are, but its wings were of such extreme grace and proportion that this steepness was a welcome and faintly acid contrast to their inevitable correctness. A correctness where line answered line and each curved statue niche owned its precise fellow. The face of the house was partly covered in ivy and partly in a fern-like growth of Good Neighbour. They were indeed mistaken who covered stone houses with creepers, but, although we may defend ourselves from committing their errors, in fact, we do not find these errors half so disagreeable as we may pretend. The back of the house was almost precisely like the front, with the occasional delusion of a blind window. Beyond was a long slip of lawn with much bedding-out, protected from the sea winds by further buttresses of fuchsia and escalonia, and between the cliffs and the sea a space of close thyme and pale flowers and paler stones. Then the low horizon.

A car came round the turn of the lawn before Miss Parker had quite crossed it and a tall, sun-burnt woman, very thin and very light on her feet, got out and came towards Miss Parker. This would be Mrs. Blundel. There was a G.B. on the back of the car too. None other could it be.

A large gay mouth painted as bright as a door, the sweetest way of bending her head when she spoke, as though it mattered whether she really saw Miss Parker or not. A little face nearly the shape of a beech leaf, lined and rather dry, brown and curling. Hydrangea eyes and dark hair. She was not old. She was not oppressively and astonish-ingly young, like Lady Bird. She was her own age which was between thirty and forty. And she was her own age which was anything you please for wit and tolerance and kindness and large experience. She had large plain hands and feet which she used with grace and circumspection. She seemed as tall as a tree and as lovely as a tree.

Miss Parker told her reverently where Lady Bird was to be found.

" I think," said Eliza (for that was her name—she had been christened Elsie, which indeed she could not bear), " that I will go into the house and have a drink first. I suppose I've driven a thousand miles since luncheon, and I see," she said, with a look at Miss Parker's gay bunches of tulips, " that Lady Bird is doing the flowers. On the whole I think it would be wise to have a drink before I go up to the garden."

Miss Parker followed her to the house murmuring confused assents. Up 'the steps—those stone steps as curved and as thin as if they had been sliced off a lemon—and in through the flat dark doorway to the house they went together.

II

" Oн, Eliza, my dear, how are you ? You look marvellous and what an amusing hat. Do you still go to that little woman of Betty's ? I think she's a robber and rather bad, but she makes lovely things for you, of course. But, my dear, you *are* painfully thin, aren't you ? "

Lady Bird was genuinely enchanted to see her guest and the more so because she considered her hat to be the last word in unsuccess, also she thought Eliza was looking both old and tired and rather ill— in fact, everything a guest ten years younger than oneself should look. And Eliza, who delighted for a limited time in Lady Bird's every mood and every absurdity, was pleased to see her hostess being every bit herself. At any rate, her greeting showed that she had not changed much. And if the tragedy of John could not quieten her, nothing but the grave ever would.

Eliza did not answer any of the remarks about her hat or her health. She kissed Lady Bird twice, lightly yet firmly. One kiss on each unbelievably smooth cheek, murmuring : " How lovely, how *lovely* the garden is looking." She then embarked her hostess on one of those ambling tours of inspection full of long pausings, bitter complaints and

12

still longer pausings for complacent boastfulness—
garden tours which are as the breath of life to
gardeners of Lady Bird's kind.

As they walked and paused and admired and
deplored, Eliza in her mind, took a journey backwards from this Lady Bird who walked beside her
to the Olivia she had known before the Great War,
which Olivia had enjoyed so much. When the war
began Olivia was pretty well at the zenith of her
beauty and stupidity, and terrifying intensity of
feeling. She was but lately married to Sir Julian
Bird. Yet not so lately as to have retained much
interest in him, or at any rate, not enough to curb
her in much promiscuous generosity throughout the
war years. She was one of those big-hearted, unrestrained women who always talked a great deal
about " giving everything." A splendid phrase,
presupposing a peculiar form of selfless chastity in
the most passionate of her entanglements. Apparently she took nothing but just gave and gave
in that public-spirited way that women had in the
Great War. Such hats as they wore and such love
as they gave. But Eliza was always a little sour
about the war and the women who enjoyed it,
because she still thought that it had devastated her
own life. In spite of all her experiences she held a
certain thread of faith about that. But that was
all such a very long time ago and so absolutely and
infinitely past—as past as Olivia's opportunities for
generosity. The values of one's life changed so
absurdly. Here was Olivia standing before a dreary

unthriving plant and complaining, as she had often done when her lovers were tiresome or faithless. . . . "And I gave it everything, *everything*, my dear. . . ." Poor Olivia, still so beautiful, so enchanting to look at. Her lovely clothes, her romantic body. Only her throat looked a little tired and perhaps her full Fra Angelico eyes ; yes, and perhaps those steel cut lines so faint and so sure between her thin short nose, and her pretty mouth.

How had Julian endured and understood and waited, and got her here at last to Ireland where he loved to be ? Where he could play at his Heraldry and breed his herd of Kerry and Dexter cattle, and fish for salmon and sea-trout, and shoot snipe and woodcock in the winter months. How had he found his courage and his patience ? Once he had said to Eliza, quoting in a defiantly pedantic way : " Not my five wits nor my five senses can dissuade one foolish heart. . . ." But that was as far as he had ever gone in confiding to Eliza to whom everybody told everything that they should have kept to themselves. And no doubt he was properly ashamed of himself. Then he had the children, John and Sheena and Mark. But could he ever get very near them ? They were too like himself. He was too intelligent to torment himself about them, but his love must make it very difficult at times. And John was coming home this evening—what a night to arrive at Silverue. " You do like a good drama, dear, you know you do," Eliza reminded herself with a certain indulgence of personal weakness. One could not know oneself too well.

She sat with Olivia on a stone bench at the end of Oliva's best border—the spot where she finally brought her guests to an admiring anchor. Indeed it was good. So much colour, and the shadows growing obviously longer, faintly more dewy, and at the end of the path there was an iron gate in the wall through which you saw birches and the untamed evening, withheld and inattentive.

"Darling," Eliza said, suddenly quiet and insistent; "tell me about John. How is he, really?"

"Oh, he's marvellously well now," Olivia said. "This voyage, you know, has done him all the good in the world. The doctor said it would. Do you know Dr. Leeson, Eliza? So attractive and so understanding. He was the only person who realised how hard it all was on *me* and he's been marvellous to me over everything. He knew I was the only person who could do anything with John, but he was so sweet explaining how it was better for *me* that I shouldn't be with him. Of course John and I have been everything to each other always. He always looks on me as his own contemporary, always—I can't think why. He tells me everything. He's rather a wonderful person, don't you think so, Eliza? I've always had the most extraordinary influence over him, why I can't think."

"I love John," Eliza said. What could one ever gather from Olivia? Why did one try? What was her justification for being, and how had she produced her divine, her enthralling children ? Of course they were dear Julian's children.

Through the iron gate Mark came running towards them down the path, hurrying, flying. Such speed and energy he showed that he ran himself out of his coat, a blue woollen coat that lay in a little coloured pool on the path behind him as he came flying towards them. All he said when he arrived was : " Wren's nest," rather surlily. But when he saw Eliza he flung himself on her, crying : " Wren's nest ! Wren's nest ! Come and see it. I'll kill you unless you come. Ah, come. Ah, come, darling. *Darling*, come. Kind Eliza, come."

" I will come," said Eliza ; " presently we will go together."

" When's presently ? "

" In the cool of the evening we will walk there together."

" We will walk there together."

" Markie, it's past your tea-time, darling. And why are you wearing such a hot shirt ? Ask Miss Parker to give you a thin one for after tea."

" Yes, my God, I'm in a hell of a sweat," said Mark, showing off sadly. When Olivia reproved him he pressed her hand to his head and his bosom to show he spoke truly. His gestures were curiously gentle, but he was only holding himself stilled for a moment—a moment for his own purpose. Eliza thought Mark was the most beautiful creature she knew. She knew no child that had his rare savage and tender quality. He was entirely conscious without being affected. To a large extent he was aware of his own power and used it cruelly or gently. He was the most moving creature ; such depths of despair were in him and such an unending ability for happiness. Such cruelty and such tenderness. Eliza had painted Mark and talked of him but it was no use, she could never pretend to get anywhere near him, really. That lovely gaze his changing eyes would show : that broad romantic brow : that grave mouth and exotic complexion : one told them over but they brought him no nearer. Absent one could not see him. He was not, because there was so much in him which was beyond grasping. And what cannot be taken in words or in any other way may be always there. Nothing in the world would have prevented Eliza from going to see the wren's nest to-night. Perhaps she was a little in love with so much beauty. She worshipped for a while with a pagan pleasure. She would be at war with time on his account that he might stay for ever seven years old. But then she had thought the same when he was six and five and four. And, anyhow, sentimentality over the ages of children was unforgivably nauseating.

" It's tea-time for everybody," Olivia said, rising a little regretfully from her seat. " Come on, Markie. Don't make Mummy speak to you again. Nip to it quickly. Be a first-time childy."

Markie looked at her, mournfully unconscious of what she might or might not mean. His eyes were now afar upon the asparagus beds. " Look at the

Nettle-dog. Look what he's done," he cried. "Ha, ha, ha!" The joke was very good.

"I've told you fifty times not to let the dogs into the kitchen garden." Olivia was really angry. "There's nothing to laugh at. You know what they do to the vegetables and it's very unhealthy. How would you like to have worms like Tiny?"

"Oh, I'm sorry, I'm sorry, Mummy." Markie's face grew smaller and whiter as if a wind blew through him. He could not bear being scolded. He would avoid it by any means, and he might have weathered this storm had it not been for the Nettle-dog who, as they arrived at the asparagus beds to eject him from the garden, committed his offence once more.

Olivia was furious. Dogs and disobedient children and asparagus and worms boiled within her, and from their stewings was distilled the edict that Markie was to go to bed at six instead of seven.

"I cannot, I cannot. John is coming back. How could I be in bed?"

"You should have thought of that before. How often have I told you what the Nettle-dog does to the asparagus and the lettuce and the cabbages. I've forbidden him to come into the garden."

Then there were tears, terrible vast tears that rolled and fell, and protestations of sorrow. "I'm sorry, I'm sorry. I've said I'm sorry."

Eliza felt shattered. She saw Olivia lose her temper and recover it, and become obstinate and a shade vindictive. It terrified her. And that she should

have such absolute power, that she should not be
ashamed to use it. So merciless a creature and one
so young that it should not realise fear. Not fear.

" I didn't do it. I didn't," he cried now
despairingly.

" Markie—look at Mummy. Are you telling
Mummy a lie ? How did he get in ? "

" He just got in himself, I promise you."

How touchingly palpable are the lies of childhood.

" Oh, Olivia, darling, but it was me. I'm so
sorry, I let him in, that dirty old Nettle-dog. It
wasn't Markie. He's speaking the truth for once
in his life."

It was Sheena, coming from nowhere in particular
towards them. Sheena stooping to pick up the
Nettle-dog, which nobody else had thought of doing,
and throwing away a whole cigarette to kiss Eliza
almost with passion, at least with a passion of
delight. Then she stood apart from them coldly, a
little afraid of her enthusiasm.

" He didn't really," she said. " Stop wailing,
Markie. Mummy knows you didn't now."

" Oh, I'm so upset," said Mark then. There was
an extraordinary tearful dignity about this assertion.
" To think she wouldn't believe me."

" Don't cry, darling, she does now."

" I will cry."

" If you cry any more I'll beat you. Yes, next
time I get you away from your kind mother."

" You know nobody but myself is allowed to beat
Markie," Olivia said firmly. " Run in to tea now,

pet one. Mummy has forgiven you. . . . One simply must be firm with them," she said as Mark ran on before them down the windings and tunnels of the fuchsia path. "Otherwise where is one? Can anybody tell me that?"

Nobody could.

Sheena walked back to the house with them. She was as blonde as a eucalyptus with elegant smoothed limbs such as they have and eyes the colour of those leaves, and gentle and Christ-like. The eyes all three children had got from their wanton mother. She painted her face absurdly and chiefly for her own entertainment, an entertainment she varied as the moods took her, and she wore quite literally ragged clothes, but took great trouble over her hair. She was nineteen and perhaps full of affectations. Olivia was very fond of her and touchingly proud of her surprising charm and success.

III

SHEENA took Eliza up to her room after tea. At Silverue there were two round halls opening one out of the other and a double, twining staircase of lovely swinging curves—two airy curves perfectly resolved in wood. A romantic staircase, perpetually pleasing. Half-way up there was a long mirror on the wall in which one could admire oneself, stepping up or stepping down, in the flattering setting of this beautiful staircase.

Eliza admired herself very much indeed, for she took great pleasure in her own rather austere proportions. But Sheena, though she was as vain as a peacock, paid no more attention to her reflection than a swan might with other matters to occupy its silly mind.

When they reached Eliza's room she went cruising round it, and in and out of the bathroom in a very preoccupied way. This was the room Eliza liked best at Silverue. Its windows looked out on the seaside of the house and it was filled with an even, salty light from the sea. It had pale grey walls with greenish prints hung on them. The chintz had a design of ships with more rigging than ship. There were several very beautiful pieces of furniture and the bed, she knew, was superb. For houses, their decoration and comfortable arrangement, Olivia had a really great genius.

Eliza went to the window and picked up a hot sea shell which somebody had left there on the sill. She sat there feeling it in her hands and considering Sheena and thinking how boring it is for the young never to be able to say what they mean, or if they do to hate themselves for saying it. To be young is to care too much. To mind with an agony of spirit. How brief, how false, how inordinate are the desires and the values of youth.

Sheena in this grey room in the sea light was to Eliza a creature exiled within herself. Bold and much afraid and most touchingly beautiful. Her defiantly disreputable clothes were such a lovely pose, those hard bare legs, that absurd red skirt with its affected patches, the dark fisherman's jersey, and a winkingly new diamond wrist-watch, that would not have disgraced the richest Jewess dining at the Berkeley, fastened outside the cuff of her jersey, all these were pathetic evidence of a great uncertainty.

" Tell me the time by your diamond clock and chain," Eliza said with gentle spite.

" It is ten minutes past six," Sheena answered, peering anxiously at her rich timepiece. " This doesn't always go very well, but it's gay, don't you think ? Rather lovely, don't you think ? "

" Indeed I do. Who gave you such a rich jewel, my sweet ? "

" Rupert did. For a nineteenth birthday present.

Don't tell Olivia because she hasn't noticed it yet and she'll be so tiresome about it when she does."

" As if she could miss it, darling. It's so—handsome."

" Oh, no, Eliza. For I wear it under my sleeve usually. I only popped it out then for you to see. And in the evening I wear it next my breast pinned to my bust bodice."

" Darling, you're *too* romantic."

" And if she ever finds it, I will say : Burma Jewel Company."

" But does she mind about Rupert ? "

" Oh, she says I'm too young to be engaged."

That lovely, prim, confident word " engaged," the word the young use about their loves, all so authentic and inevitable. Well, well.

" John will be delighted, won't he ? " Eliza said gently. She was really much more interested in talking about John than about Rupert. Rupert was such a handsome young soldier, so tiresomely the right person for Sheena to marry, although (Olivia was probably right) not just yet. " John and Rupert were always as one, weren't they ? "

" Yes, I wrote to John about it, but he didn't say very much. He wrote such funny letters, you know. Even now when he's quite well—absolutely, entirely well. But he doesn't seem the same. No rude jokes, you know. Of course he hasn't been with us for so long—would that be it ? But you know, Eliza, I wrote to him how Markie discovered a marvellous new joke, to break wind when Olivia tells him to make his bow for visitors. It was the most roaring success I've ever heard. He discovered it by accident of course, but he can do it now almost whenever he wants to, it's wonderful.''

" But wasn't John amused ? Really not ? "

" Oh, no. He wrote to me quite seriously about not making a fool of poor Markie. And you know, Eliza, if a child is a bit of a wit and no one ever laughs at their jokes, they just stop making them and get dreary, don't you agree ? I know nobody ever laughed at mine when I was little and look at me now, I ask you. I couldn't make a joke if I tried.''

" It doesn't matter. You're much sweeter as you are.''

" Oh, Eliza, you only say that to encourage me.''

" You could hardly be sweeter, I don't think.''

" Darling. And do you think I'm better looking than when you saw me last ? I look a lot older, don't I ? ''

" Yes. That's your wonderful make-up, I suppose. I can't take my eyes off it. Sheena, what time is John coming ? ''

" Eight o'clock.'' Sheena looked about her restlessly. " You must go with Markie to see his nest now if you're going, because he's to go to the station with Olivia to meet John.''

" Oh, are they going ? ''

" Yes. You know how awful it is for John the way Olivia goes on, as if they'd played together since they were children ? I thought it would be better if Markie went to meet him too. He's always such a help when Olivia is too tiresome."

" Will she want him ? "

" Oh, I've made him ask her and she couldn't say no. She's resting now and doing up her face to look more like John's elder sister ; let's go to the nest before she gets up."

" Oh, you're so bitter and cruel, Sheena, aren't you ? Must we take Miss Parker with us, do you think ? "

" No, we needn't. I do like her, you know, she's like a little hen-mouse or a little bat or a baby seal."

"All very furry, darling. What are we waiting for ? Oh, I wanted to know why you're so deadly about Olivia."

" She's a terrible woman. No reticence. Don't let's talk about her."

Outside the house they found Mark, feeding some of the dogs with Miss Parker. She was sorry when they took him away for she was feeling a bit lonely to-night, and when he had gone there was nothing left to do unless she wrote to her sister, who was in hospital with a tubercular hip. She had some very unfortunate relatives, much worse off (as she frequently recalled when she was feeling low) and in much sadder case than herself. For really, Miss Parker had little to complain about. Plenty of food, a moderately soft bed, a fascinating child to teach, a beautiful if lonely part of Ireland to live in. That was it, the loneliness, no other governess to speak to, no cinema to go to in free time. No place at all where she could run or pop in or out. To pop in and out or to run in for a chat seemed now to Miss Parker to be the sum total of bliss. " I adore country life," she had written in applying for Lady Bird's situation. Might she not have taken warning by her employer's rural name how truly rural this situation would be? But, no, she had rushed willingly upon her fate, and now she adored Mark and would find it hard to leave. This terrible feeling of aloneness, of belonging to no world at all had never oppressed her so heavily as now. With the Littles, for instance, Mrs. Little had been an invalid, and so Mr. Little had been obliged to consult her in many small matters. And with the Jarvis's, Mrs. Jarvis had made quite a confidante of Miss Parker when matters were more than strained between Mr. Jarvis and herself. But here, with the Birds, one had nothing. One lived a life betwixt and between the servants and the family. Nothing to give. Nothing given. Miss Parker more than welcomed the hundred and one extraneous tasks fastened on to her by Lady Bird. It gave her a feeling of being required, of having a little of their lives. The dogs to talk about when she and Mark came down to Sunday luncheon. The garden to discuss with Lady Bird—even though " rawther lovely " was the one and only phrase that she could ever master or use to describe the success of either a melon or a lily.

Sheena liked her and was very unjealous and helpful over Mark. But Sheena and Miss Parker had no common ground whatsoever, not even about Mark, whom Sheena thought quite perfect and Miss Parker thought a very backward and spoilt, though ravishing little boy. The pictures, which Sheena adored equally with Miss Parker, affected them each so differently as to be of little or no bridge towards any intimacy. Sheena would go into ecstasies over Photography and Good Production (she had once had an affair with a young man who took a crowd part for a week), whereas Miss Parker spent her emotions on the Stars, their satin under-clothes, their astonishing Sex Appeals and Body Urges.

Whitty, Lady Bird's maid, was quite a dear, but Miss Parker was terrified of any real intimacy with servants. She clung to her void with pathetic obstinacy. But sometimes, as on an evening like this, the bird song in the drenching woods, the sea light and the summer light of the evening, and all the beauty and all the loneliness of the world would weigh unfairly upon her. But, as on this evening, Miss Parker would not give in to any nonsense of this sort. She would retire to the schoolroom and write to her sister, read the directions for that new depilatory which had come by post to-day (in a plain cover), and set out sums for Mark to do in the morning. Perhaps she had better attack the last task first. Sitting down she composed almost insoluble problems and wrote them out in a squared exercise book, asking in her neat handwriting questions such as :

" If a man wanted to give sixteen girls a treat——"

" If two boys had three balls between them, how many——"

Better perhaps to leave the depilatory till to-night. One could deal with it best at leisure and with one's bedroom door locked. Heaven send it did not smell in the penetrating, enduring way the last had smelt.

IV

Olivia was in the hall ready to start for the station when the birds'-nesting party returned from its walk. She did look terrifyingly young and tremendously excited. Eliza wondered just how unkind John was going to be to her and how inconceivably stupid she was going to be about John.

"Hurry up, Markie! Ask Miss Parker for your blue woolly."

"Oh, I'm so hot, Mummy. Need I?"

"Odious, odious child—always too hot or too cold. Always hungry or thirsty." Sheena steered him upstairs.

Olivia turned to Eliza. Her eyes were alight. With enjoyment? With excitement? No; with consciousness of herself, seeing herself in this situation. Going to meet John—John who had been mad and was restored, his seven devils cast out. John who was so beloved by everybody, who had been such a success. She really minded about John and her pretence of intimacy with John. Now he was coming back to her and here she was ready to meet him. To think that dressing a part could make a thing like this more actual to Olivia was pathetic. The inconsequence and the obviousness of all her posturings and nonsense. How could she blind herself to the fact that they could not deceive her reasonably intelligent and spiteful offspring. They did not see even the shadow of her pretended self, only her pretences. And in her affectations she was most sincere. She had nothing else except her beauty, and that could not affect them at all. Not her children. Eliza looked at her with great pity. The poor, poor dear. There she was, changed into a pale pink tweed, brown and white shoes, and a charming, bending hat. Her face, newly painted, was as fresh and taut as a new house, and her dark Spanish chestnut hair arranged, so dexterously arranged, against the lovely hurrying line of her cheek-bone. Age could not take that, it was a bird's line—a flight—as beauty is. And could her children not be tender with her? Eliza feared not.

" Oh, Eliza, will you go and see Julian? He told them to bring the sherry into his study so that he could talk to you. I almost forgot to ask you. . . . Darling, this is a pretty marvellous moment for me, isn't it? And I have to hide everything and be so fearfully *Hallo, old man* with him."

" Yes, mind you are——"

" Don't I know the creature? He's so reserved with everybody but me. I mean he'd hate the porters or the stationmaster or anybody to see what it meant to us both, wouldn't he? Where is that child? He would come. I know John would rather have seen his little old Mum all by himself, but I couldn't say No. Markie! Mark-ie! Oh here he is—Darling, have you——?" She whispered

into Markie's ear, who shook his head like a dog.
" Well, go and do it at once."

" I can't."

" Go and try. Really, that Miss Parker, she can
see to nothing. Now I shall be late. I don't know
why I keep her. And she's quite expensive. I often
say to myself is it worth it, but then again I don't
know."

Eliza said no more. She lit a cigarette and shook
out the match as she watched Olivia jump into her
car, slam her own door and open Markie's and
re-slam it, and start off with a bounce and a crash.
She was simply seething with maternal instincts
and eternal girlishness.

" Well," thought Eliza, stepping out from the
house, " well, well. Poor John. Poor Olivia."

The gravel was gold in the setting sun, and clean
small gravel like it is near the sea, and the evening
was raving sweet with wild music. The grass was
shadowed now, and the flowers of a white rhododendron only coldly sweet for there was no full
summer's heat. Decorum, Decorum, the faint
honey pepper of her breath was chilled away. Oh,
I love warmth, thought Eliza, shivering affectedly
at the sand-coloured sky and the striped sea, and
disgusted with Decorum for disappointing her, she
went back into the house for her glass of sherry with
Julian.

For gardens and fields, rivers, seas and the songs
of birds can become at hours most distressingly
unreal, withdrawn and dismal. The spirit has

gone out of them, informing them no more. Beauty has lived and died and there is only waiting left. Houses are best then, and a glass of wine, and whenever possible an enthralling talk. What fine pleasures derive from conversation for those who employ it aright. It is at once an indulgence and a discipline.

Eliza liked talking to Julian although she was not sure after all these years that she did not rather dislike him in spite of his possessing the qualities she most admired. She liked his flexible reticence very much : the way he would gather your views on some intimate subject and yet contrive never to make you a public for his own. It was a unique defence against intimacy and she had never yet quite discovered his trick of it. How long have I known him? she thought, as she walked through the round halls that held light as though in yellow bowls ; quiet as milk in a bowl the light was, and the plumes of white genistas in their copper buckets were as quiet in the light as the Eastern jars of benign and restrained line and colour which were arranged here and there and always in the right places (like Julian's comments on life).

How long had Eliza known Julian? How long had she been bewitched by him? How often had she betrayed herself to him? How often had he restored her to herself? He never gave back for he never allowed himself to take. He was mean about taking. He was as able not to take as he was able to wait and keep a thing he valued through all

vicissitudes. As he had valued Olivia, as he had
kept her for himself at the last. Eliza had loved
Julian. It had been long ago and rather bitter, but
not valueless to her—although it had been only an
alley, lovely but blind, where she had walked alone
to the end and turned back to walk out into her own
life again—a desolate but instructive experience.
Funny Julian. Sweet, unkind Julian, who required
no romantic woman nearer than the very edges of
his life. Not depressingly austere, but himself and
true. Or was he himself? Was his life not one long
pretence at being himself? Well, if so, his pretence
seemed to occupy him very completely.

"Julian," Eliza said, opening the door of his room.
One turned left down a passage from the inner
hall with its curving mahogany doors to get to
Julian's room (his Sanctum, Olivia called it).
"Hullo, Julian, how are you?"

Greetings of any sort are mainly futile, futile
whether they mean nothing or anything.

Julian was sitting in a window tying a sea-trout
fly by the sea-light and the daylight. A vice was
screwed into the edge of the sill and a confusion of
bright feathers like a Sitwell poem lay on the sill.
Julian attached a pair of tweezers to the end of his
waxed silk and arranged a chair for Eliza. "Sit
where I can see you," he said. He never wasted
his time on idiotic greetings. He gave her a glass of
sherry and a cigarette and returned to the con-
struction of his fly without so much as a glance at
her. It was hard. Intercourse with Julian was

always a little pernickety ; one must not forget this. Difficult if one expected too much. Good if one expected nothing at all.

" I must finish this," he said, " I want to have it for John to-night. It's a bit early for evening fishing, but I expect he would like it. I would if I was him, poor darling."

Julian was always so successfully impersonal about his children. And so womanly.

Eliza said, " Go on, Julian, please. I have a mass to tell you."

" What an enthralling gossip you are. Go on, darling, please." Julian smiled at her and fell again to the wedding of bright feathers.

So Eliza told him of this and that. Who loved who and who paid. A tiny scandal of the turf. A friendship gone. The results of a party. The success of her exhibition. Who had bought her pictures and why. A picture she had bought and why. A horse she had sold. A woman she had disappointed. All nonsense, and all very entertaining as a woman can only be entertaining when she minds about her audience. When she will make that lovely effort to put life and a twist into all she tells about and the result, though slight, is a complete and finished thing.

While she talked and grew a little gayer and more quickened in herself towards the end of her second glass of sherry, Eliza looked again and anew on Julian as she always did when they met again, as she always would probably. Tenderly at his tender hands ; with the same old surprise at his obstinate mouth and cruel secret eyes with their flying line of eyebrow. His fair rather dismal hair was no thinner and very little greyer than it had been for the last twenty years—and that was never very thick. He was as obstinate and insolent and set apart to himself as ever. As preposterously thin. As entirely defined, and no doubt as difficult to cope with in every possible way. One could not discuss John's return with him any more than one had discussed John's departure. And yet there was a sort of a shelter in Julian. Were one in difficulties of any alarming kind, even the fact that one loved him would never prevent one from going to him for help and for advice and for something that only Julian could give his friends, even when their spiritual or financial relief was quite beyond him. He would compete with situations entirely out of his power to assuage or alleviate. He might even compete successfully with John, his own child.

"Well, now, that's done," said Julian, picking his fly out of the vice and holding it up to the light for his own considerate admiration. "And very lovely I think it is. I don't suppose John will think much of it. He ties an infinitely better fly than I do. But there it is. He won't like to hurt my feelings by refusing to go out and fish the sea-pool to-night, will he, Eliza ? "

Julian found escapes for people. Even for John to-night an escape from Olivia, who would pursue him, exuding tenderness and contemporary under-

standing. Julian would help him to escape from
Olivia who hated the river at night, for it was nearly
always cold and the wind would blow in from the
sea should one go a-fishing and make an hour a hell
and a wreck of her complexion. No, the affectation
of enjoying fishing was almost entirely beyond her.
She would not pursue him there.

This curious room of Julian's occupied Eliza for
a moment while she was silent. Like he was, it was
tender and cruel. He had given an asylum here
to things he laughed at and valued not at all.
There was the strangest confusion here in the way of
furniture and ornament possible to imagine. All
the sofas that had been superseded in other parts of
the house seemed to have gathered themselves
here in ungainly hordes. Julian's bookcases which
took up nearly two sides of the room were filled
with old German novels, volumes of Ruskin (heavily
scored by his sisters in the passages where they
discovered themselves most nearly affected). Many
of his children's school books—marking the date
when the schoolroom had again become a nursery
for Markie—and much more unconsidered flotsam
had found its way in here. Julian's own books on
Heraldry and Cattle Breeding were mostly piled
upon the army of sofas. There were four very lovely
chairs which Olivia thought aloud and in vain
would look much better in the drawing-room.
But she never tried to rob him of that touching relic
of the Great Exhibition, 1869—a pink wax lady,
curiously draped in fur and feathers, and encased

in a dome of glass, neatly labelled " Florida Squaw, Great Exhibition, 1869." Nor as a matter of fact would Julian have parted with her any more than he would have parted with the chairs. She was so comely and pathetic, having all the nicer characteristics of the wax fruit of that date and much more gaiety. There was a fair sprinkling of stags' antlers on the walls, and many other decaying trophies of sport both at home and abroad—foxes' masks and tiger skins frilled with red flannel and stuffed sea birds. Not that these last were so very sporting, but there had been an uncle who was a keen ornithologist in the days when ornithologists did more than observe and take notes and photographs. There were many black tin boxes full of mysterious papers, notes that Julian compiled about Heraldry chiefly, or records of the Kerry herd, and black tin boxes full of feathers and mice and moths.

Julian moved among this deplorable confusion with entire ease and comfort, found what he wanted when he wanted it and where he expected to find it, and never showed any signs of distress at the discomfort with which he was surrounded. " If this was an attractive room," he said to Eliza once, " would I for one moment be left alone in it ? No ! Well, there you are," and he looked about him at his protective gods—the angular sofas, the gulls, the tiger skins, the lovely wax model of the Florida Squaw, the pre-1914 novels, the German books and his sisters' girlish enthusiasm for Ruskin—with a certain amount of gratitude and a certain amount of vanity, for who but he had maintained and protected them, perceiving potential saviours in them all. He never stopped to observe them without admiring his own forethought which amounted, he considered, almost to vision.

" And how long are you going to stay with us, Eliza ? " he asked, varnishing the head of his fly with a pin dipped in a little bottle of varnish. " A month, anyway. Ah, at least a month."

" No, Julian. I must be off to paint a portrait of a fat child long before a month is over."

" I never heard such nonsense. You've got to stay with us now. You know how much we need you now." Julian would not say any more than that. It was surprising that he had said so much. And Eliza knew that he needed her. She knew her own use and power with her friends. She loved and she was of use to them. They loved her for her use but not for her love. She was a Romantic Woman who knew the horrors of Romance too well. A Romantic Woman who timed her emotions and kept them in hand. Sweet Eliza, who was valued but not greatly beloved. She said to Julian :

" Of course, Julian, as long as you like. Of course, I *want* to stay," although that portrait of the fat child was worth seventy-five pounds to her. Not that this counted. It had gone from her mental calculations entirely. Julian needed her for something, not for herself in the smallest way, but for something she could do. Well, and so she would. To be there and to help about John. That was what

was needed. Whether she could help or not. But
at least to be there. If she could not help John,
perhaps, sometimes life is kind, she could help
Julian. But life had never given her that. Life had
never really been very kind yet. It might take a
turn. Then it was not very kind to Julian—and
his tolerance had been called by a very ugly name
once—and his child had gone mad. But was whole
again, they said. His lovely John. His dearest
child.

Surely they would be back from the station soon
now. " I think," Eliza said, " I'll go and have my
bath." She seemed again like a tree. She was so
tall and of such a gentle growth. And her painted
face was as quiet in the evening light as an old
woman's face by candle light. Lovely and very
quiet.

" Thank you so much, dear Eliza, for saying
you'll stay," Julian said to her. Showing he knew
that it had mattered. It was not nothing.

Eliza said, " Dear, but it's lovely for me," and she
went away leaving Julian to everything that was
more important than she was. To dressing flies
for his mad son. To waiting for his faithless, cruel
wife. To his Life in which she had no smallest
part. Well, so long as one knew where one was,
nothing hurt one. Only the unexpected wounds and
defeats.

V

To reach the bathroom Sheena passed the open door of the schoolroom where Miss Parker would sit most evenings waiting for her supper to come up with some interest, for she was as greedy as a bird, and waiting for a few moments' chatter with Sheena which she valued very much. Markie would be in bed waiting for " good-nights," alert to wrest the last possibility from the day. Miss Parker was divided in her mind between the labour of quelling his turbulence and the pleasures of a little talk with those who came far more to see him than her. Sheena, even on the nights when Markie was asleep, always stayed and talked, or read the letters in the back of *Home Chat* and the *Woman's Own Monthly* which asked what should a girl do under almost any circumstances and were signed, " Worried Blue Eyes," " Puzzled," and sometimes " Anxious."

They were not all made up of kindness on Sheena's part, these nightly conversations, for on the whole she rather liked Miss Parker, adored *Home Chat* and the *Woman's Own* and sometimes found the problems at the back not at all unlike her own Above all, Sheena enjoyed the atmosphere of worship with which the air of the schoolroom was so fully charged.

The schoolroom was a little dusky at this hour. Its window did not look out to sea but back to the gardens and the hills. Markie's empty glass of milk was usually sitting on the table looking rather sordid and waiting to go down when Miss Parker's supper came up. Schoolrooms often look a little dingy. However gay their chintzes and wallpapers, there is so often that dreary photograph of Mummy in her court dress and feathers, and Daddy looking extremely sporting and pompous in his hunting cap, and not infrequently rather big in the neck and jowly. Why photographs of that most becoming headwear should so often produce this effect it is hard to say, but so it is.

Miss Parker had written a cheerful letter to her sister and completed her series of problems for Markie's solving on the morrow. Now she had nothing left to look forward to but her supper and the exploration of her depilatory and Sheena's evening visit.

Sheena came in and said, " I expect I'm going to be very late for dinner. I mustn't stay a moment." She seemed excited and estranged, and when she was in one of these moods Miss Parker drew no benefit from her at all. In any case she was far enough off at the best of times, beyond the edge of beyond, but when she went out and up in the air like this Miss Parker could not contend at all. She felt very flat and alone. A very sad little governess.

She said, " Markie was so excited at seeing his

brother again. I could hardly get him to bed at all."

" Oh, yes," Sheena said inattentively. She went to the door. "Shall I go and say good-night to him now? I think I will. Good-night, Miss Parker."

And Miss Parker was left alone again with the empty glass of milk and the rather inky table and the photographs of other people's families, while the evening advanced softly in finger-lengths nearer to the dark. Needless to say, she was disappointed. Sheena was usually so sweet and full of jokes. She would even tell Miss Parker a discreetly rude story every now and then. But to-night she was gone away, and Miss Parker could not but perceive that, although she was more excited than sad, she was not happy. Was she frightened? She seemed so unsure, as if an unfamiliar strain had suddenly been put on her.

Markie was lying in bed in that false dark in which children must sleep. He looked very exotic and disturbing.

" I have a sixpence in me bed," he said, " some-where."

" I can't feel anything in your bed except your dog."

" Filthy brute. I hate her. Full o' fleas." How wildly he defended himself from any parade of affection.

" I don't know where your sixpence is unless Mouse has eaten it."

" Do you think she has, Sheena ? Well, if she has——" Markie made rather a coarse comment on his probable recovery of the coin.

Sheena said, " Well, that would be only natural. But why is your hand so tightly shut ? Little one, open your hand."

" Oh, Sheena, Sheena."

" Of course, I knew it was there all the time," Sheena said. " You're not one to lose sixpence. Who gave it to you ? "

" John. I have a nice bunch o' flowers on my dressing-table," he said languidly. And then, for it was too unimportant, " Take them if you like." He was so off-hand with his gifts. How well he would give when he was older.

Sheena said, " I would like. What a handsome bouquet. I suppose you stole them from the station-master's garden. Why didn't you give them to Olivia ? "

" Silly bitch. Why should I give her my flowers ? "

Sheena said, " Well, good-night, sweetest one." She didn't reprove him at all. She never did. Why should she ? And he was usually so right.

He kissed her carelessly. Then he clasped her wildly, " Sheena, Sheena, don't leave me. Don't leave me alone with this blind mouse of a dog. What good is she ? "

" You have Parker near you too. My darling, I must go." It hurt Sheena quite definitely every night to say good-night to the little boy. He was so tenderly reproachful at his eternal failure to keep her. His effort and his acceptance seemed to her very touching, although she knew how entirely unreal they were. A lovely piece of drama to keep her for a moment more. And not even her so much as the life of the day.

Sheena was very late coming down to dinner. She seemed so idle and insincere in her white dress, with a faint ribbon in her hair and her gentle painted face. John felt very strange with her.

John was going out fishing after dinner. He had only changed into a green jersey and a different pair of flannel trousers. He was terribly inclined to put everybody at their ease, Eliza thought. And to talk about his careful doctor's house as the asylum, and to say things like, " Even when I was cracked—barking——" at which old Byrne, the butler, flinched almost perceptibly. Eliza did not like it. There was too much defence about it all. For Julian's sake she did not want it. Julian was so sweet talking about fishing or racing, when John would go rasping off about his fellow lunatics and their curious obsessions. Laughing, but coming back. Eliza resented John's insistent frankness for Julian and through him for Olivia, sitting there so silly and bereft of comment at the other end of the table. Olivia, whose fond boast it was that John told her all and everything, hated his confidence to include not only the rest of the family, but the servants. Poor Olivia, it was one of her children's old defences to tell her everything they chose to reveal in public. Eliza knew that. But to-night she found it all rather cruel and hurtful.

And John was more than ever like John, with a curious unlikeness to himself which all this clamour could not shelter. He had come back to them, and they must not think he wanted any nonsense about nervous breakdowns and the like. It made things much worse for him. And if he defended himself from worse so wildly, the present must hold some terror of soul for him past imagination. Eliza wondered where he found refuge. She wondered if he had a refuge at all. Dear John, she thought, he has that unsteadiness about him which makes even his appearance a little unreal, a little boring. Could Olivia see it? Or Sheena? Or Julian? Olivia probably thought he was better looking than ever before, and she had always had a particular adoration for his translation of herself into himself. It was not a question of calling back the lovely April of her prime. She saw him now, each passing day, herself and her present echo. A great deal of her brother and sister obsession was involved in this pose of mind, and with it this pretence of confidence where there was so less than little.

John was very like Olivia to look at. He had her little nose and fine line of jaw and cheek bones and his hair grew with the same pretty spring, but it was dark and not rusty chestnut like hers. His eyes were not hers either. He was the only child who had escaped those eyes. His eyes were bold, but troubled, and quite untrusting of anybody. They were grey eyes, and very melancholy when they forgot to be light and defensive. There was a portrait at Silverue which was very like him, a picture of a pale and dissipated · great-grandfather with wild eyes, but John did not look dissipated. If anything, there was an air of untried austerity, an escaping from pleasure about him, which was as misleading as his likeness to his mother.

Eliza saw that all day they been waiting, Sheena and Olivia and Julian, for something they were afraid of, and now it was worse than they had expected. They had each prepared a different soft acceptance for John. And John came back to turn a strange, completely sane, but changed face to them all. He turned his face away and gave them nothing. But in what lonely coldness must his feet be set. Eliza longed to talk to him, to quieten him from this extravagance of feeling. But everything she thought of seemed so futile, so unconnected with all that had mattered to him.

I saw your lovely girl friend, Desna, walking down Bond Street on Thursday—— What was the use of that——

Hubert Curry rode a lot of winners last season, didn't he ? That Starling must be a useful horse—— John had been away sea-voyaging. How should he know or care what Hubert rode or owned.

In the end everybody spoke together. Sheena said, leaning forward to John across the table, " Oh, Rupert bought such a nice horse the other day. He's a nice gay little horse. Of course, I never really looked at him. He might be a dreadful looking horse. Shall we go over to-morrow ? "

And John had hardly time to agree before Olivia was off :

" Boy, darling—" that awful habit of calling him " Boy," and it always sounded so rehearsed, though why ?—" you know I have a shocking thing to break to you. The garden is open for the Jubilee Nurse fund on Thursday, and I must have you to look after the games. Clock golf, you know, darling. Only you must see people don't cheat."

" Who cheats ? "

" All Sheena's friends cheat wildly and think it so amusing. And then some one from the Town makes a good serious score and they're furious."

" You live in terror of the town and its Beady Bonnets. Which of my friends cheats, anyway ? "

" Well, look at Rupert last year."

" Rupert does not cheat about anything," Sheena said with venomous dignity. " He only came to your disgusting fête because you badgered him so. That was why."

Julian was saying to John—" then I put up a Lee Blue and the brutes wouldn't look at that——" this was a longish fishing story which lasted well through the savoury and until dessert had been put on the table and the servants had gone. And then suddenly there was quietness in the room, and for a minute or two no more pretences of anything, for any purpose.

Eliza saw Sheena touch that embedded watch or

where approximately it might lie—a tender torture—
and glance at the clock. No doubt she had one of
these abandoned girlish assignments with Rupert,
which she would lie herself black in the face to keep,
and come speeding home then, enchanted.

Julian poured himself out a glass of port very
steadily and considerately and sent the decanter
round. Eliza saw that both Julian and Olivia were
watching John at that moment. They wanted to
see if he would have a glass of port or not. He was
not supposed to drink. Oh, but this watching—
Why is a watching so sly and destructive? John
saw them, of course. He said, " Not even a glass of
port, Olivia. Very unsteadying." It was cruel of
him to say it. Julian put a gentle hand on the table
with a sudden regretted movement, and Olivia
looked away from John and towards him for
comfort. But Julian was making no more errors of
that sort.

Eliza knew it was more than time for her to be the
woman her friends required her to be, the woman
who helped them with the right word. The woman
who loved them. But Eliza's tongue was not always
as ready to speak as her heart was to understand.
Now she said, " John, give me one of your cigarettes.
I can't help it, I don't like Julian's."

" Of course I will, Eliza." His hands were so
like Julian's, with the difference that they were not
quiet. Lovely, intolerant, nervous hands.

Julian was teasing Sheena and Olivia was complaining about some sort of fruit that Byrne had

forgotten to tell her had run out, when Eliza's cigarette was lighted.

"What a lovely jersey, John. I'd give you big money for it."

"Darling, you may have it. I'd love you to have it." Suddenly John was entirely himself and sweet again. And it was with the idea of giving.

"I would like it. I do think it's charming. Where did you find it? It's so nice."

"A woman on the cruise made it for me. She thought I was enthralling till one day some one told her the difference between a keeper and a valet. After that there was a distinct drawing aside of skirts."

"Oh, John, darling, how terribly funny you are. Don't make me laugh any more. You've been so marvellous all through dinner." Now what made Eliza say this cracked little piece, speaking very low, leaning towards John, a little breathlessly.

"Oh, one's got to play, hasn't one?" John made a superb pretence. It was a confession of being grand. It was an admission to Eliza of a certain affectation of bitterness, but if he affected this bitterness he hid—What did he hide?

Eliza slid him a look of complete inquiry and complete interest. It was a look alive with sympathy and with a setting aside of real importances till a better moment.

John thought, "I had forgotten what a darling person Eliza is. I'm glad she's here."

"And, oh, mummy, do you mind if I take your

car after dinner ? " This was Sheena, uncertain but careless.

" Where do you want to go ? "

" I'm going to the pictures in Killabeg with Cuckoo and Cissy."

" You'll be late."

" Not for the Big Picture."

" No. Perhaps not. I might come too. Would you like to go to the pictures, Eliza ? "

Nobody missed Sheena's agonised eyes.

" Well, no, you know. I don't think I want to go," Eliza said. " Must we ? "

" No, no, darling, of course not."

" You're certain you wouldn't like to come ? " Sheena said, now that the danger was over she had visibly relaxed. " Perhaps I'd better fly then—may I ? " She stood up in her white dress in the evening light and the candle light. There seemed to be a dividing air about her between them—the old, and the old and the sly, and the experienced, and the hurt—and Sheena, who kept her distance from them, an enraptured creature. She was gone then in her soft dress as soft as a white owl, and gone as certainly as an owl will slide its flight out of knowledge in a moment. She had left them.

" She's so sly," Olivia was complaining. " Why couldn't she say where she's going ? She must know we all know. When I was her age I was quite frank and open. None of this deceitfulness. Of course, I was extraordinarily innocent for my age. When I married Julian——"

" Olivia, don't you think we might make a move ? You could continue your girlish confidences to Eliza in the drawing-room. John wants to fish."

" Oh, all right. Boy, darling, I don't think I'll come down with you to the river to-night. It's a bit cold for the old girl, isn't it ? Come and say nightie-byes to me, won't you."

" I may be awfully late."

" Never mind, childy, wake me up."

They went out together, Olivia clasping Eliza's long thin brown arm with her plump hands. They looked like a woodcock and a white pigeon. Rather an exotic woodcock and rather a trimmed and worldly white pigeon.

Of course, it was too early for the sea trout. John went out of the house through back ways and passages to the rod-room, which had the laundry on one side of it and the gruesome larder on the other and a narrow deeply worn path, inevitably hedged by fuchsias, leading from its door down to the back avenue and its white sea stones. No doubt it was too early for sea trout. But no doubt also that the more he kept out of their way the better pleased they would be. No doubt they would find many improbable occupations such as this for him. He could hear Olivia having a good heart to heart with that old Doctor over him and what he was to do : and what he was to think about ; what interests were to be provided ; what was to be talked about and what left unsaid. Could they not leave one alone ? Cease from their plans and their interference? Whatever they did they would not get near one now. One was alone, after all this. Given back to oneself now, but not to them. Never again the same to others, John supposed. He did not care. Not if they would leave him, cease their touchings and withdrawings. He had shown them that he didn't mind, that it didn't hurt or embarrass him to talk about that time—well, then——

In the rod-room, coldly and devastatingly the same as he had always known it, John shut the door and waited for a moment almost without thought. I don't mind. You're not lonely because you're alone, he protested. I'm all right if I keep quiet. All right. I'm *quite* all right. It's only for a second I feel a bit wretched. Was it this room being so inevitably the same that had made him feel terrible for a moment, so divided from all he had a right to ask of life? The same shelf of dog's medicines. The same row over row of rod-rests, and the rods one knew so familiarly lying on them one above another. The fuchsias half-darkening the windows, and Boody with yet another litter of healthy and illegitimate puppies in the box in the corner. All these things were rather drearily the same as they had always been. That was it. That was why they hurt him so much.

Somebody had put up John's rod for him (again, could they not leave him alone and let him see to his own things?); they had even decided what flies he was to fish. Well, it might interest them to know that John was not going to wet one of those selected

to-night. In any case, he remembered again it was
all nonsense fishing for sea trout before the end of
May. Just an idea to get him out of the house.
Make things easy. Occupy his time They were all
so bloody tactful. Curse them.

Boody came to him, leaving her pups with that
air of bored disdain he knew so well. Flicking out
from among their demands on her and leaving
them thrusting and squirming in their straw. There
was a faint gleam of the old hardy Boody through all
her gross maternity. Boody the brave little one, the
tender and dear one. He made a fuss about her
for a moment and looked at her babies gently, then
he picked up his rod and landing net and went out
of the farther door and set his feet on the deep
sheltered path towards the sea, feeling mended at
heart for the time being.

VI

Sheena had left her car at the crossing of two mountainy roads ; flat rock came through the road and six walls met and turned corners here. Above the cross the mountains ran darkly up into the pale air and below the cross the little fields spun their touching patterns down towards the sea.

Sheena and Rupert had met here to-night— Sheena dashing the door of her car open and across the road like a flash the moment his car appeared. For she never would be sufficiently mistress of herself to keep him waiting. Supposing he thought she wasn't coming and went away ? However, she distrusted neither Rupert nor herself, so she was not coy or missish, and nearly always ten minutes at least early for assignments.

She flew across the road now, the tail of her dress like a white columbine flower upside down below her long tweed coat, and was shut into Rupert's car in a moment.

" I'm five minutes too soon," Rupert said, looking at her sideways.

" And I'm ten minutes too soon. I thought I'd never see you again."

" I escaped before the end of dinner too."

" So did I, before dinner was over."

" Oh, how lovely to see you."

" Oh, so lovely to see you."

" Where shall we go ? To our own place ? "

" Yes."

" Where's Mrs. Cooney, Sheena ? "

" Interestin'. She has the shutty-ups, poor little girl."

" Poor little sweet. Mr. Cooney's here. Cooney, boy, aren't you ? "

" Oh, little sweet dogs, how are you ? Did you go fishing to-day, Rupert ? Did you do any good ? "

" Yes, I got one fish."

" On what ? "

" On a tiny hairy olive."

" Oh, darling, I'm so glad. Nobody else got any to-day. John's gone out to take a crack at the sea trout."

" It's a bit early, isn't it ? How's John, Sheena ? "

" Oh, he's marvellous. Quite all right, you know. Only I thought he was just a tiny bit being grand at dinner."

" What do you mean—being grand ? "

" Oh, he would keep on and on about everything. About his breakdown and all that, you know."

" What ? he talked about it ? My God, I thought one would pretend it hadn't happened. Poor old boy ! Are you sure he's quite steady again, Sheena ? "

" Oh, yes. Only—I don't know, Rupert—he's different "

" Different ? "

" Oh, darling, you know how he was always so sweet and—stop me if I'm saying something silly— always so near one. And now he seems a thousand miles off and so hard and so wretched. No, I remember when John first went to his Preparatory School. The first holidays he came back I was so mad to see him, all our jokes and plans and things I had ready for him, and then he arrived and he was different. Quite, quite another person, and he had grand new jokes I didn't know about."

" Of course, he was bound to be different. All little boys are."

" Yes, but don't you see, this time it's the same, only it's not new jokes he has."

" You'll see he'll be all right," Rupert said. " John was always the best person in the world, and so dam' brave. He'll get over this."

" Yes, he will, won't he ? "

" Yes, he will."

Rupert stopped the car. They were at a great height over the sea now, but there seemed to be still the same height of mountain behind them. And no sky. They were mountain enfolded. All the sky dropped to the sea to the lost pale horizon below them and before them. Back in the mountains the heather was burning and along the farther mountains that were nearer the sea fires burnt too. Strange and romantic, fire on the mountains on a summer night. And the sea white and quiet and without waves or life.

Rupert and Sheena got out of their car and leaned

their elbows on the round dark stones of the road wall. Side by side they stood looking down on the smoke of little houses : on the dwarfed obscurity of woods, airy and gentle ; on the little stony fields and the nearer green of the bracken. And the foxgloves—their lovely strides of colour were below them, lost in the summer night, watching far up in the mountains.

" I like here, Rupert."

" So do I, my sweet."

Sheena was very quiet and grave. They talked gently about how lovely everything would be when they were married. How Rupert would not stop her from riding in points-to-points. Nor she him. How many children they would have. Markie. Miss Parker's beard. Sheena's rock garden. Rupert's horses. Sheena's horses. Mr. Cooney. Mrs. Cooney. How many children they would have. How many children Sheena and Rupert would have. Their sexes. Fishing. Hunting. Fox-hunting. Rabbiting.

And then Mr. Cooney was lost. The little brute had gone off hunting—and they rapt in the still evening. They called him high. They called him low. They commanded. They entreated. He made no response. A little dog was lost in the mountains. Then indeed was Love forgotten and ghastly thoughts of brave little dogs never seen again overcame them. Little dogs lost in mountain earths, held up in wicked angles of Buried grey stone. Little dogs starved and entreating and calling vainly on their gods.

They walked up a hazel-grove full of rabbit holes, calling and waiting to listen. Stars bloomed sullenly out of the sky, but no little dog came or answered. No hunting cry was heard on the hills. He was lost. He was gone. Far and wide they called and searched for him.

" Sheena, you'll play hell to your dress."

" Oh, darling, as if it mattered." Pieces of that white romantic gown hung here and there on briars and stones and bushes, and still they searched and called in vain and went back at last to the car. " For not unless you had three punctures at least," Rupert said, " you couldn't be as late as this."

" Oh, I'll steal in. She's only thinking about John to-night."

" You'd be amazed how you'd occur to her mind if she thought you weren't home yet."

" Yes, I suppose that's true. But I can't go till we find the little one. Oh, look, Rupert. I have an idea. Blow the horn."

They blew the horn——

They blew the horn——

And they blew the horn——

They waited. And presently a brown dog that had once been a white dog came hurrying down from the hills, dropped into the road and came mimbling and mambling, covered in shame towards the car— covered in shame and confusion and penitence— an evil and cursed little dog and nuisance, but with all that, a lost dog that was found again. They were glad to see him.

" Oh, wicked little man, come to me. Do you promise never to be lost again ? "

" Never again ? "

" Oh, so naughty and so dirty and such a bloody nuisance."

" Ah, I'm safe now, don't be unkind to me."

They drove down the road again to Sheena's car and they stood together at the cross roads with the night sea near to them and the mountains apart again, and here Rupert kissed her as a child might kiss a tender bird. For he was afraid and she was beyond anything to Rupert, so being young he was perhaps bound to make mistakes about her. Though not perhaps, one might think, quite such stupid mistakes as to kiss her as a child might kiss a tender bird.

Sheena delayed beyond his kiss for a second. No. Not half a second. And she was back in Olivia's car again. She let down the window nearest him and leaned out her head to kiss him again. This time a gay kiss, a little kiss that did not matter a bit. But there was something in her withholden. Something quite unconnected with that gay kiss and belonging to the moment before, and that was what gave her this quickened needful loveliness.

" You'll come with John to-morrow ? " Rupert was seized with a sudden small despair at her going. " Do you promise me, dear Sheena ? You won't let any one stop you. It is so important. And I want you to see this horse."

" Yes, I'll come. I must go now. Oh, how I hate going——"

" Good-night, my sweet."

" Good-night, my sweet."

Sheena drove home at high speed, feeling wildly happy. She had reason to be. If you are twenty and in love and beloved, if you have a share of beauty and good health and are a kind and brave creature and not too wildly imaginative, you have a great chance of happiness. And Sheena had all these reasons for happiness and more. She was one of those excitable creatures who delight in the Chase, and in the winter months pursue it with ardour. She was one of those who feel tenderly and ridiculously about their horses—to the edge of boring any other but themselves on this inexhaustible topic. (For, let it be faced and admitted, other people's horses, their ailments, temperaments and achievements are incredibly tiresome. We suffer their recital only that we may, in our turn, have the luxury of an attentive ear when our turn arrives to tell and set forth the prowess of our equine possessions.) Besides being brave, so ridiculously brave as to be the despair of many a knowledgeable and hardy sporting sister, Sheena was industrious and of a very active turn of mind. She would embark unhesitatingly on the most appalling projects such as : the running of gymkhanas ; theatricals for just causes ; the making of gardens ; (their chief reason for being to make a garden as unlike Olivia's as possible) ; the breeding of ferrets—but this last was beyond her quite. Ferrets she bought, but induce them to breed she could not. No, she could not. Although a kind of wild success crowned much of her activity this feat was beyond her.

Sheena disliked Olivia very much. Here her tenderness fell short and stopped. She was not even tolerant of her. It was not a case of not caring. She took her dislike of Olivia quite seriously, even going so far as to try to be fair to her, which showed that dislike had gone quite beyond any equitable view of the matter. She loathed Olivia's affectations and posings and lyings and misrepresentations of anything that mattered. She could lie herself, of course, and often did, but she had no poses. She was brutally, terrifyingly candid. She took and she gave where she wished. But Olivia took and gave so consciously. She had no integrity whatever. This was what Sheena realised most keenly, although she knew nothing at all about her mother's life. Not one of the things that Eliza knew were known to Sheena. And the sad thing was that Olivia really and truly was fond of Sheena and proud of her, and took a keen delight in buying her lovely clothes and seeing her virginal triumphs. In thinking to herself : So was I once. So I loved and schemed. Her condemnation of Sheena at dinner to-night had been in its fashion a sort of praise. She had had no smallest intention of going with the child when she suggested this to Eliza. She was a little anxious about Sheena and Rupert. This was the first thing that had mattered at all to Sheena. How could

Olivia realise the surprising truth about Sheena's
and Rupert's love? There was a gravity and
decision about their love that she had never known.
It could wait.

Sheena was fond of Julian. She was very fond of
him. His distance and fairness were very attractive
to her, and she trusted in him. He was a truly
kind person and so gentle and interested, he might
at moments be a sympathetic stranger, not one's
father who knew how young and dreary one really
was, and knew one's motives and enthusiasms
too well to question whence they came or where
they led. He was a person who could view
Endeavour without seeing the motive behind it or
the disaster in store and follow its course with
enthusiasm or sympathy. Indeed, Sheena was fond
of Julian.

Sheena had learnt to accept Julian's attitude of
defence towards Olivia. His standing between her
and her own idiocies and between her and their
children's unkindness. It was no good questioning
it. There it was. And one could often work round
Julian and get the inside turn of Olivia. So long as
he knew she suspected no conspiracy or understanding between any of them against her. But he would
sacrifice any of them or any of their schemes rather
than hurt her. For he loved her best. They all
knew this. But Julian knew something that mattered
about living, and he was kind and gentle to them
all. Dearest Papa, Sheena thought as she slid the
car as quietly as possible into the garage. If there

was any question to-morrow as to the hour of her
return, he could be trusted to have heard a car
being put to bed by eleven. Sheena clasped her
dark coat round her and went slipping through
the night into the house. It was the end of this
adventure, and, ah, she sighed for the next.

VII

ELIZA had spent rather a bleak sort of evening. She heard Sheena coming in and wondered once more at the elaborate subterfuge of the young. There was Sheena holding her breath as it were in one hand and her shoes in the other. So attentive to these details, so absorbed in the thought of her silent progress through the night house that, even after she had crashed once into the banisters and once into what, from its direction, sounded remarkably like Olivia's door, between these disasters she continued to go softly as a young mouse might go.

Eliza permitted herself a sigh for those extravagant, romantic, nerve-shattering moments known best to maiden virtue. Moments when one went softly with a beating heart and a desperate longing to gasp and giggle. But may not. Moments of divine hysteria when one flung oneself upon one's own safe bed and shook with laughter to think of the narrow margin by which disaster was avoided, laughed till one's face ached and one's body felt limp and tired of giggling. And then with solemn speed to bed, so owlishly trustful of one's own resource and sagacity. So entirely certain that one was queen of this or any other situation.

Eliza permitted herself to sigh again before she

turned on the light beside her bed. She had most thoughtfully extinguished it at the first sounds of Sheena's elaborate advance. It was tough on the poor child to know that some one was quite certainly awake and heard her, as that line of light beneath the door must inform even her sublime confidence.

Eliza picked up the book beside her and read :

" But thy eternal summer shall not fade,
  Nor lose possession of that fair thou owest,
  Nor shall death boast thou wanderest in his
    shade,
  When in eternal lines to time thou growest."

Was that Sheena ? It seemed so now, but then the young, the unsatisfied, the seeking young, are so fantastically romantical it is unfair to classify or label them in any way. To an imaginative person over thirty years of age they are tiresomely enthralling : tiresome, or enthralling. To Eliza they were enthralling. And when their feet were set like John's were set in bitter adversity it was nearly more than one's heart could bear. But Eliza was entirely too romantic, and forever deceived herself as to the depth and meanings of other people's passions or tragedies.

She had passed a splendid evening with Olivia. ". . . She's a *lady*, you know, so of course she knows which colours go with which." Olivia was looking at patterns of material destined for an evening gown for Sheena.

"Does it always follow, darling? How interesting." Eliza was glad anyhow that they had escaped from the tale of Olivia's wedded innocence. In spite of having heard it many times and only heard Olivia's side of the story, she could never abandon the conviction that it must have been infinitely worse for Julian than for Olivia. "And is she a good dressmaker?"

"She's quite good enough for a young girl." Olivia's own pullet-like curves were deceivingly flattered by the most expensive and subtle mind's devisings.

"Do you choose all Sheena's clothes, Olivia?"

"Well, she has an allowance of her own and she spends that herself—rather disastrously I'm afraid. But I buy a good many of her evening dresses. I love buying clothes for her."

Eliza had been startled by this extreme sincerity. "Did you give her the white dress she had on to-night? It was good. If I had designed it I'd have called it Evening Lilac and left the fact that it was white to take its chance."

"I don't quite follow you."

"No, darling. But it's such a sentimental dress!"

"I thought it was rather good style."

"Perfect. How lovely to be so right by accident."

"I suppose I have a sort of instinct for the right clothes. I remember when I was quite a young girl people used to think me marvellously dressed. I was always being asked the name of my dressmaker. I remember a very pretty dress I had. I wore it at

Ascot one day and people raved about it. It was pale blue georgette with wide sleeves to the elbow and a tiny fringe of blue and white beads. It was made with a kind of tunic and a wide belt of itself and the skirt was knife-pleated. It really was lovely."

"Yes, I think I remember it. You had great success in it."

"Oh, had I? I don't remember that, perhaps I had. I never knew why men liked me, I suppose because I never pursued them. But I had really rather a good hat I wore with that dress, I remember. Dark blue straw, very wide, with a wreath of blue flowers. And I wore pink malmaison carnations and long white kid gloves and black suede shoes with paste buckles."

Olivia saw nothing grotesque in the recital of these dead fineries. She spoke of them quite simply. Calling them back to life as beautiful, as indeed they had been then. Perhaps Olivia did not look back with a general horror on all dead Fashions, accepting without reserve their fantastic memories as others did, because she had lent her own beauty to each fashion and so saw only that. No doubt even when draped in the blue tunic fringed with blue and white beads, Olivia had been herself and lovelier than other women who wore the same trying type of garment fringed with almost the same beads. She had been lovelier and she remembered that. And then there was not the least doubt she had a particular gift for seeing and making beauty.

This grey room where they were sitting, a room
avoiding colour without achieving coldness, how had
Olivia, with her startling commonplaces of mind,
made a room like this? So remote. So gentle. It
was a perfect room for china and glass and lovely
pieces, and it embraced Olivia as it did another
lovely piece. It was a room that liked and flattered
women, as pearls flatter women. Eliza respected
Olivia for this room. She would like to have thought
of it herself. But she would not praise it now to her,
for if she did the same Olivia who had chosen
Sheena's perfectly romantic dress to-day, and
recalled with equal pleasure the horror she herself
had worn at a long past Ascot, could accept Eliza's
pleasure in this room while her memory and her
tongue wandered contentedly to the pink and white
dreadfulness of some dead inspiration in the shape
of a bedroom. " Do you remember what a success
it was? And everybody said it was perfectly
charming."

Eliza and Olivia were sitting one at each side of
a neat fire of coal which burnt brightly in its iron
basket grate set very high and elegantly. A faintly
raised plaque on which was a still more faintly
raised group of marble nymphs decorated the
centre of the mantelpiece. There was a dignity
and grace about this group with which Eliza and
Olivia, sitting opposite to one another in their
chairs with this lovely mantelpiece between them,
seemed to have a definite connection. Eliza was
making a piece of tapestry and Olivia was sewing

too. So they sat bending towards one another and joining, as it were, the two ends of a regular design. A long thin fender stool between them was covered with a faded strip of tapestry.

"You look like a book plate," Julian said, coming in and sitting himself down in the sofa opposite to them, "my dear Mrs. Bennett, and (yes indeed) my dear Eliza."

"Oh, don't mind him, Eliza. He goes on like that, you know. I don't know what he means, but I never pay the smallest attention to him. Perhaps he's in wine? Are you intoxicated, Julian? I suppose you've had a nice crack at the Cointreau. I thought you'd gone down to the river with poor John."

"No—to everything you say." Julian picked up a paper and began to read, quite lost to Olivia's absurdities for the rest of the evening.

"What is your attitude about Sheena and Rupert?" Eliza asked. "I gathered you were being perhaps not very enthusiastic. And why? I should have thought it was an excellent thing——" An excellent thing—this wild romance. If Sheena could have understood her and known about Excellent Things. But now she was talking to Olivia.

"Oh, well, Sheena's so young and very young for her age, I think, although she's so sly. I'm not putting my foot down in any way, but I'd rather she waited and met more people. Monica Brompton is going to take her about next year. I would.

But really, as Julian says, we're so poor and the
garden takes up so much of one's time, and of
course she does have great fun. There are lots of
young people here. And then it's been so awful
about John, it's put everything else out of my head,
I'm afraid."

Julian said, " You know, Eliza, I don't want to
be hard on the girl, but I'd rather for her own sake
she waited till it had all simmered down about
John. Not that I intend to take up a stand in the
matter, but there it is. I don't know what Rupert's
family think about it all. I've always thought Jack
Lamfield a very tiresome man. Really a horrible
man. Do you know his cousin, James ? "

" No."

" How fortunate for you. But I'm very fond of
Rupert."

" He's so good-looking," Olivia said. " Sheena's
like me in that. I always felt romantic about tall
dark men. Even if I did marry a little fair one."

" He is very decorative," Eliza agreed. " Those
high, wide cheekbones. Very good drawing, I
always think."

" Oh, darling, don't be so tiresomely Bloomsbury.
I like his grey eyes and his black eyelashes and his
wonderful figure and his charming clothes. And I'm
sure that's what Sheena likes too. And then he rides
so nicely. And he's such a good judge of a horse.
And they tell me they think a lot of his polo in the
regiment. And he's a good fisherman. And a good
shot. And he'll have Owenstown some day—it's a

house I've always longed to see as I should like it to be."

" Perhaps you'll only see it as Sheena would like it to be."

" Oh, Julian, that's what I said. I only want the child to have more confidence in me. And to be less deceitful. And to be happy."

"——To be happy. But not just yet," Eliza said softly. " Oh, the poor young."

Julian shot her a sharp look, and Olivia began to fuss about sipping a glass of hot water and lemon juice. So it was near bedtime. Near Olivia's bed-time, anyhow, for she seldom relaxed her rule of bed by 10.20. She could as easily have cut off her hand as abandoned one of the thousand and one rules of health which underpinned her shockingly youthful appearance. What does she keep it up for ? Eliza asked herself again. Why this continual struggle ? For whatever the success, at the cost of how much effort was it achieved ? She has no lovers now and seems most happy to have replaced them by her garden. The countryside adore her for her placidity and kindness ; and even beyond her stupidity and selfishness. When she does make a joke she makes the sort of joke they've heard before and they like that. None of this vital part of her life depends on her looks. Nothing depends now on this terrific sustaining effort. One of these days she'll crack up under the strain. The exercises, the baths, the tonics and the cruel, cruel dieting. This discipline the silly old wanton inflicts upon herself

is more harsh than that which any novice in any
nunnery is asked to endure. Such constant, never-
ceasing effort. . . . I'm so tired I could drop
forever into sleep or death—but no. First I must
roll my eyes twelve times to the right. Then twelve
times to the left. I must blink rapidly twelve times.
Pause, and do it all again. I must turn my neck so
many dozen times this way and that way. I must
lie on my back across a hard chair with my head
down to conquer that terrifying incipient sagging
beneath chin and jaw. Oh, what endurance !
How remarkable and how frequent and how tough
are the natures that can keep up the struggle,
finding it worth while to the last. Eliza's hands and
her sewing dropped limp and effortless on her knees
as this renewed thought struck her. Who am I
to consider it ? she pondered on. I am thirty-five
years of age, and I look neither older nor younger.
I have been loved (though not so much nor so often
as people think), I have learnt the right colour
to put on my mouth, and I quite often buy the right
clothes. I have charm, I know, and a sort of wit
that is outside myself. I can't be sure of it. Nor is
my life ever completely real to me because I love
Julian till I die. I wonder whether it would have
been at all different if Luke hadn't been killed.
I shouldn't have married James and divorced him,
or gone to bed with people I didn't much mind
about. But I'm certain I'd still have loved Julian.

Olivia had supped the last drop of her hot water.
She was folding up her work things and yawning

a tiny yawn and belching a tiny belch and trailing
divinely across the room to look out of the curtained
window and wonder whether it would rain. She
was still standing with the folds of the curtain
upheld in one hand when the door opened and John
came in.

John came in and walked over to stand with his
back to the fire. John with his face rather white and
cold, and his mouth not mattering—hard and still.
That high dark collar round his neck and his eyes
trying to see a joke.

" Hullo, boy, my darling, did you do any good ? "
Olivia came studiedly across the room again. She
stood beside John looking up at him with inquiring
tenderness. " A lovely trout for my brekky ? "

" When did you start eating breakfast again ?
I thought you never did." John was determined
to be nasty and tiresome.

" Oh, I know, darling—just a tiny glass of orange
juice and a Rye Vita, d'you remember ? But I
could have trouty for my luncheon."

Julian said, " Did you get a fish, John ? " He was
gentle and grave, but John was to answer a question,
and not with questions, either.

" No, I didn't. It's absurdly early for the sea
trout, isn't it ? I caught three small Brownies, but
I put them back. I'm so tired. I don't know why.
I think I'll go to bed now. My face feels like yours,
Olivia—slipping just the least bit. I'll go to bed."

He was sorry then, for Olivia looked quite stricken
at the idea of her face slipping. She put her hand

up to it in a surprised and rather touching gesture. Eliza thought something twisted in John with the effort he was going to make before he said, " Come upstairs, Olivia. It's past your bedtime and your face really will slip if you miss that. And I couldn't bear it."

Eliza said, " Good-night, John," as he went away after Olivia—Olivia an undulating length of silver cord. There was a sweetness and a hollowness in her voice into which you could put what you chose or nothing.

" Good-night, Eliza, darling. It's so lovely you're here."

" Yes. It's lovely you're here." Julian came back to his sofa.

Now that they had both gone and left them alone —Julian and Eliza, those late bed-timers—Eliza felt herself farther than usual away from him. She knew that Julian realised why John had come in early. He had intended to say good-night to Olivia then and escape, dreading that soft inexorable demand for a good-night which she had laid on him. He intended to show that he perceived and disregarded Julian's motive in sending him down to the river. Julian could keep his motives and his kindness to himself. John was broken and embittered but he wanted no kindness. Julian must realise this. All these frightful helping hands—it was too much after everything else. And then to yield. He'd had a wounding crack at Olivia and then kissed her and softened, to expose himself to the full welter of her maternal chumishness. It had been a bad evening for him. And he had taken it both badly and bravely.

"The poor child," Julian said ; "the poor little boy. He's not going to be very good about it, is he?"

"To-night was terrible," Eliza said. She lay back in her chair staring at her large feet gracefully crossed before her. Her long thin arms were crossed behind her head. She was all crosses, no curves. But there was some wild length of beauty in her. As one perceives this in the exquisite gauntness of a heron, so in the same way it was apparent in Eliza. It could not fail one. Julian was devoted to Eliza. He valued this quality in her and her loving sympathy and her sweet changing face. He valued her because she was herself, and because, as he knew, she was silly enough to love him and wise enough to know that this romantic friendship of theirs was as much as he would ever need from her. No less and certainly no more.

"Well," said Julian, "let us hope we shall all feel more normal to-morrow. We were simply ghastly at dinner to-night, weren't we? How did you like my fishing story?"

"I always hate fishing stories. They remind me of old men whining and babbling and dribbling on and on."

"Well, isn't it strange, I think even all fishers loathe each other's stories. They only attend if they must."

" I do think Sheena is looking lovely. I keep on saying so, but I do think she is."

" Yes, isn't she a lovely girl now? And so nice. I'm devoted to her, you know, Eliza."

" How impersonal you can be."

" Ah, it's only affectation. You know I'm the most affected creature. I cherish my affectations like Olivia cherishes her face. I wouldn't let them slip for anything. I couldn't bear to be transparent. Do you think I am? "

" Clear as crystal, dearest Julian. An open book."

" How unkind of you to say that. And you know I cannot endure you to be unkind to me. Always tender, that's what you must be. It's not enough that you must always help me, like you are doing now. You must always be kind to me too."

" Yes, indeed." Eliza knew a level and unencouraging answer was now the due response in this queer game. " It's not what one's loving friends *do* for one that counts in the least, is it? What they take matters far more—to be a good taker, Julian, is a fine thing to be."

" I'm a good taker, I think."

" Yes, I think you are. Admirable."

" You sound as though I was very complacent."

" Complacent? Well, now, how deceiving is the human voice. You're the least complacent person known to me."

On the contrary, how revealing is the human voice, thought Julian. Darling Eliza, and I'm so fond of her, the sweet.

They sat silently for a little while. Eliza did not look once towards Julian. She knew his idle way of sitting and the gentle drop of his hands. He was the least fidgety, the most unbusy person. God help all Romantic Women, thought Eliza suddenly, catching hold of herself. All Unbeloved Women. And pity them.

After this little Litany she felt better, and presently thought it was time for her too to go to bed. She reminded herself she had motored a million miles to-day. Yes. To Julian, and now she would leave him in a sort of blind obstinacy.

". . . You don't want to go to bed yet, surely ? "

" Ah, but I'm as tired. I'm as tired as an old hen."

" You're all right, darling Eliza ? You've got everything you want up there ? I'll look in and see. Servants are so awful."

" No. I've got everything. Don't bother, Julian. Good-night."

" Good-night, then. But must you go ? Well, good-night."

Eliza went upstairs thinking : I shall look out at the June sea now and that will give me great pleasure. When she got to her room she leant out of her window for some time looking and listening. Monotonous, distant, quite uncaring, the sea's whisperings smote on and on. Past to-night and pain and all time into quietness. Eliza felt steadied and chilled from all her unreasonable fever soon, and her mind turned gladly to the fact that she really was tired, dead tired, and only very faintly unhappy now.

On her pillow was a neatly folded dark object. Eliza considered it with an utterly blank mind. At last it struck her as curious that a housemaid of Olivia's should have put out a dark knitted garment for one of Olivia's lady guests to sleep in. Not quite natural surely. She picked it up and switched on the light by her bedside. But this was not hers. No, it was John's jersey—the jersey she had praised lightly at dinner-time and that he had promised lightly to give. And he had taken it off and folded it up and put it here for her. Was nothing left to John now, slight and unimportant? This was unbearably sad and sweet—that he should have remembered and been so glad to give, John who all his life had taken gaily, to give in this way, remembering a little humbly and laying a present on Eliza's pillow like a young child. It was, she thought, one of the most touching and unhappy things she had ever known. For John to do a strange, gentle, unnecessary thing like this how deeply changed he must be. Eliza held John's jersey against her cheek half-inclined to tears. But she remembered in time that she was a romantic woman and so quenched them. She went to bed then much happier for herself but gravely concerned for John.

VIII

WHEN John went down to fish after dinner he met a man called Nicholas of the Rocks or Nick o' Rocks by most people.

Nicholas of the Rocks or Nick (as he may now be called with less sound and drama) was a queer man. He was lonely, for he lived by himself in a painfully white cottage on the extreme point of a low and rocky peninsula. His small and narrow farm running back behind his house was not at all a model product of neatness or industry, because Nick was of a sporting turn of mind and he put a day's shooting or a day's fishing or a day's beagling after hares in the mountains far and away before the exigencies of his farming. But although most through-other over the farming he was very clean and particular, in fact, both exacting and fussy, over his house.

The Bird children all knew Nick's house well. You could stand at one door and look straight through it to the sea or stand at the sea door and look straight back into the mountains. It was practically surrounded by the heavy shelter of fuchsia hedges—nearly as high as the house itself, and it was through a high, narrow slit that you saw the sea and through a high, narrow slit the mountains. Nick seemed fond of his house and always kept it as bright as a clean button inside. He had

never married a wife to do this or anything else for
him. Although he was nearly forty years of age and
several nice and suitable girls had been proffered
to him in marriage in his time, he had not taken a
wife. It was not that he was at all misogynistic
about women, for he could be very gay and free
with them, and in his sailoring life no doubt he had
encountered all sorts. But since he had inherited
this place from an aunt, the thought of a woman
did not seem to trouble him much more than the
farm. Like that it was subservient to a day's fishing
or shooting or hunting in the mountains. He had
his lobster pots and his net. And he had his higher
cunning as a fisher of salmon and his skill in shooting
snipe or woodcock. He was a very dear friend of
the Bird family, so kept most other poachers off their
ill-preserved game, whether such swam or flew. He
was the first person, except Markie, that John had
been really pleased to see since he came home. He
liked to see Nick again, and his light wild eyes as
quick as a bird's, and his dark strong hair with a
curl in it and a dash of grey. He never looked quite
human or like other people. He lived too much
alone. There was a kind of curlew sadness about
him, or perhaps more the sadness of a woodcock,
for there was nothing faëry about Nick, as there is
about a curlew. He was cosier than that, but sad.
He was vain too. John had often seen him pretend
to pick up a fallen snipe when he had fired and
missed, and thought some ill-disposed person might
have been a witness. And he was vain of his looks

too, and kept himself only a little less clean than his house, and shaved himself with praiseworthy regularity considering what a lonely sort of life he led.

He met John in the Fuchsia Walk on the way to the river and the sea.

" I heard tell you were expected back to-day, Master John," he said. " So I was anxious to see you. What way are you ? " He tapped his own head and glanced inquiringly at John. " All troubles past, please God."

" I think so," John said, shaking him by the hand. " I'm loosed out of my madhouse in any case."

" Oh, fie to that, Master John. That's an ugly word. 'Twas no madhouse but a doctor's care for you."

" Well, it's all much of a muchness so far as I can see. People think the same of you after one as the other."

" Well, that's true too," Nick admitted—not very comfortingly perhaps, but not as if it were any great matter either. A small thing but not to be quite ignored. " And what is it all," he said, " in the course of time ? The water in that river below," said Nick, " isn't as quick to change and forget as are the people's minds. And you were always beyond thinking, Master John, of what one would say or what another would say."

They were walking nearer to the sea now and the evening light was the same now over the land and over the sea, not as in the daytime when the

difference would be strangely marked. Now there
was a level flow of light. Quiet pigeon-like colours
were steeped in the sea and the turning birds were
as white as old lime wash. The noise of the waves
too was a quiet pigeon-breasted noise, and the
turning of the river water sweet and deep, and
without any vulgar brawling. The roughest streams
were quiet and the few dark flats delayed themselves
under the stoop of fuchsias that grew in the banks
as willows do, delayed and flowed on, carrying red
flowers to the sea.

The flying winds and the quiet sky, the bird-
breasted sea and the dark river—John had never
needed to add praise to his acceptance of their being.
He did not consciously enjoy them. He was too
much theirs. He had known the river too long in
all her hours. Since he was a little boy struggling, as
Markie struggled now, with a nasty butt of a rod
on days evilly disposed towards young fishers when
his ambition almost despaired and his soul felt faint
within him, the river had left the mark of those
days upon him. He could remember crying as he
fished those sullen waters that would yield him up
no prey. He could remember that far better than
he could recall the madness and the glory of the
death of his first trout. How he had prayed that
day—to all his nurserymaid's gods—to Jesus, to
Mary and to Joseph. And to his own more aristo-
cratic god, that rather dreary Our Father ch'art in
Heaven. No one was there to help or witness when,
unable longer to withstand the temptation of seeing

his fish, his own fish, captured from the waters, dead upon the bank at his feet, he had lifted his rod and whirled that trout from the river to the grass behind him in one savage unorthodox second of absolute determination—those days and other days and nights, all partaking now of the same lost quality. No, John thought, the river hasn't changed, not towards me. She was never very kind. She is not less unkind now. He felt the same as he had felt about Nick. One need not be defensive, they did not pity or understand or mind very much.

During that quiet and not particularly hopeful evening Nick sometimes sat on the bank afar off meddling with casts and flies or smoking a cigarette by himself and sometimes on the bank beside John gossiping idly of this or that—of salmon, or snipe or the price of a greyhound, or he would fish a cast or two now and then. He was there. He was as impersonal as the night itself. John loved his being there. Such company was very pleasant, as familiar and yet as changing as the streams he knew so infinitely well, and the deep pools and the flats, and the rocks and the black, owl-shaped curls of water in this little river. He knew the fishing of each yard of this water and Nick, who knew it as well, liked to see him take every advantage of the secrets they shared together. It was a common thing between them.

They stood together chatting and talking after John had given up fishing. It was as good as dark now and the river was black and the sea pallid and

tender and the air was tender too. All wind had
dropped. The air was as quiet as the inside of a
cup. It struck John surprisingly how cosy it was to
be here talking to Nick, his evening's fishing over
and himself a little tired. It was lovely in some ways
to be home again. " Yes, we'll go out with the lobster
pots on Wednesday. Shall we take Master Markie?
Ah, yes, Nick. He'd like that."

" Each day he said to me : ' Master John'll be
home on Monday, Nick.' He was out of his mind
to see you. ' God blast it, Nick,' he says. ' Will it
ever be Monday?' . . . He's fishing away here
always. We should get him a better rod. The poor
child is persecuted with that owld yoke he has."

" If I gave you the joints of my old Castle Connel,
Nick, you could contrive a little light one for him ? "

" I might be able. If I'd knewsed where to put
my hand on that I'd have captured it."

" Are you going back to your house now ? "

" I am. My old bitch is sick. I must go give her
a bit of company."

" So's Miss Sheena's bitch. I'd like to walk up
to your house with you, Nick, and have a talk."

" Ah, do."

" I suppose I'd better get back. They'll expect
me above."

" Well, maybe so. Good-night, Master John."

And John had walked home through the dark,
alone and quite happy. And then he had turned
bad like that in the drawing-room, and spent a
fierce unavailing ten minutes in Olivia's room,

fiddling about at her dressing-table, and asking to
be shown her new evening gowns, and being
sophisticated and brotherly, and admiring all to
keep her away from himself. Suddenly saying :
" Good-night, darling. It's lovely to be back. It's
lovely to see you looking so lovely." And flying out
of her room before she could forget Olivia and begin
to be emotional about John, ruining and destroying
him for hours.

It was not till he was in bed that he thought of
Eliza and her cool destructive voice and her sweetness. Something about her was like Nick. She did
not even accept things. She asked questions about
them which made them seem so past—like an
operation one has done with. She was his friend
not his relation, smirched over with that terrible
fog of familiarity. She was clear to him and rather
exciting and like an interesting map of a place not
known. She was quite important enough for him
to want to get out of bed and fold up his jersey and
put it on her pillow. On her pillow because then,
perhaps, she would see and claim it before a devastatingly intelligent housemaid recognised and
took it back to his room in the morning. She would
like it no doubt. He went to bed almost comforted
back to the frame of mind he had known with
Nick on the river. Quite soon he slept. He was not
feigning sleep when Olivia (before she smeared on
her mud-mask) tiptoed in to see him.

IX

AT one o'clock everybody in the house except Miss
Parker and Sheena was sound asleep. Sheena was
awake, lying in a divine romantic lull, her loving
thoughts more with herself than with Rupert, but
her thoughts of him through all thought. Sheena
was almost entirely happy. Through her and over
her she was conscious of a state of happiness.
Sheena was young enough and without experience,
she could reach a stage in love like this and rest
there like a travelling salmon in a pool. She was for
the moment complete and as completely happy as
she would be until she slept with Rupert, when this
unfevered sweetness of life would be with her again.
Sometimes, as when she had kissed him good-night
this evening on the side of the mountains, an ardour
she could not measure was in her for him. But she
was a virgin creature in her mind and when these
moments with him were past they did not trouble
her remembrances or her thoughts at all. They did
not leave her unsatisfied or disturbed. They were
past. She was happy. She would know them again,
and she was happy. No one could live in the
present moment as Sheena could. Nobody could
be so realistic, for she was alive to the moment with
an unconscious integrity. She possessed much

spiritual industry. Her mind was not lying in a
dead water of past hours or future hours, what she
had done or would do. It was there with her all the
time, and she had a quick and ready use of it.
Although seldom surprisingly brilliant Sheena was
never a bore, and she was kind (although not to
Olivia), but to others she could be very kind unless
she chose, and then she could be very naughty.
Very naughty indeed.

Julian had never forgotten the first time she had
made him quite aware of her grown-up mind. It
was at a terrible luncheon party which Olivia had
forced her daughter to attend, to which Sheena had
gone fuming, with a ladder in her stocking and a
lovely drooping hat on her head. She had sat
beside a smooth, young-old man at luncheon whose
conversational efforts she found very tiresome.
Olivia was sitting opposite to her young daughter
and observed her eating with enormous rather
slothful greed and paying so little attention to the
remarks of her neighbour that Olivia longed to kick
her into good manners. This was no way for a young
girl to go on. No way at all. And Raymond, who
was really trying for once—and with a stupid child
like this—would soon weary of his efforts and in no
time at all would put it about that Olivia's unfortunate débutante daughter was as stupid as her
mother. For Olivia was well aware he did not like
her. Luncheon progressed, as Sunday luncheons
eventually do (although there never seems any real
reason why their vast and glorious boredom should

ever lift), and still Sheena continued to enjoy her
food, but to show little interest in anything else.
And still Raymond, determined now not to own
defeat of his indefeatable charm to this beautiful
young bore, tried to find a chord to strike to which
some sure response was due. Ultimately a stray
note from the far end of the table made its faint echo
in his brain. Had he not been told that Sheena was
a skilled and exquisite fisher? He had indeed. It
was her thing. And now success perhaps at last was
his. He was quite fond of talking about fishing
although he was a poor fisher himself.

"Do you fish?" he asked her reverently.

Sheena helped herself to an unfair amount of
asparagus before she answered slowly—a slurred
voice from her half-consciousness.

"I don't know," she said.

Julian heard as well as Olivia. He was perfectly
delighted. Never had he seen such a rout of the
gay, dreary Raymond. It was superb. It was
magnificent. And unanswerable. But Sheena had
not required an answer. She was attending to her
asparagus in that typical dedication of the moment,
to the moment which people like Raymond had
never known—would never know about.

Olivia had been both shocked and abashed and
complained to Julian a great deal and only just
saved herself from apologising to Raymond. Julian
at the risk of not being understood had explained
to her at length what he thought about it all and
left Olivia with a respect for her daughter that she

had not known about before. In fact, now that she came to think of it (now that it had been put word by word into her brain), she allowed that she gave Sheena full marks. " Raymond's always been spiteful about me. And how he's ageing—making these stupendous efforts about young girls. . . ." That was to show how affected and tiresome Sheena could well be on occasions. And powerfully affected too, for she was really an enthusiastic young girl and adored success. It was quite true she was a lovely fisher, like all the Birds, and did not a bit mind boring people with tales of some of the salmon she had caught. But she went enough within herself to refrain from making successes with people like Raymond. She had no feelings towards them and she had needed to exasperate Olivia. How little did she know that Julian had heard and sniggered and turned this to her account after all. One does not expect answers like this of life when one is so young.

X

Nor, when one is Miss Parker's age, does one expect great results from any depilatory. However largely advertised. However highly paid for. Used with whatever trembling of the soul and carefulness. Still one does not hope too much. One does not dare.

But at least one cannot foresee an hour earlier, an hour in time, that one will be lying in bed with tears pouring down a blistered and still bearded face. To have foreseen this—ah, to be as one was just an hour ago.

As twelve midnight struck Miss Parker had climbed out of bed, full of busy optimism. She had turned on her light and read the directions round a small sordid little black bottle for the tenth time since it had arrived in its plain cover this morning. Very well. It was all too simple. One did this and one did that, and the results were such and such. She took one glance at the portrait of a hirsute lady at the top corner of the leaflet and another at the pale nymph at the bottom corner. Yes, it was all too simple.

Trembling a little, although she affected an immense calm to herself, Miss Parker applied to her upper lip and chin this potion distilled from limbecks foul as hell within. Goodness, how it smelt!

Not that she minded this in the greater issue at stake, but there was that horrid Dora who might come in and sniff disparagingly in the morning. Well, if Miss Parker had a beard, Dora had spots. And in the morning Miss Parker's beard would be gone and Dora's spots would remain. Miss Parker gave a little skip in her nightgown—for she was a girlish creature in some ways. A faint air came in through the window blowing chill through Miss Parker's nightgown. But she scarcely felt it. So absorbed was she in what she was doing.

Presently her upper lip began to stiffen and her chin began to stiffen too. So the potion worked. Miss Parker glanced again at the part of the directions that applied to time, longing already for the moment when " with a swab of cotton wool or a soft sponge " she would gently wipe away " Totex " and with it that embarrassing growth of hair.

Now her chin grew uncomfortably stiff. Now it smarted almost unbearably. She scarcely felt this, and if she did, looked on the symptoms as further satisfactory evidence. It burned now, but did she care ? No. She exulted. And the wind from the sea blew through her white nightgown bellying it about her and she was unconscious of cold. Only a fevered trembling of expectation was in her, almost a certainty now as she glanced at her watch, and the burning became almost unbearable, like scalding leeches, could such things be.

Miss Parker was a very conscientious girl. She waited for the last possible moment directed for the strongest possible growth of hair (a growth only conceivable to some early Italian master with a most florid conception of the Crucifixion) to disappear. She waited for this minute to tick past before she seized her swab of cotton wool and swabbed with gentle vigour at her agonising face.

She would not look. She washed and washed, deferring the glorious moment, deferring this climax in a sort of fierce ecstasy of expectation. After so much pain something simply must have happened.

And then the most dreadful thing happened. Miss Parker looked in the glass—a moment of rapturous acceptance before her, before she became sternly practical with cold cream. She looked in the glass standing there in the draught in her nightgown and shaking with excitement. And as she looked tears filled her eyes, terrible, angry despairing tears that seemed to be distilled out of her very bones (for she was a sensible little thing and cried but seldom), and these tears flowed down her face, flowed and fell upon her still bearded face, and on her breast, and on her hands that clutched the edge of the dressing-table as she leaned towards her glass looking at this sad and shocking she. Not only was the beard still there in all its hated profusion, but now it sprouted from a malignant and poisoned-looking face.

All this was too much. Too much. Miss Parker sobbed on. The hour was late and she was tired. Emotionally it had been an exhausting crisis. She was cold now, cold as a stone and her heart cold as a stone within her, and her hands trembling with

cold. Angry and frightened, she shut her window
against the little sea wind and gathered herself up
to deal with her distorted face and with the sickening
deadly smells that Dora was not to sniff at in the
morning. So disheartened was she that for a
moment she debated with herself whether she would
or would not fulfil this last plan of hers. But old
habit—that slight nervousness of other people's
servants of which she could never cure herself—
prevailed. She went tiptoeing down the passage
with her basin between her hands.

At last she was back in her bed. Poor Miss Parker,
all her tears were shed. She lay very straight and
cold in her narrow bed. Miss Parker should have
known about despair by now. But although she had
known nights almost like this before, she never
seemed able to realise that her beard positively
throve on depilatories. And to-morrow she would
have to face Dora and the world with spots as well.
"Could I say I am ill?" Miss Parker wondered
desperately. "No, I suppose not." She lay quiet
in the darkness touching her face now and then
with hatred and pity.

XI

Sheena brought John with her to see Rupert the next day.

Rupert, when he was home on leave as he was now, lived with his uncle and aunt at a place called Owenstown, about thirty-five miles from Silverue. The mountains and an arm of the sea lay between Sheena and her love Rupert, and a long thirty-five miles it often seemed to her, speeding along to her love in the plains. The mountain road was the most beautiful besides being the shortest, but it was not a road designed for a loving young girl in a hurry. John told Sheena this several times as they drove along.

"Ah, you don't know how awful it is for me," Sheena said. "How you do fuss and go on. Now if you were me, jumping out of your body to see Rupert—as I am."

John said no more about her bad driving after that. For she had shown him good enough cause to swallow his nerves and his tremors, he considered. What would it be like to feel again as Sheena did—alive in one person? Not truly alive away from that person. John had loved often, though not seriously, but he had always managed to persuade himself of height and depth and disaster in the least of his amatory adventures. He was not persuaded either, but convinced. For self-persuasion would imply an understanding of himself which John had never had. But he understood well enough the reality in Sheena, and because he was so fond of her he was glad. He knew that Rupert could be trusted to accept without betrayal a creature as real and as lovely as Sheena. If she had not been so lovely her earnestness could have endangered her happiness more easily and more deeply. John did not truly perceive all this and hold it word by word in his mind but he was aware of it through his knowing of Sheena. Sheena who shut her eyes and her teeth and jumped off the tops of garden walls when she was a child. Sheena who would lie for hours in an agony of stillness watching birds or little foxes playing, impervious to cold or any discomfort, untouched in her faithfulness to the present. And she was so brave and persistent. If she did a thing badly she did not seem to identify herself with its present ill-doing, but with the vision of the thing done well. She was full of brave endeavouring. For the protection of this state she affected moods of aimlessness in which too, she was happy. And never brisk. Dear creature. Dear Sheena.

There was a tennis party at Owenstown to-day, one of the first of the year. Rupert's two sisters had given this party—not that they were fond of tennis— but they did not mind how badly they played and enjoyed parties of any sort. This was the time of year for tennis parties. Had there been a season of the year for skipping parties, or parties for bowling hoops, they would have given one of these too, at the right time and skipped and bowled with the best.

Rupert's eldest sister Silene looked like an enormous, a vast, an overwhelming angel. She was tall and enormously fat and gloriously fair with viper-curling yellow hair and a wonderful skin (although this was not quite what it had been what with her troubled life and constantly drinking gin). She did not like her husband very much, and spent most of her time staying about with her friends and relations who all loved her although she was a crashing bore when she was drunk.

Rupert's other sister, Kirsty, was not a bit like Silene. She was unmarried still and a little sad about this, but really felt it most at awful moments when the wheels of her motor car punctured and she could not work the jack. Then—oh, then, for a strong and faithful man who drove with one wherever one went (or even for a little weak man who came sometimes and understood about jacks). But, leaving the marriage question out of it, Kirsty was a lovely girl and it was hard to understand why, if she wanted one, she had not got a man. There are so many girls of this sort that it is difficult to account for them. And Kirsty was a charmer too, with a ready tongue and a tiny little sweet face and long legs, and an enormous bosom and an enormous voice in the back of her throat. She was very fond of Silene but enjoyed nothing more than telling good, but disparaging stories about her. She was a little given to the production of amateur theatricals. We all have our faults and perhaps this was her worst.

They both adored Rupert and thought there was nowhere such an enthralling young man. They looked on all girls that he favoured with kindly but searching criticism. They were big-hearted girls and wanted the very best for their romantic brother.

Why was Rupert romantic? Partly because he looked romantic, which really means nothing at all. Partly because he did dangerous and skilful things well. But neither of these given things imply romance. Romance is a quality some people have the power of keeping within themselves. A power to be alone and secret. Rupert had this and with it he had a great simplicity of spirit. His jokes were simple and his primary outlook on life was a Keep It Clean Young British Soldier Woman and Children First outlook that some people might find offensively wholesome and other people might find of lovely importance, promising great comfort and peace.

"How are you, Sheena? And John, my dear, how nice to see you." Rupert's, Silene's and Kirsty's aunt came out of her water-garden, paddling along like a penguin. "You're almost the first arrivals," she said. "Rupert and the girls are playing a set with Mr. Borrows. The poor little man likes to get his eye in before people come—the parish doesn't give him much time for tennis, does it?"

"No, does it," Sheena agreed harmlessly.

"How is the water-garden, Aunt Louisa?" John said. She was no relation whatever, but they always

called her that. " Any more nice new bits and pieces
since I've been away ? "

Aunt Louisa, the she-penguin, shot him a suspicious
look and cleared her throat repressively. Surely he
was not going to start about that—that sinister
" Being away."

Just for a second John forgot to feel amused and
a terrible desire took him to flee from this party
and from all these people who could neither understand nor accept anything. Just for an instant he
was aware of exactly how Aunt Louisa felt. But she's
sane and I'm mad—this was his sad protest. Because
I've been a tiny bit mad, just enough mad to make
me know sanity from madness, I am forever put in a
mental servitude to penguins with fat stomachs and
no brains. Then, mercifully, a sense of her absurdity
closed upon him again.

" Any good bits and pieces ? " he repeated easily.

" Well, I've just got some new bronze pots which
are rather fun." Aunt Louisa did adore talking
about her water-garden, even to chaps like John
who we all knew had been a bit unsteady (poor
darling), and so awful for Olivia (poor darling too).
" Come and see them."

They stepped down flights of granite steps with
two granite balls at the top and the bottom of every
meanest flight, into the dreadful complexity of Aunt
Louisa's water-garden. This garden was designed
with all the ingenuity of a formless mind. There
was something almost invigorating in its awful
failure to please. The whole thing was really the

most stupendous failure. There was nothing about
it that anybody could possibly commend. Even
Aunt Louisa wondered about it a little at times, but
she would still any query in her mind by buying
another pot of bronze or stone or alabaster and
disposing it in some fresh nook. Or she would buy
another couple of Cyprus and pop them in somewhere. And there was always room for a new
nymph, cherub, or bird-bath, and the establishment
of these would reinstate both her interest and her
confidence in her garden and herself. After all, grey
stone and Nepita, water and pink water lilies—
what could be more pretty and attractive? And it
was marvellous how well palms did here in the mild
winters. Yes, palms were here too, in all their want
of propriety to any Irish garden. Everything that
should not be was here. Balustradings in profusion
entwined by pink rambler roses, impatiently waiting
to burst into flower. Terra-cotta pots full of
geraniums and lobelia flanking bronze Buddhas and
stone bridges. No country was omitted in this rich
horticultural mixture. Japan, Thibet, China, Venice,
Greece, not a country or town that had not yielded
its dash of inspiration to some mood of Aunt Louisa's
vigorous mind.

In these days when so many people have such
successions of good ideas about gardens and put
them into execution with such practical efficiency,
it comes as a kind of inverted pleasure to see a
really good gross unbelievable muddle like this.
Sheena and Rupert were not in any way precise in

their gardening notions, but at the same time Aunt
Louisa's W.G. (as they called it) gave them a
sensation of horror they much enjoyed and took
great credit to themselves for experiencing. . . .
"Would anybody like to see the water-garden?
It's looking *rather* lovely . . ." On this invitation
they were usually among the first to spring to their
feet.

During John's absence Sheena had kept him well
posted with details of any particularly nice improve-
ment in the W.G., so he was now able to inquire
backwards into a year's progress in an intimate way
which delighted Aunt Louisa. Soon they were all
embarked on a calm ocean of mutual pleasure.

Sheena was glad that John should enjoy himself so
much, but she found herself in a state of exasperated
patience. It was very trying for a girl to be now
so near her love and yet to see him not, nor hear him
speak. The minutes seemed chained to the minutes
by Aunt Louisa's earnest pleasure and John's
rapturous pauses at many admired points. Sheena
went trailing along with them, knocking her feet
together like a really bored, tired child. Her face
was as a stone, without aim or expression, while
she knew her one immediate desire was to see
Rupert. And she was half-afraid to leave these ones
and go alone to see Rupert because she knew the
girls would come at her, saying this and that,
thinking this and that.

"Darling Sheena——"

"No, we're only knocking up. You must play."

("Not one moment could she wait.")

("Really, these quite young girls. No reticence. Isn't it terrifying.")

Sheena grew cowardly as well as impatient. To tell the truth, she was afraid of her more experienced contemporaries and often without words for them at all, which she minded about most unnecessarily.

Soon more guests arrived to swell the party and Sheena and John were lost among them, speaking to this one and that one without much reason or meaning, as they walked back along the twisting, paved paths, and up and down the flights of steps leading from the W.G. to the house and the tennis courts. Sheena was walking with a determined old grandmother who still enjoyed a nice game of lawn tennis and had in her day been one of the brightest tennis stars in the country. Although these days were long past now, for she really was an old lady, yet she stepped boldly on to every tennis court in the country and could still—as she put it—hold her own. She was the terror of all the more timid young girls who had the misfortune to partner her in a ladies' four, for she really could set about them and abuse them with great severity for their inactivity and awkwardness. She had indeed been known to reduce an earnest and unskilled young player to tears.

" Run ! " she would cry as a nasty little ball came tipping back just over the net. " You should start sooner," she would say, as her partner came slinking back to her place with another point lost. She had a devastating " I know you can't help being a fool and spoiling my fun, but at least you might try " way of sending up two more balls at the conclusion of a double fault, perfected in years of play in tournaments long past, but never forgotten by Mrs. Critchley. Sheena did not mind her a bit, but then Sheena played tennis quite well enough to escape the worst of Mrs. Critchley's odious superiority. The person who really hated her was Silene, for she was the only person who had ever succeeded in making Silene feel that playing tennis badly mattered. That she was of lesser, meaner clay and did not count much because of this want in her. Silene would not play with or against Mrs. Critchley, and hated even watching her on the court. There was something about the adequacy of her steady, hideous and almost undefeatable smiting of every ball that came near her which infuriated Silene.

Well, Sheena walked back with Mrs. Critchley, who had a long story to unfold about her eldest grandchild and the pony club, and somewhere in the middle of the story she met Rupert, who came walking straight towards her and stood by her side contented. And Sheena was contented too. Her day was made now. She had seen him. That would do for the present. They stood together in the patchy shadow by the seats, where rugs and jerseys and boxes of white tennis balls lay brightly, for a very little while. Then the girls came, Silene and Kirsty, making up sets. People kept saying : But I'm terribly bad. Well, you know the form. I haven't played tennis for five years. This is the first time I've played tennis this year. My shoes are too small. I can't extend myself. May I borrow this racquet? Thank you so much. Are you sure you don't mind? What a perfectly bloody racquet. Oh, it's a *lovely* racquet. I like a light racquet. Thank you so much—— Well, shall we begin? Which side do you like? . . . They had gone farther away now. Aunt Louisa said: "*Would* anybody care to see the water-garden? It's looking *rather* lovely."

The occupants of the benches and the deck-chairs rose reluctantly to their feet.

Ownestown—quite apart from its water-garden—was the most charming old house imaginable. It had Dignity and Peace and Beauty like the speech in *Cavalcade*, and like only a very few Irish houses It had been built early in the reign of Anne, and only added to in the more dignified of the succeeding periods of architecture. Luckily it had survived successive sad times of fire and terror. Perhaps through this survival it had been endowed with some of the qualities seen in marriages that have stood through terrifying difficulty for some cause that counted, and in their endurance have achieved a state which mattered, meant a great deal, and was in a strange way more exciting in its truth and tried steadfastness than any romantic yielding to Fate or Love can be.

Owenstown was built away from the mountains

where Sheena and John lived, and a fox-hunting country lay round it—a very delightful country where Rupert and his sisters loved to pursue the chase as their predecessors had done before them. And as their fathers had been so were they : ardent supporters of fox-hunting. Generous subscribers. Brave and knowing riders to hounds. Sometimes more brave than knowing. Sometimes more knowing than brave. There were belts of woodland near the house, strong and well-preserved covert for foxes, and the house looked through them down a length of vale where good sound grass land and banks nicely tempered to the ardour of the brave or the fears of the shaken had convinced many a young man and many an old one that there was no sport like fox-hunting. And no colour like red, some one was bound to add, although that should have gone first.

The only people already mentioned by name as attending this party are Mrs. Critchley, Sheena, John, and Mr. Burrows besides their hosts, Aunt Louisa, Rupert, Silene and Kirsty. But besides them again there was an argumentative young man called Geoffrey Cruise who was a Master of Fox-hounds. He was very popular for, besides being a fair sort of huntsman and as brave as a lion, he was a bachelor and could yodel like an angel or the finest Alpine man imaginable. All the girls simply adored him, but he was careful about preserving his single state and only had affairs with people of Silene's age and disposition. He was too kind-hearted to madden young girls and do no more about them, and he could not possibly afford both a wife and a pack of hounds.

Then there was Uncle Jack, Aunt Louisa's husband, who was very tall and weighed round about sixteen stone. For his weight he had been an extraordinarily brilliant man to hounds in his day. All his contemporaries said so still. He was a great racing enthusiast too, and knowledgeable about food and wine and many other forms of pleasure. He was greedy in an intelligent way and much regretted how in age appetite dies. Besides, he had a really good brain and was a good judge of many things besides racing.

An earnest and respectable young man called Archie and his gay wife, Jane, completed the party. Archie had once been very gay too, but since his marriage with Jane he had taken life seriously by the throat and choked all the fun out of it. One settled down. One had done with rude talk and gross jokes. Other things mattered. Very soon Jane would leave him and that would matter too. His life would be broken up then.

Later in the afternoon people came wandering into the house for tea, avoiding the people they didn't want, for even in a party as small as this one there were cliques and factions who must drink their thin Chinese tea and eat their tomato sandwiches and chocolate cake apart if possible. Cruise and Silene together. Archie and Kirsty. Jane saying the most impossible things to the enthralled Mr. Burrows. John and Rupert and Sheena and Mrs.

Critchley together. John who had been playing tennis badly as Mrs. Critchley's partner felt almost as furiously despairing as one of her young girls. He kept on failing to feel as amused as he should have felt about himself and other people. It was all :

" You remember that really fast hunt from Crop-thorne Beg ? I rode him that day and he carried me great. . . . Oh, of course not, no, of course not. You were abroad then."

(No, I wasn't. I was in a madhouse. But one must not say that. Very embarrassing for people.) It was a case of saying : Oh, yes, and oh, no, a good deal. How exhausting and boring to oneself was this awful brightness and eagerness. And people persevered so. And so kindly. They were deter-mined to ignore anything difficult and their deter-mination was only equalled by their stupidity, for apparently they could not think of any subject fit to talk about that had not its roots in that fatal blank period when John was " away " or " abroad," or " in foreign parts." There was a hideous fascina-tion in the way they entangled and disentangled themselves, but it all left John feeling as tired as a dog and aching vaguely with his own gay replies.

At last something happened which welded each person in the room into a part of one protesting whole. Kirsty began to talk about a play she wanted to produce at a concert that was to be held for the local benefit of fox-hunting. For her play she must have actors.

" You'll act, Jane."

" I'd do anything in reason for you, Kirsty, but, you know, act I can't."

" Of course you can. It's only a tiny part. You've only got three words to say. Or you can be the servant girl."

" Oh, really? Thanks so much. What a nice part. But I'm afraid I'll be away."

" Make it a pantry boy and let Cruise take the part."

" Oh, no. We can't waste Cruise in a dreary part like that."

" Kirsty, you're a terrible woman, and how I love you, but I'm not going to get up and make a feck of myself on any stage, even for you."

" But Cruise could do a yodelling turn behind the curtain."

" Yes, I'd do that. I wouldn't mind."

" But is there any Alpine fun in your play, Kirsty? "

" Couldn't the pantry boy yodel? He could yodel to excite the butler. Why not? "

" But there isn't really even a pantry boy. We just thought of him."

" What *is* your play, Kirsty? " Archie was inclined towards earnest helpfulness.

" It's a marvellous piece. A girl I know wrote it and lots of big people have been simply staggered by it."

" Darling, don't be so grand and stage. How many people are there in it? "

" Thirteen."

" Thirteen ? It's preposterous. You'd never get so many people together at once, would you ? "

" I'll produce for you."

" Yes, Cruise can produce."

" No, Cruise. You be quiet."

" Why must I be quiet ? We're going great. Somebody must produce. You can't run a stable without a head man."

" Why should you produce ? "

" I knew a grand girl once who acted quite a lot."

" Is this a funny play, or sad, or what sort of play ? Is it vulgar ? "

" Oh, it's sad as hell."

" But that's no good, Kirsty. No one is going to pay money to see a show like that. You must find another, Sweetness. That's a bloody awful idea. You haven't got a chance, Sweetness. I'm just telling you first."

" Oh, please don't be tiresome and difficult, Cruise, even if you did once rattle with an actress. It's absurd. You don't know. And I've copied out every word of every part for everybody. It nearly killed me. It must go now or I shall cry my eyes out. My dear, the fatigue ! "

Archie was struck by the horror of all this. He felt they were all being unduly and childishly frivolous. Besides, he didn't mind acting. Getting up on a stage and making a bloody fool of yourself, he called it. All the same, he liked doing it. And fancy poor Kirsty writing away like that. This was all for the good of fox-hunting too. It must have due support.

" We must all lie up, chaps. It's mean not to after Kirsty copying out every word of the thing."

" You've often written a letter and torn it up again, haven't you ? "

" Yes, Cruise, old boy, but one must be fair to Kirsty."

" Oh, this fairness to Kirsty. Just because Kirsty chooses to be a bloody obstinate pig and jump over a cliff we all have to follow her like a lot of Gadarene swine. She's bitten off more than she can chew, that's the length of it."

" Why not have a Miracle Play with the swine going over the edge ? " But no one paid the smallest attention to Mr. Burrows's suggestion. Soon Kirsty had produced pieces of paper closely covered in her tidy handwriting and pinned together by safety pins. People read bits to themselves and bits to each other, making rude jokes and sniggering.

Archie said at last, defiantly : " It's a marvellous play."

Silene said : " Yes, and if one single person puts a word in wrong the whole show is—is messed up so far as I can see. And, anyhow, they're all amateurs—they'll all dry up."

" Why not cut it out and have a boxing turn ? "

" The gentility of the town wouldn't like that."

" Have a cycling turn."

" I might as well get up on the stage and hiccup."

" The cast is preposterous. You can't have

thirteen people on the stage. They'll never turn up."

"Look at Jane there. Off like hell because she doesn't like her part, and we're left without the servant girl."

"That's a pretty rotten thing to say about me. As if I minded what sort of lousy part I had."

"I know, pet. You're a lovely girl. Come to Cruise. I don't know why you live with your husband. You and I won't act. They're all lousy. You're quite right."

Archie said, with studied temperance : "Well, my suggestion is — cut down the cast. Thirteen people aren't necessary."

Cruise said, suddenly determined to madden Archie : "Thirteen is the whole point of the play."

"You've missed the point of the whole thing utterly, old man, if you think that. Thirteen's got nothing whatever to say to it."

"Well, if you think you're capable of being Somerset Maugham and Barrie, and cutting the bloody thing in half, I don't. How can it be a success ? Cut yourself in half and see how much success you'll have."

"All I mean is we must lie up with Kirsty."

"You can't lie up with a sinking ship. The thing's impossible."

Some one said : "How are we going to make up thirteen people ? We have to make up the nigger troupe and produce them, haven't we ? "

Some one else said : "That's a table in this play.

What about that? Half the people will have their
backs to the audience."

Archie had taken the play on his shoulders now.
It was no longer Kirsty's. " Oh, we'll get over that.
We'll manage it somehow."

" Yes, you go out there and dig deep enough,
Archie. You'll find something."

" That's not at all the point. Don't be so stupid,
old man. It's not funny."

" All right then. Go into the village and buy
shovels and hire men to dig. That's the case
exactly."

" Don't torment Archie, Cruise. Archie is a kind
white man."

Archie grew quiet and dignified. He did not like
Silene joining with Cruise against him. It was not
fair. None of them could give anything a chance.
Not anything that mattered. And Kirsty had not
seemed at all grateful for his support and assistance.
She seemed to have lost interest in the matter now.
Archie never could understand why, as soon as a
project was eagerly sponsored by himself, it went
bad on everybody, and even opposition and per-
secution could hardly envenom it again. One
expected Cruise to be irresponsible and contrary
about a thing like this principally because it gave him
a chance to argue ; but other people, who didn't
like arguing and rather enjoyed acting, why
shouldn't they show enthusiasm and lie up with
Kirsty? No guts. No loyalty. No initiative. They
were all rotten. They went wandering off to the

tennis courts again, and Kirsty gathered up her scattered play and gave it all to Cruise, saying : " Read it, darling, and say if it really is hopeless. Do you mind doing this ? " Again Archie felt enraged and hopeless. Cruise took the play quite seriously and put it in his car, saying : " Yes. I'll tell you what I think. It might do."

Rupert and Sheena escaped with some difficulty from the tennis. Silene and Kirsty had shown throughout the afternoon the most perverse ingenuity in putting them in different sets and in having one or other of them constantly on the court. They wanted to temporise over all this. They had a reason. Last night there had been a discussion in Silene's room. John had figured largely in the discussion. John and Sheena and Rupert, and a great-grand-father of Rupert's who everybody said had been brilliant to eccentricity and had died of a fever (an unnamed fever), while making the Grand Tour in foreign parts. But Silene and Kirsty knew that he had jumped into the Rhine in his nightshirt, as mad as a hatter, and his swollen corpse had been fished out by William Brown, his faithful valet, and Tom O'Brien, the coachman who drove the carriage and thought very little of the hired post-horses ; and very little of Europe compared to Ireland ; and very little of people with as much money as his master for jumping into the Rhine. He was a man who lessened everything he thought of, but he was capable of keeping his mouth shut and so was William Brown. Their descendants lived on very comfortable good farms—the proceeds of faithfulness and discretion in their great-grandparents.

Silene and Kirsty knew all about this, but it had never troubled them till now. Rupert knew about it too, but it had not troubled him yet. He would not have allowed it to trouble him in any case. Nor would his loving sisters. But they were going to trouble Sheena about it one of these days. She was a sensible child and they would put it to her quite plainly that what with poor John so sadly unsteady and Rupert's grandfather jumping into the Rhine, Rupert's and Sheena's children might throw back to something most awkward. One had to face these things. One could not be unconscious and sentimental over them.

Kirsty and Silene did not really mind facing them. They were like Archie about the acting. They thought something ought to be done and they did not mind doing it. They felt that they were the people to put things right. Of course Sheena was a dear child. They were very fond of Sheena. But she was only a child and of no great charm or importance. Just a lovely little silly. And she would recover from this in a short time and marry somebody else with a good strong common pedigree and all would be well for her in the end. Silene (who had resorted to extreme measures in her day to avoid the procreation of children) and Kirsty (who had only distantly contemplated the same measures) were full of thoughtful care for the future generation. They sat there in their pink satin nightgowns with

brown lace on their enormous bosoms and they felt
this to be right. Silene, who always managed to
hold nightly conversations when she was in her own
bed, lifted up a temperate hot-water bottle and
placed it comfortingly upon her stomach.

" How far do you think they've gone, really?
Sheena and Rupert ? "

" Oh, nothing. Just a very little love and lots of
talk about their dogs."

" Yes, I do think that too. Nothing, really."

" Oh, nothing, really."

This was when Sheena and Rupert were in the
mountains looking and calling wildly for Mr.
Cooney. And it shows how right Kirsty was. Now
they had escaped these sisters and were walking
together up to the castle field to look at Rupert's
new horse.

" Is this a racing horse or a saddle horse we're
going to see ? "

" Darling, it's a grand hunting horse. How do
you think I can afford to keep more than two horses
in training ? Of course it's a saddle horse."

" Of course. I'm so silly."

The castle field had no castle near it, but a big
moat where kings were buried, and below the moat
a gorse covert where a famous breed of foxes
habited and reared their children now in great
peace and comfort, and heaps of leisure to teach
them to be straight-necked and to smell strong like
all their uncles and aunts, and to enjoy their gallant
deaths when the proper time came.

From the moat, which Sheena and Rupert were crossing on their way to Rupert's horse, you could in the winter months see a hunt with great ease, safety and enjoyment. They stopped there now, looking down at the covert and out across the country recalling many pleasant days and their excessive perils. They looked down the valley and back towards Sheena's mountains and then again at one another. There were ash trees growing in the moat. Young ash. The green of their leaves was in Sheena's eyes, and the black of their keys and all the gentleness of the evening was in her eyes. She looked so tender this evening and so much older than nineteen. If it had not been for these things and because he was quite aware of something that crossed and thwarted him in Silene's and Kirsty's conduct of their tennis party to-day, Rupert might not have kissed her here, and again, and so he might not have laid up so much rapture and so much unhappiness for them both.

It was the evening and it was the feeling that they had escaped something together, something that they would have to go back to, that caused Rupert to kiss Sheena as he had not kissed her. And why had he not so kissed her? Time lost. Time gone. And she so gay and so eager about it.

"Oh, sweet Sheena—I'd do anything in the world for you, my dear sweet one."

"I know you would. I must kiss you. I must give you a tiny kiss of my own now. . . . Oh, the *time*, my darling, the time."

" The time ? Yes, isn't it awful and we haven't been away a minute and now it's seven o'clock, and you haven't seen this horse yet."

" I must see him and I must get back too. What shall I do ? "

" They're certain to be miles away, the horses, they always are. But I do want you to see him."

" Come on then, let's go and see him. After all," said Sheena with a sudden steadying sense of proportion, " what does it matter if we are a bit late ? "

" And I want you never to leave me."

" I never will. I'm lost without you."

" It's awful how much it matters, isn't it ? " Rupert sighed and kissed her thumb-nail and got up pulling her on to her feet. So love was over for the moment. Over but with them. It was strange, Sheena thought, how blandly one accepted a happiness from life such as one had not known could be. If one considered it, it was too much to realise. One nearly suffered in the thought of it. If one was alone perhaps it would seem more true. Now it was beyond her. And before this she thought she had loved. She knew she had loved. Poor Sheena. Poor silly. She had better laugh at herself now.

They found Rupert's horse at last. Of course he was in the farthest possible corner of the farthest possible field, but at length they found him with three others well known to Sheena. Two good hunters and a hoary villainous pony that Rupert had had when he was little. Idle, inquisitive, gross summer horses moving in the evening shelter of a hill, the sun on their fat ribs, grass ticks in their noses and blisters on their legs. How awful they looked. One's love embraced them for their winter's bravery. Rupert's new purchase Sheena liked very much. She praised him for this and that, and Rupert crabbed him here and there. But only that she might disagree and praise the more, for really he thought he had bought a very nice horse and was delighted with him and with himself.

They walked up the hill then and away from the horses for it was far more than time to go back and leave each other. On the side of the hill was a chestnut tree with the air dark and enclosed within its branches. Its low branches rubbed by horses and cattle, and the ground was very dry and rough below the tree's shelter. Here they kissed again, not so gaily, for there is a desperation about these little partings. Below them Rupert's horses moved in the light, and the burdened may trees were heavy as though snow weighed them down to within their own shadows. There was a deepness in everything and on Sheena's mountains fires burned slowly, and the gorse in the fox-covert below where they stood— the colour of the gorse was as heavy as its own scent.

" You must leave me ? "

" Yes. I must go."

" This is getting beyond me, you know."

" Yes. I know."

" Sweetness, you can't know."

" My God, I do know."

John and Silene and Kirsty and Cruise had played
their last rather dreary game of tennis before Rupert
and Sheena returned. They had searched petulantly
enough for lost balls and walked back through the
water-garden (and in this lovely evening even the
W.G. contrived to look sentimental, if not romantic)
to the house to drink a little gin before they parted.

John was quite aware of Kirsty's and Silene's
annoyance at the disappearance of Sheena and
Rupert. So they did not like this love between
Sheena and Rupert. It was very strange of them.
But he had known them long enough to realise that
they were unhappy, and it was not in their power to
see happiness in others without some idea to destroy.
This was not fair to them. Nor quite true. But John
felt it to be very true this evening. He feared for
Sheena a little but not much. She was beyond
them, he thought.

Another thing which struck him was how nice
Cruise was. Besides Eliza and Nick he was the only
person who had not pursued John with evasion. He
said to him : " You were with old Donald Leeson,
weren't you ? " That was the Doctor who had kept
John. " I was there once for nearly two months.
I had a fall riding a horse of Jack Norton's at
Towcester, and I was as mad as a hatter after it.
He put me right. I think he's a wonderful man.
Did you like him ? "

John had liked him very much. So they talked
about him for a while and about the " Permanent
Inmate," who thought he was Edward VII., and the

frightfulness of Miss Leeson with her portable wire-
less and other things that were very clear to John
and seemed so much lessened by speaking of them
to Cruise. Lessened but not past. For he had hated
to-day more than he allowed to himself even. He
had been frightened by himself, by his realisation
of the stupidity and horror of these kind people
whom he had before found sufficient. He was so
fatigued by his own gaiety and unreality that his
brain and his eyes felt quite stiff and he hated
himself with an exhausted disgust.

Sheena and Rupert came back at last. They were
unembarrassed and unapologetic, quite sure and
distant within themselves. The determined chill of
the girls' good-byes did not seem to matter at all.
Sheena was so much more powerful than they were
this evening. For the time being this world was
hers. She could have commanded anything and it
was hers because so much was hers.

" Good-bye, Silene. I enjoyed your party so
much."

" Good-bye. I'm so glad. Cruise, you're staying
to dinner, aren't you ? "

" Good-bye, Kirsty. Will you come and play
tennis on Thursday ? You know that awful garden
fête is on."

" I'm so sorry, Sheena. Rupert and I've promised
to play tennis at Ballyhackett on Thursday."

" Oh."

" I'm coming to the fête, Sheena. I promised
your mother I'd work some game for her."

"Well, Rupert, of course you'll do as you like, but is it not a tiny bit unkind to Clare Hackett? You particularly said you'd go, you know."

"Clare won't mind."

"Oh, well. Good-night, Sheena. Good-bye, John." Kirsty left, saying : "I must have a bath."

Rupert and Sheena did not say good-bye at all. No doubt they had made some future plan. John felt an acute envy for people with future plans. They seemed the only thing to him at the moment. He drove home. Sheena leaned back beside him singing to herself. She did not sing very well. In fact, the poor girl could scarcely get one note in tune, so she only sang when she was wildly confident and happy. John knew this about her. Presently she grew quieter and her singing was finished.

It was lovely driving back to the mountains, and in the evening there was a colder exciting air when the fat valley lands were left behind. The hills were ribbed with stone. Stone like heron's feathers in the glass green of the bracken. And stone made all the walls, and there was a hunger about the hills, a need that would never be fulfilled, something within them and hid from them. Sheena, John knew, was at peace here, feeling her joy more warmly in these lonely places. But poor John knew about their despair. Like the mountains he would never find something. It was not a thing he had lost but a thing he had never found.

"Did you ever want to hurt a car, Sheena? Drive like this—and like this." John accelerated and

braked monstrously. "Go on, you bitch." He
changed gear in a very motoring way. Then he
changed the subject. "It was a good party, I
thought, did you, darling? And wasn't the garden
marvellous? It was lovely for me, not having seen
it for a year. She's done a lot. How sweet Rupert is."

"Oh, John, he is a sweet. Don't you think so
when you see him again?"

"Yes, I do. I didn't talk to him very much, of
course. I couldn't to-day, could I?"

"No. Tennis parties are so awful like that. One
oughtn't to go to them, really."

They were driving along the cliff road now, the
deep sea on their left hand. A little girl was driving
two small black cows along the narrow road. She
had blackberry coloured eyes and a blackberry
coloured mouth in a white face, and she had a
charmingly free way of walking. It was a pleasure
to see her there in the evening, and gone behind
them into the evening. John had stopped the car
to let her pass them with her cows. He had stopped
where foxgloves grew down into the road and raised
their lovely correct structures far up into the hills.

"Oh, *foxgloves*," said John. In a moment he was
quite satisfied. Sheena was aware of them too, but
vaguely dreaming. Not with that true sharp pleasure
but as a part of her joy. They drove on.

XII

OLIVIA always had plenty to tell of her day and
how she had spent its hours. Where she had
succeeded. Where she had been thwarted. Why
she had done this and when she had said that. She
sat discoursing to Sheena and John as they ate their
dinner, after everybody else had finished. They paid
her as much attention as they could reasonably
spare from themselves and from their food.

". . . And, my dear, I don't know what to say
to her. It's too awful if she's going to have spots
like that as well as a beard. She may give them to
Markie. It's so horrid to think he kisses her. I don't
know how to tell him not to. Could I say to her
quite kindly that I'm thinking of getting a French
girl for Markie, or a Swiss? Do you remember
Agatha's Swiss governess, Sheena?"

" No."

" She used to sit up half the night doing the most
wonderful work on Agatha's underclothes. I wish
I could get Markie a governess like that."

" She died of consumption."

" Did she? So she did. And she must have
positively *lived* in Switzerland. I do dislike unhealthy people."

" Sheena, how can you eat that filthy savoury.
It's made o' cheese."

" Don't you like that savoury, boy ? Remind me
to tell them not to have it again."

" Oh, I don't mind. It's affectation." John began
to eat some at once.

" How were Kirsty and Silene ? Is Silene still
there pursuing Geoffrey Cruise ? "

" Cruise is cracked about Silene," Sheena said
defensively and for no reason.

" Was she looking nice ? What was she wearing ? "

" Oh, a tennis dress."

" Darling, I didn't think she'd be wearing a
bathing dress. What sort of tennis dress ? "

" A sprigged muslin," said John, with vicious
intention to be uninforming.

" Sprigged ? Boy ! Muslin ? You funny old
thing ! What was she wearing, Sheena ? "

" A pink dress with a string round the waist. She
looked like two wet jellies in a bag tied in the
middle," Sheena said distinctly and unkindly.

" Oh, Sheena, the poor sweet—did she really ?
I'm sure she did. Really how a young girl like that
can let her figure go as she has, it's beyond
me."

" It's beyond her too, I suppose. John, don't eat
the last piece of ginger. It's mine. Ah, John, you
greedy sod."

" All right, sweetie. I'm getting it for you."

" Let John have it, Sheena. There's masses more
ginger. I can't think why that fool Byrne doesn't
send it up. Ring for it."

" Oh, no, Mummy. I don't want more ginger.

It gives me the wind. Here, Sheena, bitchie, you have it."

" All the same, ring. These servants are too slack to breathe."

" But we don't want ginger, Olivia. How you do fuss and go on."

" You're both so tiresome and greedy, and then when I do my best for you, you aren't a bit grateful."

" Oh, darling, do leave us alone. We aren't doing you any harm."

Olivia felt a sudden want of defence against them which she did not often experience. She wished she had not left Julian and Eliza in the library to come in here and be matey with two such uncompanionable creatures.

" Who else was at the party ? " she asked. It was easier to stay than to go now.

" Mrs. Critchley. Mr. Burrows. Archie and Jane. Cruise. Silene. Kirsty. Rupert. Sheena. John. I think that's all. And Aunt Louisa and the Colonel."

" How were you playing, John ? "

" Shocking."

" And Sheena ? "

" Oh, shocking."

" Heaven knows I spent enough money on your tennis, Sheena. All the extra coaching I paid for."

" I never was much of a girl with the games mistress. She wouldn't bother about me. She had her favourites."

" You don't know what you're talking about."

" Well, I'm only telling you."

"All the same, you ought to take your tennis more seriously. So much depends on it for a girl."

"What depends on it exactly?"

"Oh, it's important. And that reminds me, John, I do wish you'd play cricket with Markie. That's another thing Miss Parker is hopeless about. I do wish I could get a nice Swiss girl."

"But cricket bores poor Markie so much. He simply hates it. I've tried before."

"That was a year ago. He's a year older now and he ought to like playing cricket. Anyhow, you might try."

XIII

THESE evenings with Julian Eliza enjoyed in rather
a perilous sort of way. She was so near unhappiness
and so near happiness when she was with him. She
was either lost or found. That was what it was like.
To-night she was found. It was a night when they
had many things in their minds to tell about that
each knew the other would appreciate, and this is
great happiness. Last night Eliza had suffered,
feeling very sad for Julian about the strain of John's
return. She had been keyed up at seeing him again
and too much alive within herself for her mind to
work slowly enough to be true. Everything had been
a shade distorted, not quite in focus. But to-night
she had found her ease with him. It is always
something like this seeing people one minds about
again. Meeting again is a death to familiarity. For
a little time all power is quenched and that lovely
intimacy only breathed in absence is gone, and
there is nothing yet established to take its place.
Sooner or later, or perhaps never, a level is found
again, built in the past and the present time and
future time. To-night Eliza had found this level
which mattered so much and so she was able to
experience really the pleasure of being with Julian
again. Yesterday she had only been aware that

there were moments when she should have felt glad
or sad, but now she was glad or sad or amused, she
was part of these feelings without being aware and
so apart from them.

Julian had been quite happy with her last night
because he did not mind so much as she did. His
feeling for her was not balanced finely and dangerously like hers for him. He expected a great deal
from Eliza and put aside all that did not matter
to him as not mattering to her either. It was much
the simplest and best thing to do, and he did it so
wisely and gently that Eliza could almost think at
times that it was she who did it. They gossiped now
very amiably.

" Can you understand creatures like Silene and
Kirsty, Eliza? Will Sheena become like them, will
you tell me? "

" I don't think so. I'm terrified of girls like that.
So rude and so lovely."

" I'd like to see them well discountenanced."

" So would I, Julian. Nothing could give me
purer pleasure. But there you are—a creaking old
bag like myself would criticise successful young girls."

" How could any one call Kirsty a lovely young
girl? She's over-sexed and spiteful, I think."

" I never wanted to paint Silene and she is so
lovely."

" Let's tear them some more."

" Oh, Julian, it's too easy for us. We would do
much better to be old and kind."

" We would, wouldn't we? "

" Old we may be—though I won't allow it really, not for you, anyhow. But we'll never be really kind, I suppose."

" My beady bonnet will wag and the jet will fly until I die, I promise you."

" Gossip and arranging the flowers, I'll be able to keep alive for those."

" How divinely Olivia does flowers, don't you think so ? Of course it's quite unconscious in her, I suppose. Look at those white iris."

White iris, a flight of moonstruck birds. Olivia had really achieved something that counted in their flinging attitudes. Did Julian think this was unconscious in her ? Or did he think it was an expression of some forever latent truth ? Something within her that she was just true to. Something not forsworn and betrayed through acting its presence. Eliza knew it was a quality aside from Olivia entirely, the same as her genius for rooms and houses and having bought that white gown for Sheena. Could Julian doubt this ? He did doubt it and held her so much dearer because of not knowing for certain. Eliza wished he had left her out of their consideration to-night. Olivia and the things one could not dispute about her. She mattered too much.

" Yes, how lovely. Truly lovely." Her eyes wandered from the flowers. She felt discomfited. They were so wildly right indeed. " Julian, what ancestress is that girl in the white dress ? "

" A great-great-aunt of mine. Jane Sheena

Curran. She's a bit like Sheena, don't you think?
Only so offensively girlish and tiresome."

Julian spoke in the cold particular voice he kept
for ancestors and Kerry cattle. He really was
interested in both these subjects and spoke of them
very rarely. It was a voice as definite as the writing
a diamond makes on a window pane. So afterwards Eliza remembered particularly what he had
said.

"Yes, it is like her. Why have I never noticed
it before, I wonder? It's not a very good picture, is
it? It's as careful as a copy. No life at all!"

"I'm rather fond of it. I had it cleaned the other
day. It used to be in my room, but Olivia wanted
it here. It's so absurdly like Sheena. I'm sorry you
don't like it, but I don't mind, really."

"No, I don't, you know."

"Sometimes I'm quite thankful I don't know as
much about pictures as you do. It must spoil a
great deal of your enjoyment."

Eliza was taken aback. It was such an inconceivably stupid remark. She could not believe
that it was Julian who had made it. And it had
been spoken in a dull obstinate voice, unfamiliar
and unaccountable to her. It was an extraordinarily
bad picture too, and Julian, who had a feeling about
such things, and a little knowledge, must know this.
She was not merely being difficult about it. Well,
well, how can one ever know where one may put
one's feet. This was strange.

Sheena came wandering in. The tilted, unknowing way she had of walking always pleased and amused Eliza. Julian liked it too.

" Come here, poppit, and don't be so grand and up the air. What was it like ? "

Sheena went over and sat on a piece of Julian's chair, but she did not tell him anything. She only smiled and yawned and finally coughed.

" Well, you are an entertaining girl I will say. Can't you even tell me how the W.G. was looking ? You and John are so remarkably precious and Bloomsbury about it. Tell me all. I want to know. Has Silene had a dash at her hair lately ? "

" Yes, it's looking wonderful. And Kirsty wants us all to act in one of her plays."

" Oh, you must. I do like Kirsty's plays. Do you remember when Silene knelt on the aspirin bottle and cut herself to the bone. That was grand."

" Oh, Julian, and she was so brave."

" My dear, it was her big moment. She stole the act. And what else did you gather ? I'm glad about the play. But tell me more."

" Silene had to play with Mrs. Critchley in a ladies' four, and Mrs. Critchley maddened her."

" That's most interesting too. I'd like to have seen that. And was the garden looking ' rather lovely ' ? "

" Yes, but we ought to have seen it last month, of course."

" Yes, Miss Draper. Go on."

" I think I'll go to bed."

" I think I would if I were you. You're not much

fun for us. Girls must be bright and entertaining, even if they feel as tired as dogs."

" I'm as tired as two dogs."

" You don't look tired exactly," said Julian, considering her.

" Oh, I am. Good-night. Good-night, Eliza, my darling. Did you have a nice afternoon, my darling ? "

" Lovely. With Markie."

" Oh, lovely for you. With Markie. Good-night."

". . . Does she look tired, Eliza ? "

Eliza laughed. " No," she said deeply.

" Yes, I agree with you. Wouldn't you like a drink ? I think I would, though."

Olivia and John passed by the open window, strolling together in evening. It was nearly dark now. Only the sea was pale and the narrow pond at the end of the house like a spear in its low water, a long light spear fallen on the ground. They walked away towards it. Olivia's voice was muted to the hour. John's was exact—a ten o'clock in the morning voice. Eliza felt rather disheartened for him. Could they not leave him alone. No, of course not.

XIV

WHEN Mark woke up his day began at once. He kicked his dog, the Mouse, to show her how little he cared. He got up and put on his dressing-gown (because you were always sent back for your dressing-gown), also his blue bedroom boots, and went off down the passage in a bold sort of way. He felt very powerful in himself in the mornings. " I'll just wake up this poor bloody Parker," he muttered. " Terrible woman to sleep."

Poor bloody Parker was asleep still, curled up in a furry ball with her face hidden. Markie looked at her for some time. He put his hand out towards her and put it back again in his dressing-gown pocket. He did not feel quite so resolute about waking people up as he had done a few minutes before. He moved about her room taking a look at her now and then, but still she lay sleeping in the half-light. Not a stir out of her. Then he saw his dog, Mrs. Mouse, looking at him in a nasty sort of way. A " cowardly little sod, aren't you ? " sort of look. So with that he gathered himself and struck Parker a savage blow between the shoulder blades. He kept telling himself : " I hit her a terrible crack. God, I hope I haven't quinched the woman." But she only stirred and turned in her bed like a hare in its form. This was both a relief and a disappointment.

He left her room in rather a hurry. His sense of importance was satisfied and the entire incompleteness of his achievement did not trouble him at all. He had proved himself to himself pretty early in the morning. That was a terrible blow he had struck. He thought of different kinds of blows, of the queer solid knocking sound Nick made when he hit a fish on the base of its skull to kill it. He thought of the shape of a trout, and he felt angry and miserable thinking how little a distance he could fish. " Damn rod's *useless*," he muttered. He would go and see John. He went vigilantly down the passage. One never knew quite where one was. It was the sort of hour it might be any time at all, and people said : " Do you know the time ? Go back to your bed at once." The banisters and steps up and down looked strange. He tied the cord of his dressing-gown again, giving himself a business-like sensation of confidence and reality.

John's room. It was blindingly light. Not like Parker's and his own with the blinds half-way down and the curtains drawn. This was the right way to sleep, like everything John did, it was right. Mark took a look at the whiteness of the sea, very calm and with the dark lines of currents like pulling strings to be seen. No ship. The sea is good for children to live beside. There they see things and look afar for things. He turned back to John. John was sleeping as fast as Miss Parker. But so differently —Miss Parker lay curled up like a mouse—a cosy, if a sad, she-mouse. John slept despairingly. His arms outside in the coldness of night and morning, the palms of his hands so touching, so seldom seen. His eyelids lightly, lightly shut. Poor John. No peace about his sleeping.

It was all one to Markie, Miss Parker slept, John slept. If Miss Parker was asleep it meant nothing particular. If John was asleep it must be the wrong time of the morning for sport. Markie took off his dressing-gown and got quietly into bed beside John. As quietly as possible. Mummy Mouse started to fuss. He pulled her up, breathing savagely, and kicked her down to the bottom of the bed. John woke up. He said : " Markie, you're a terrible fellow, Markie. Go asleep now like a good child." He was gone again into that deep, impenetrable coma of one's elders. Markie was an imitative child. He flung his arms outside the bedclothes, each as John's were, and even in this unfamiliar position he soon slept again.

That part of the day was lost soon—gone and forgotten in the hours that passed, as long as days these hours, between waking and dressing, and washing your ears, and screaming the place down, eating your breakfast and visiting women who ate their breakfasts in bed, and eating bacon off their trays, and pouring them out second cups of tea with great dash, but not much assurance, and down-stairs to the dining-room at high speed.

" How fast was I going ? *No*. When I came in, John, how fast would I be ? Twenty-five miles ? Forty-one ? "

" Not fast enough to warm yourself."

" Oh, John, I'll kill you."

Julian moved his hands defensively for Mark. " I would have said you were doing a good thirty-five, and at least forty down stairs. You're a great boy to go down stairs."

Little boys are so clean and romantic in the morning, they have been awake so long in their other nursery life—the tedious necessary life from which they can only be rescued from time to time, from an hour to the next, by the saviours who love them. Julian felt tenderly and sadly towards Mark, poor boy, so soon to be delivered over to that furry little despot upstairs. And on this gay day, God help him, with the sea outside the windows and a world of pleasures at his feet. Poor sweet. He gave a kiss to lovely Markie, waiting only for a moment, hanging within his arm.

" Please, can I ? Can I, Daddy ? Can I ? "

Could he, what ? This exotic child might certainly do as he pleased, for Julian would forbid him nothing, now or ever. What did the child want ? He raised his eyes to John for help.

" May he come with Nick and me lobster potting ? Olivia won't mind ? "

" When ? This afternoon ? "

" Yes. This afternoon."

" Yes, why shouldn't he go ? "

" I don't know. I didn't know if he might."

" Yes, of course you can, child."

Olivia came in and sat down in the morning sun.

She looked most beautiful, rested and complete. She moved the tulips on the table, changing them so little but entirely. There was not one smoother nor brighter than her face. She had had her breakfast upstairs. Now she would read her monstrous correspondence. First she called Markie to her and kissed his cheek. (He turned his jaw to her.) And whispered. Whisper. Whisper.

"Yes, I have," said Markie loudly.

"Why do you always ask him that?" John said. "Of course you always used to ask us, I remember, and very embarrassing it was."

"And most tiresome for me. Of all the constipated little monkeys you were the most troublesome." Olivia showed a sudden flash of morning spirit. Then she began to open her letters. So did the others, perhaps a little impeded in their understanding by the pieces Olivia read out to them mercilessly from her own letters. She had a distracting way of doing this without any explanatory preface. And she would comment on something unexplained and wait for an intelligent rejoinder to her comment. It was like this : "'If I may come to you on the 25th it would be simply lovely, but do put me off if this doesn't suit you.' I wonder if I want her then? She's such a crashing bore, isn't she? But I'd like her to see the border now it's so good. She was so informing about telling me everything I did wrong before it thickened up—— *Eighteen pounds*—it's absolutely ridiculous. And he didn't manage to straighten them at all. They were just as bad before she went to him. Ought I to write and say I won't pay it, Julian? "

" Yes, I certainly should if you have any grounds to." This was a reply which Julian had found covered most possibilities and saved him from purposeless mental strain. Only hours afterwards it would occur to him that a speech like this referred to a dentist's abortive efforts with Sheena's front teeth.

". . . These cow-testing people are really too dreary. Shall I let them? I don't think I will. Or I expect this is for you, really. I wouldn't have anything to say to it if I was you. . . . I wonder whose this writing is? Isn't it just like Aunt Fanny's, Julian? John, don't you think it's extraordinarily like Aunt Fanny's? I wonder who it's from? These sickening Irish post-marks, one never can tell, can one? . . . Now I do call that absolutely monstrous. I always disliked the woman and it only shows one ought to trust one's instincts and not be kind to people. May Henscastle told me what she was when she first came into the country and she was right. May's a bit coarse at times (I think she thinks rudeness is attractive to men), but she's right this time. It's the only word for her. John, don't you think it's past words? "

" I do indeed. What's she done? " John asked before he could think better of his rashness.

" She's opened her garden for the Jubilee nurses on the same day as mine. And I fixed the date months ago. It's my date. I'll write to the people

in Dublin and get them to compel her to alter it—
and a fortune-teller. My dear, I wonder if she's
booked Mrs. Cousins from Kiljennet post office?
It would be just like her. But I'll settle her—well,
isn't this infuriating? One thing after another.
Of course they can't charge duty on it, can they?
I was most careful to sew the name of a Dublin firm
into the back before I sent it over. I never heard
such a thing. This country gets more impossible
to live in every day, but this is beyond anything.
Really, these Customs, you never know where you
are with them and it takes years off your life. To
think of my lovely coat lying there ruined by sea
water and horrible men and probably their wives
will wear it, I heard some awful story about that
the other day. It was Sue who told me. I absolutely
must rescue it or I'll never be able to wear it again.
What shall I do about it? And when you think
what mink costs—— Markie! You're not to eat
biscuits between meals. How often have you been
told? If you disobey me over that again I shall
tell Miss Parker you're to walk round by Woodenstown Cross this afternoon along the cement road.
Put down that biscuit. No, you're not to eat
another crumb. In fact, I think in any case you'd
better walk by Woodenstown, then you could leave
a note for Mrs. Cousins at Kiljennet. It's not at all
a bad idea having a fortune-teller. I think I'll try
it. Every little helps, doesn't it? So remind me."

Both Julian and John were aware here of their
profound respect for Markie because he refrained

entirely from wailing about his afternoon plans for the sea. His own granted pleasure. His face grew a little pale and he leaned his wide, romantic brow against John's arm. But he spoke no word of anxious dismay, precipitated no wordy crisis. When he raised his head John thought he looked at Olivia in a peculiar long way. If he had had a good knife and freedom to act he might have stuck it into her, ending her senseless tyranny and shouting as he killed her, as he had screamed when he killed his first rabbit. John could see him now running in on the wounded rabbit and beating its soft belly with his fists, crying: " Killed. Killed." And a blood lust mounted in him and a sort of terror.

Mark had a real disregard for them all. He had a savage sense of Mark, only Mark. And then in the evening, tired and so beautiful, one was afraid of him. He would say: " Kiss me. Only trust me and kiss me, John. Trust me and kiss me." And then bite. Bite John to hurt him. John thought: " If I can remember Mark when I am old and very weak and greedy it may give me a moment of real feeling, of real pain. Mark, seven years old, so lovely in everything he does, when he is greedy, when he is brave, when he is sly, when he is frightened. How can I endure that he should change at all ? " Mark riding his pony—mad for speed, a single desire for this possessing him. Faster, John, you idle sod. Faster. Faster. Screaming and biting his pony when it napped and whipped round with him. Some of his terrible passions of remorse

John would remember when he was old, passions that would come on him when he had seriously damaged a loved one, crying then, " Hurt me. Please, hurt me." And when the silly beloved refused, striking his own head, tears streaming down his face. And with all this he was able to disguise his own truest emotions. He was dangerously able to keep a secret, if he knew that secret would suffer a change in its telling. He could keep a thing entirely within himself, denying it vehemently and keeping it for his own alone. That and his exact memory, with a true and imaginative connection of ideas, were the powerful things about Mark that John treated with great respect.

And now this pale creature must go away for those interminable hours of morning lessons, with his hope of the day shaken in him. Miss Parker put her head round the door now to sound that dreadful bright determined note which struck for durance, that, " Come along, come along, Markie." John in his own day had always felt a cold despair in his stomach when he heard it. Now he felt Markie lean more heavily against him and he bent nearer, whispering to him, " It's all right, Markie, I promise you."

Markie did not even turn one of those insufferably touching looks on John, looks that asked for assurance against all contrary chances in this dangerous day. He put down his head and ran out of the room before he could provoke further disaster and retribution.

Olivia tore up her letters sharply, such of them as

needed no further thought. A little wind went backing across the sea, backwards across a grey bird's breast. The sun was gone and the joy gone out of the hour. No heat was in the light at all. It came in through the windows pale and without kindness. The long day was young and sour with a twist in it for ugliness.

John looked over the room at a picture of Mad Harry Bird, his great-great-grandfather. Even Lawrence, with all his urbanity, had not contrived to make Mad Harry's portrait the respectable pompous and elegant portrait of a gentleman that it should have been. Mad Harry had not jumped into the Rhine as Silene's and Kirsty's ancestor had done. He had confined his eccentricities to beating his wives, torturing cats, and keeping his daughters' heads shaved like billiard balls till their most probable marriageable days were past. That is to say, until they were quite twenty-five years of age. Towards the end of his life he took a great dislike to living in Silverue itself, so built himself a house in a tree where he would compel his wife to come and sleep with him, sometimes keeping her up the tree for days together, while his pale bald daughters fluttered fearfully about the house, too cowed by the unbelievable custom of their days to make the best of these intervals of freedom. Although Silverue was not haunted by any ghost, some of the terror of these unfortunate girls and some of their unhappiness could still be felt at quiet hours. No part of the house was entirely free from it. But it was as ineffective as their lives had been.

John did not care much for looking at Mad Harry. His portrait gave one a bad feeling of his extreme power and loneliness. A really bad feeling. One might be one of his three poor daughters as one looked at it, and in any case one was his great-great-grandson, of his blood and name. For a long time that picture had been in Julian's room, but Olivia, feeling that to be no place for a Lawrence, had removed it to hang in a good light where all could see. John saw it a good deal oftener than he wanted to these days, but he was severe with himself on the subject and occasionally facetious, taking quite a lot of trouble to treat the matter lightly in his mind. But he did not like Mad Harry's eyes. They were everywhere in the room. He was not quite able to ignore them.

XV

ALL that morning John felt dreary and sad. He occupied himself savagely, and yet he could not fill his mind with real thought of what he was doing. Whatever he did was accomplished with a futile ease and speed that left time only in his hands, hours of time, hours till luncheon time, interminable hollow hours. He had put all his fishing tackle in order, meddling with it fondly, he had tied a fly for evening fishing, he had read the paper, he had failed to persuade Sheena to bathe with him and bathed alone. He lay now in the sand and sun and sharp grasses. He should have been quieter in himself, but he was not.

Eliza came down to the sea. She stood suddenly between John and the sea and the sky like an immense poster of the tallest possible woman. Her tiny brown face was a mile away from him. She was wearing John's green jersey. Sea gulls screeched in the distance behind her, somewhere near the level of her waist. She sat down, becoming real and undistorted, changing into dear Eliza beside him. She had a nice bag of sweets in her hand which she had bought at the post office for Markie. John was very fond of sweets, especially after bathing. He ate one gladly and lay down again. The space of time before him shrank away; it was not long enough to have Eliza here to himself, lying in the sun and full of conversation. Probably she had cigarettes in her bag too.

" What were you doing walking along the shore by yourself ? "

" Cooling my ardour."

" Nonsense."

" Giving my new jersey a breath of air then."

" It looks lovely, doesn't it ? "

" I love it. It makes me appear to have a bosom like Silene's. I have been so proud all the morning looking down at them."

" Oh, no, Eliza, you can't compare your bosoms and Silene's. Those Royal udders, darling. You aren't in the same class."

" Well, don't dishearten me about them this morning. I think they're looking fine."

" They are gay."

" I must heat my back," Eliza said, lying down in another way and giving up her calm shoulders to the sun. She rolled up her sleeves and laid her face down on her arms. John felt the sun was better. He lay closer to the hot sand.

" Darling, it must be luncheon time. What is the time ? " Eliza asked at length.

" It's not time to move, I know. Give me another of Markie's sweets."

" But the poor little boy."

" As if he'd mind. He's the one creature who loves me."

"How grand you're being. Little Lord Fauntle-
roy's bitter and dissipated uncle. . . . A little
child's love. . . ."

"You're so unkind, darling, Eliza. But it's
lovely to be with you. How long will you stay here
with us?"

"Quite a time. Until I can bear it no more and
then I go back to my whoring life in London,
saying, 'Farewell, thou art too dear for my
possessing.' Do you ever read the Sonnets?"

"Which Sonnets?"

"And like enough thou knowest thy estimate.
What you miss in your ignorance. Do dress yourself,
John. Olivia will be so cross with us if we are really
late."

"You don't mind Olivia."

"I do think it's uncivilised to be really late for
meals in other people's houses."

"Now you're being the perfect guest, the true
country house visitor."

"It's not that. But I will not lose my friends by
stupid rudeness. When you are older, dear, and
wiser, you will treat your mother more politely,
and then perhaps you will enjoy her society as much
as I do now."

"Oh, well, don't miss a minute of it. Don't let
me make you. Give me my trousers. You've
ruined them lying on them."

"Nonsense." How unsteadily John had flared
up. Hours would not put him right with himself
again. Eliza lay on her back waiting for him to

put on his socks and his trousers and other clothes, and wondering in her own mind how to get back with him to the quietness they had reached before Olivia's name had been mentioned.

XVI

MISS PARKER had spent a difficult morning. Markie
had been inattentive and mournful over his lessons.
Miss Parker had a pain that caused her to feel grey
all over and rather tempersome and shaky. Dora
had been impertinent about two handkerchiefs
which Miss Parker knew perfectly well ought
to have come back from the laundry. She had let
her eyes rest heavily upon Miss Parker's beard while
she spoke, until Miss Parker could hardly govern
the itch in her hand which prompted her to raise
it to her chin and shelter herself from those eyes'
unkindness. Mercifully the shameful spots were
partly cured and partly obscured by the undisturbed
luxuriance upon her lip and chin.

Markie had irritated her almost past bearing by
his determined refusal to solve that old problem
about the man and sixteen girls. When the problem
was set in terms of one, two or even three girls he
would unhesitatingly produce the right answer.
But could he see it in relation to the sixteen? He
could not and would not.

Miss Parker felt a terrible nervous sadness creeping
in upon her and overwhelming her like a tide as
she washed Markie's hands and her own and
combed his smooth hair and her own (harsh with

one cheap wave on top of another) before luncheon.
She took two aspirins and a glass of remarkably
chilly water and felt worse. She even considered
the possibility of staying upstairs and not coming
down to luncheon at all, but quickly put this
preposterous idea out of her head. It would require
altogether too much explanation and excuse. So,
as the gong rang, Miss Parker and Markie proceeded
straight to the dining-room, as was their habit, and
waited for the rest of the family to appear.

Markie swung on the chairs and tormented Byrne,
and showed Mrs. Mouse the delicious food he and
not she was going to eat, and Miss Parker reproved
him mechanically but not violently for everything
he said and did, while Byrne smiled upon him
indulgently, for he spoilt Mark in the most shameless
way and rather enjoyed undermining the governess
in a good-humoured way. To-day Miss Parker did
not much mind ; she had never felt less inclined
towards self-assertion. She suddenly wondered what
Byrne would look like if she said to him now, " Oh,
Byrne, give me some gin or some port." But
actually she would no more have made this not very
extraordinary request than she would have jumped
out of a train going at speed. It was outside her
conception of life to ask for what she wanted or to
take what she wanted. So she waited there,
trembling a little, feeling ill and chilly and repeating,
" Don't, Markie," over and over again.

Soon everybody came in to luncheon, Lady
Bird and Sheena and Sir Julian, and not much later

John and Eliza. They all sat down and ate large quantities of very good food in a careless greedy way, most unlike the way Miss Parker had been taught to eat, and which she vainly tried to instil into Markie. But, no. He ate just like the rest of them. Not as if his food was important, but as if he himself was immensely important.

Lady Bird was full of ideas about her garden fête. She had discussed and re-discussed them through many meal-times lately, but now that the date approached so closely and a rival threatened, her enthusiasm knew no bounds. There was a venom in it and a searching activity that spared not the smallest detail nor the least person who might be made of use to her on or before the big day.

Towards the end of the meal she fell into a muse, her eyes on Miss Parker. She was wondering how best to employ the hours of Miss Parker's afternoon. Whether she should help to fertilise the melons ; dress the dogs in sulphur and train oil ; walk to Kiljennet post office with the message to Mrs. Cousins ; wash the flower vases ; or pack up the books for the library. Some of these jobs could be combined and some could not. It was a nice problem to decide how best to divide a willing usefulness with time. Kiljennet post office and dressing the dogs might just be fitted in, but dressing the dogs and fertilising the melons—no.

John said, " How are you going, Markie ? "

The accepted answer to this question was, " I'm going great." Markie made it with pleasure.

" Well, hurry up with your pudding or the little
boy'll be left behind. Nick and John will go
without him."

" Oh, John, John——"

" No, I won't really. Take your time."

" Markie has a little job to do for me this afternoon," Olivia said brightly and firmly. " Have you
forgotten, darling ? Mummy said you and Miss
Parker were to walk to Kiljennet, didn't she ? "
Kiljennet it shall be, she decided, and perhaps the
flower vases and the dogs after tea.

Markie raised his eyes from his plate and looked
with gentle inquiry from Julian to John. They must
speak for him. They did. They said, " But we
promised Markie at breakfast-time that he could go
lobstering this afternoon."

" That was before he was naughty and disobedient
about the biscuits. I told him then he was to go to
Kiljennet, and besides I want Mrs. Cousins to get
this message. It's most important."

" Perhaps Miss Parker would go with the message
if we took Markie with us."

" Miss Parker is to go with Markie. I won't have
him out in the boat without her."

" Oh, Olivia, you know he often goes alone with
us."

" Yes, and always catches a chill because none of
you can make him put on a woollie in time. No, if
Markie goes, Miss Parker must go too."

Miss Parker smiled wanly. Really she was in too
much despair to speak. The walk to Kiljennet

would have been bad enough, but the thought of the sea was appalling. Was there no help for her? She looked at John and saw his vexed face. No doubt the last thing he wanted was her company. Realising this so plainly she was conscious of only a very faint resentment, in fact of none at all. She looked at Markie and saw two things in his anxious changing eyes. He wished that she should stay at home and he feared that if she did he might not be allowed to go to sea at all to-day. His fear was the greater of the two, and his eyes changed again to sorrow that was very moving. She looked at Lady Bird and knew that she at least was determined to thwart everybody she could.

Eliza said, bending down the table towards Olivia, " I asked the Sybil in the G.P.O. this morning whether she was going to the Kellery fête, and she *is*. Isn't it frightful for you, Olivia ? "

Olivia was really angry and entirely distracted from the employment of either Markie's or Miss Parker's afternoon hours. She talked a great deal about Disloyalty and Common Drops and Bad Blood and Jealousy, Lack of Common Decency, and again Disloyalty, Bad Blood, Jealousy and Common Drops. She fell then with renewed vigour into plans for outdoing her rival. Every moment a new distraction and amusement was to be provided for the faithful who should attend the Silverue fête in preference to that held at Kellery. Boats should take the faithful to the islands at the modest tariff of one shilling a head.

" They'll see the puffins giving terrible love out of themselves," Sheena said ; " it's worth more than a shilling, isn't it, John ? "

" Oh, it'll madden your Beady Bonnets, Olivia."

" My dear, so nice for them. You never think about their drab lives. And then I think we'll get people to lend their cars and charge a shilling for a drive up to the Nine Stones and back. Who would lend cars ? George White. Mrs. Crockett. The Jeffries. Rupert. . . ."

Sheena saw a dreadful thing happening. She saw Rupert for the day given up to driving parties from the town up and down the mountains to the Nine Stones and back again. She said :

" Well, Olivia, can we ? I mean it means if ever anybody wanted to borrow our cars we couldn't say no. And you wouldn't even let Silene drive yours five miles back from the station once."

" Because I considered it a bad precedent. Besides, it was only a matter of convenience."

" Yes. Not your convenience."

" Certainly, I don't want everybody driving my car. Now I would be exceedingly loth to lend it to Rupert."

" And why ? " John asked. Everybody was getting involved rather angrily into this argument.

" Well, he's so reckless and stupid. Tearing about the roads. He's sure to have a bad smash one day."

" Yes, but what you have to look at is how long has he been driving without having an accident ? "

" I don't care. I wouldn't care to have him driving my car."

" If you borrow other people's cars you must lend your own. I would rather lend a car to Rupert than to you any day."

" No. I will not lend my car to Rupert."

Julian said pacifically, " Well, but Rupert is very unlikely to want the car. He has three cars of his own. The question is : Shall we borrow cars to drive your town friends up the mountain on Thursday ? Of course, it means you must expect the countryside to wait by dozens in the avenue daily to borrow ours—but still. Do we want cars on Thursday enough to risk it ? Wouldn't the three cars here be enough ? "

" Well, and who is going to drive them ? Johnson is playing his melodeon in the band."

" I should say the band would do just as well without Johnson's melodeon."

" But I ask you, how can I tell him that ? Sheena is in charge of the ices. I shall want John with me, and in any case Johnson couldn't drive three cars at once."

" You wouldn't know what Johnson would do. He's a very enterprising man."

" Oh, it's all very well for all of you. You take no interest except to see how unhelpful you can be."

" Oh, darling, we're awfully keen. Don't be silly. We'll all lie up. Come on now, Markie. What about Miss Parker ? "

Miss Parker looked for her instructions to Lady Bird, and Lady Bird nodded go.

Of course, it was remarkably silly of Miss Parker not to say : I feel ill. I have a pain or a headache, she might have said. I am very often sea-sick and really I cannot go. I shall be a nuisance to everybody, and I will suffer agonies both mental and physical myself. Give me a glass of port and a hot water bottle and let me lie down on my bed for the after-noon. I will wake a giantess of industry at tea-time, and after tea I will wash the dogs, weed the rock garden, fertilise the melons or run back and forwards to Kiljennet post office just as often as anybody wants me to. But it was utterly and completely impossible for her to say anything at all like this. She could no more have said it than she could have taken off all her clothes there and then and danced a jig in the middle of the dining-room table. She was completely unfree within herself. All she said was, " Come along, Markie," and went upstairs to find the woollies and waterproofs and rubber hats and gum boots which Lady Bird ordained should be worn upon the sea no matter what the weather was like.

There followed after this for Miss Parker an hour and a half of complete horror. She felt very unreal to herself as she walked down to the sea between the fuchsias. The bright sea and the bright field before her to cross, the long and unkind afternoon before her to cross. Markie ran on, striking his backside with his heels as he ran, a thing he thought himself pretty clever to do. John walked in front of her smoking a cigarette and carrying a basket with tea in it, and Miss Parker brought up the tail of the procession carrying a collection of coats and woollies and encouraging Mrs. Mouse (who disliked the sea almost as she did) with cheerful little cries for if she slipped back to the house Miss Parker knew that the start of the expedition would be delayed until Mark had found her again. Miss Parker was not feeling very grand, but definitely not quite so ill as she had done before luncheon. However, before long this was to be changed.

Nick and Mark were standing together on the landing-stage talking to each other when John and Miss Parker appeared with their baskets and bundles.

It had never even remotely occurred to Miss Parker that Nick was the most enthralling and engaging man possible to look at as well as to talk to. Eliza had said when she first saw him, " I think Nick is the most wonderful and attractive looking man. I feel quite moved by him, but then I am very easily moved." Miss Parker divided the men she knew into three lots. Those she found enthralling but beyond her, such as Rupert or Douglas Fairbanks Junior ; those she found enthralling and within reach but possibly not within her reach, such as the gay young man in the R.A.M.C. who had stirred her sister to a frenzy of romantic excitement before he returned (without her sister) to India and presently ceased even to write letters.

And those that she lumped together as the Lower Classes, putting Johnson, the chauffeur, and Byrne, the butler, and the boy in the grocer's shop and Nick (that sporting man of leisure) all into the same unknowing corner of her mind. She often wondered why it was that Lady Bird, who was distressingly particular in many ways about Markie, made not the least objection to his spending as much of his time as he could contrive in Nick's company, nor did she protest about the distressing accent and curious expressions that Markie picked up from his low-class friend.

Miss Parker was quite accustomed to a feeling of being the superfluous member of a party, but this afternoon, as she scrambled uncomfortably into the boat, she was aware of a triple animosity which depressed her more than usual. Nobody wanted her to be there and she really was of no possible service to anybody, for John and Nick were entirely capable of dealing with Markie. As capable as they would be helpless to deal with her when she was prostrated by pain and sickness, as she expected very shortly to be. Nor did she deceive herself. For very soon she had passed through that interval of hope which precedes an interval of determination which precedes that awful yielding to the body's needs, promising so much relief and productive of so little but exhaustion and despair.

It really was awful for Miss Parker. She soon became oblivious of Markie's fascinated staring and of John and Nick's low-voiced and irritable

discussion in the end of the boat farthest from her.
She was as sick as she could possibly be, and between
one thing and another felt pretty near death.
Somebody very kindly covered her up in an old
oilskin when she was shaking with cold and tied
the woollie that Markie ought to have been wearing
round her neck for a muffler. She looked up and
saw that it was Nick, and felt very grateful to him for
this and for his gentle undisgusted face. She thanked
him with the genuine gratitude the sick feel towards
the merciful, but soon she had thrown off both coat
and muffler in a fresh hideous tide of horror and
sickness.

She discovered afterwards that it was John's idea
landing her on one of the bird islands and proceeding
without her. At the time she felt too far gone even
to envisage the comfort of land beneath her feet
once more. When the boat stopped she thought
they must have reached the lobster pots or net or
whatever they were looking for, and she was
surprised from her misery almost into lively
embarrassment when John encouraged her to step
out of the boat and into Nick's arms who stood over
his knees in water ready to carry her ashore.

" You'll be all right now, miss," Nick kept telling
her as he waded carefully to the stony shore.
" You lie quiet a while and you won't know yourself.
Ah, God help you," he said as he set her down, " it's
not upon the sea you should be at all."

How ardently she agreed with him. Staggering
with weakness and misery she said, " Tell Master

John how sorry I am, and please see that Master
Mark puts his coat on before it gets cold."

"Well, what about Master John?" Nick said
slightingly. "Sure the like o' this could happen any
of us. I'll mind Master Mark now as good as yourself
would."

"Yes, I know you will," Miss Parker said faintly.
She leant back against the sureness and comfort of
the place where he had set her down, and there she
wished she might die and know no further suffering.
Fool, weak fool, that she had been not to have
spoken up and refused to embark herself on this
hideous expedition. She would be in much worse
trouble now, but that seemed quite infinitely remote
and inconsiderable at the moment. Her present
sad case was as much as she could think
about.

Presently, all by herself in the afternoon, Miss
Parker felt a sense of betterness coming over her.
The boat was gone and she was more alone perhaps
than she had ever been in her life. And because she
was for once without people she was less lonely.
For it was the loneliness of being with people that
Miss Parker knew about, not the divine aloneness
of being by herself. She knew nothing at all about
that. O last delight I know I am alone. Mr. Remy
de Gourmont could have explained nothing to her
because she was so ignorant of even the earliest
fundamentals.

Now she was alone and feeling better, aware
again of warmth and the exquisite comfort of pain

ceasing. Aware of the flight of birds and the little cries of waves and the heat of the sun. But most of all, the only physical pleasure she knew, that of pain ceasing. That, and eating and sleeping she really enjoyed, for she had been born with a capability for pleasure that it was as well she knew nothing about. She had never been drunk and she had never loved anybody. In the sun she slept. The bright day had turned merciful as Nick had been. Not far off and unhelpful like John and Markie, signs of all her dim life. Miss Parker swallowed and slept in the kinder day and woke feeling renewed and wondering what she should do now. If she had been Sheena she would have gone to watch the puffins at their comical love-making, but since she was Miss Parker this was hardly an aspect of ornithology which she found either diverting or instructive.

There were wild flowers on the islands, thrift and thyme and this and that, and a sweet air, and little paths made by God knew what, like fox tracks through the tufted flowers, but where were the foxes? Lichened rocks and white stones and white birds and thyme like a springing cage under your feet to walk on. Islands are so romantic and so guarded. Nobody knows.

Into the emptiness of Miss Parker's body and spirit this thin air was coming. And yet it could not. She was too impossible. She knew too little of any possibility in life. She had never been gay. She had never been wanton. She must never know sadness so, nor the extreme romance of little islands and to be alone in them.

Soon she knew it was late. Past tea-time. Past dinner-time. The sky changed, and the sea changed, . and the flight of birds was different, and the kind air as cold as life. She sat on the beach, an expectant she-seal. And she knew reality, thinking herself forgotten. Tears ran down her face, and if she had been the she-seal she looked so like, she would have wailed her grief aloud, squatting there on a rock with sea birds flying about her and the long black oilskin coat coming down over her hands like fins, and over her feet. Poor little governess, poor little beggar, and they really had forgotten her.

XVII

THE fact was they had only partly forgotten her. They had forgotten her until the tides were doing the wrong thing for getting near the islands in their boat. By then it was Markie's bed-time and John very prudently considered that it would be wiser and better to have Markie home in time and fetch his governess later on. Olivia would be cross enough at their return without Miss Parker, but she would be a great deal more tempersome if the reunited party returned two hours beyond its proper time.

Markie had spent a most enjoyable afternoon. He had caught two fish, a pollock and a rock cod, and he squatted in the bottom of the boat now handling them affectionately and talking a great deal about fishing. Nick and John listened to him with proper attention and respect and answered all his questions faithfully. At last even Mark grew tired of talking and working and meddling and putting everything in order, he sat against John with his tired face to the wind and made no protest about wearing his waterproof. That languor was on him in which John found him so moving. As on a lovely day beauty seems in the evening to dwell, a separate bloom, an air apart, so on this child when he was quiet at last. No dead child could be so far off.

John was rather tired too. He felt more completely

quiet in himself than he had done yet. He felt gentle and satisfied. Being with Nick one worked because one must. One talked because one wished. And one was silent when one needed silence. And being with Markie again was more pleasure than he had remembered. Markie and Nick and Eliza—they were the people he needed. Not even Sheena, because she was too happy now. He had wanted so much to see her again, and now he was half afraid of her. She had found a thing since he had gone that held her away until, perhaps, it should be complete. Then Sheena would be on his level again. Now she had a thing too much her own. This return to Sheena had been sad for John.

* * * * * *

Miss Parker on her island was much too sensible a girl to cry very much. But when hour after hour passed by and still nobody came back for her she certainly felt most forlorn. She felt cold too, and by degrees grew more and more miserable and conscious of her unhappy state. It was fantastic that she should be here by herself on an island with night coming on and the cries of sea birds round her and colour changing into no colour at all, no romantic evening sea but a coldness and a loss wherever she looked. Miss Parker tried very hard to be sensible and practical, but in spite of herself an hysterical despair set in on her spirit and the most unlikely things seemed quite natural and bound to happen. Nick and John and Mark had all been drowned so no one would ever come and rescue her. Their bodies would float on the eighth day and people would say how strange and how tiresome that Miss Parker's body would not float too. It would occur to nobody to look for her bones on this island. It was not even the island where Lady Bird intended to transport her garden visitors on Thursday. That was a mile away, and in any case Thursday was five days off. By that time Miss Parker would be nearly if not quite dead from exposure and hunger, and much too weak to shout. Of course, it was absurd to go on like this. Of course, they would come for her. But why had they not come back by this? Miss Parker walked a little wildly up and down the pebbly strip of beach, staring out to sea and back to Ireland. She could see the summer fires in the mountains and the clear faint line of the mountains, wild as they were, she thought they looked secure and familiar now. If I was on the top of the highest mountain, thought Miss Parker miserably, I could walk down to some little house where they would give me a nice cup of tea and show me the way to go home. But there is no help for me here. . . . Perhaps nobody has been drowned. Perhaps it is just their cruel thoughtlessness. I'm only the governess. I don't matter. It will be quite a good joke when it occurs to them that they've forgotten me. The true sadness of being herself had never struck Miss Parker till now. She had always forbidden herself such silly and morbid thoughts (except perhaps at the most private moments when depilatories guaranteed safe, harmless and efficient went wrong), but how could she ever be more alone than now? She was so lonely as to be really past her tears. She went back to the little corner where Nick had left her and sat down there again shivering and despairing—a weak, soured little shrew mouse, forgotten as she thought by all, and colder than she had ever been in her life.

So Nick found her when the tide was at last right for him to take her off from the island. He had come back alone to fetch her, for John had not wished to aggravate his mother more than necessary by being late for dinner, nor had been over anxious to assist at the transport of the queasy Miss Parker from her island to the mainland. Nick had not found him very difficult to persuade of his super-fluity to this second trip.

Nick was the sort of man who really did not bear Miss Parker any ill feeling for all the trouble she was causing him. A thing like this was neither here nor there with him. It was to be done and he would take his time to do it without fuss or disturbance of any sort. A sea-sick governess could be dealt with by him as neatly and efficiently as he could deal with a calving cow or a boat in a storm. One equipped oneself to deal with these things, and they caused one neither trouble nor embarrassment.

He had not, however, expected to find Miss Parker quite so shaken in herself nor so dazedly grateful for his coming as she seemed to be. He saw her crouching there, a shapeless little heap of misery, under the tent of his stiff coat and called out to her as he walked up the beach. She did not answer, and when he came near he could hear her sniffing and sobbing and was reminded forcibly of one of those sad seals who wailed near his house at night. It was as if one of them had become half a woman, a woman in more than her crying. And for one of the Silverue governesses, that succession of robot instructresses, to strike Nick as human was not stranger than if one of his seals came crying to his door for love.

Those governesses, whose surveillance he had helped all the children in turn to escape, Nick looked on them (if he ever troubled to look at all) as on a breed apart—apart even from speculation, a pitiful breed towards whom he felt if anything a grand contempt, as one who has towards one who has nothing at all. He had no familiar ground with them as with Sheena and her equals in age and state. In his consortings with such he was in every way that mattered wiser and more able. He had taught Sheena to fish and to shoot and she was his friend. Many of Sheena's friends and Julian's had been his friends in the same way. It was not because he had known her since she was so little that Nick had this familiarity with Sheena. But of all those governesses which he treated with so much politeness, never had there been one with whom he had enjoyed the meanest pleasures of conversation.

Now this girl was trying to stop her crying, and struggling on to her feet, and thanking him. He had never given more than the most slighting thought to the looks of any one of these unreal women, but now the pitiful ugliness and weakness of this one struck him. She had become alive again as if a seal had come to human life and asked at his door. It really was only comparable to this.

Nick spoke to her reassuringly, much as he would have done to a seal. He was glad he had thought of putting a little bottle of whisky in his pocket for her. He handed it out to her now saying, "Take a sip at this every now and then. It will keep off the sea-sickness."

Miss Parker was too far gone to disobey any order. She sipped and sipped and soon she felt unbelievably restored.

The comfort, the divine comfort, of being found and looked after again. Nick's perfunctory arrangements for her comfort bore a significance which was as true to her as it mattered little to him. This was the antithesis of all the last hours. Alone without food and shelter. A man and a little boat to take her home. Pain, cold and despair. Comfort and heat from the drink which she continued to sip obediently and an exhilaration of spirit in which she denied to herself even that she had cried.

Never had Miss Parker known anything so near to delight as this return.

She threw herself back at her ease in this little boat come for her transport only. She counted the stars in the sky and laughed because she found them so difficult to count. She observed the mountain fires and the thought of them went through her with sharp delight. " Fire on the mountains. Run, boys, run." That was in a poem she had taught to Markie lately, but then she had not known its wild intention. Miss Parker felt very far from herself. She bit her thumb to convince herself of reality and felt her teeth very plainly and importantly. This did not convince her of reality at all ; only that she was rescued and comforted. There was a new aspect to everything. Sounds mattered so much. She knew exactly what they meant. Comfort was six times more good. She got more good out of everything. Nick's quiet doings in the boat enthralled her. She saw their purpose before they were complete. She could have accomplished such things herself with ease. She said to Nick, " I had better news of my sister yesterday. My sister is better."

" I'm glad of that," said he, looking at her closely. " Is she very sick ? "

" Tuber — tubercuar — Tuberercular.   *T.B.*," finished Miss Parker in a loud brave voice. She was not going to be beaten by a word like that.

" Isn't that sad ? " Nick's voice was very reassuring. " And she a young girl too, I dare say."

Miss Parker found herself telling him her sister's age and her own age and a great deal about their lives before Father died, and of the misfortunes that had befallen them since. To talk at ease like this upon the sea in a little boat was to Miss Parker a new and wonderful experience. For once she was not bound and tied in her own sense of superiority or inferiority. She uttered the thoughts that came into her head and to do so was complete pleasure.

Nick listened to her and made gentle answers as though he were speaking to Markie. Inwardly he now wondered how wise he had been to hand over the whisky bottle as he had done. A drop like that, he kept assuring himself, couldn't upset a child. Yet he could not escape from the conviction that it had certainly brought a strange change over Miss Parker. She was become a woman all of a sudden, and proudly female. He told her to sleep as he would have advised Markie to do, and she obeyed him, her foolish talk ceasing with a queer gentle obedience that touched him surprisingly.

Nick was conscious of finding himself in a faintly awkward predicament. He had left Master Markie's governess upon an island. He had failed to rescue her until the middle of the night. And now he had made her more than a little drunk. To say the least of it the situation would require some explanation when it came to her Ladyship's ears, and Nick had a horror of any form of explanation. It occurred to him that Miss Parker might be in serious trouble over the matter too, and this thought distressed him. After all she had told him to-night of her own and her sister's circumstances, the occupation of Master Markie's governess had more reality to his mind. It would matter to him now if this poor drunken little governess lost so comfortable a situation, and through his kindly meant efforts for her assistance.

When they reached the dark small quay under

his house, Nick woke her up, hoping very much that she had now quite slept off her potations. She woke up quite cosily and naturally. It was only too clear that, for the moment, the limitations and restrictions of her governess existence were gone. Nick felt that had Lady Bird been awaiting her there with a reprimand Miss Parker would have gathered herself up and given as good as she got. She was in no state to be confronted with her employer. What between sleep and whisky Nick was obliged to lift her out of the boat and put her sitting upon a rock while he tied up his boat and wondered what he had better do next. He thought perhaps he would go and find John and let him bring a car down the bosheen and fetch her away in that. In the meantime he would bring her to his house and make her a cup of strong tea in the hopes that this would have a sobering effect upon her.

Miss Parker agreed gaily enough to this plan. Was it not what she had thought of as the ultimate point of safety, only an hour or two ago—a nice cup of tea. Yes, a nice cup of tea. That was what she needed. She went bumbling happily along by Nick's side up the path from the sea to his house. Now and then he caught her elbow to steady her and now and then she caught at the pocket of his coat to steady herself. This sea-sickness had a very weakening effect on a girl. A very strange effect indeed. She did not feel at all herself. Yet she knew she was her real self, her own self that she had never found yet. She was very happy to sit on a chair in Nick's kitchen, the night sea and those dreadful islands behind her, the shut door and the fuchsia hedges and all this kindness between her and that desolation. She was happy to see the fire burn up when he turned the wheel beside it. The thought of Lady Bird and who had put Markie to bed had long ceased to torment her. All she wanted now was a nice cup of tea.

When the kettle had boiled Nick made a pot of tea in the gentle, unhasty way in which he was so well used. He cut her a piece of bread and butter, too, for he hoped that this might soak up the whisky in her empty inside. She was delighted with her tea and bread and butter and felt only cosy now. None of that lovely unsteadiness. Soon it occurred to her as a very sensible thought that she should make her way back to Silverue and her bed. She was loth to leave Nick's house, but the idea of her bed was very comfortable.

Nick agreed readily to her proposals for departure. "But," said he, "I will walk up to the house with you." After all it might be better not to wake John and create more disturbance than necessary over this unfortunate return. He began to hope that with luck the whisky drinking might be forever a secret between himself and Miss Parker. A secret between himself and one of the Silverue governesses —a very strange thing to take place.

Miss Parker made no silly objections to his company on the way back. It was one of the comforts that had been sent her to balance those other dreadful moments. When she said good-night she thanked him freely for all his kindness and said she feared he must be very tired.

" No, indeed," said Nick, " many a time I'd give the night on the sea."

" Ah, but you'd be fishing then, I dare say, not rescuing sea-sick women ? " said Miss Parker, conversationally. They were standing at a side door of Silverue and he wished very much she would stop talking and go quietly in to her bed.

" Good-night, miss," he said, and turning round he walked away from the big pale face of the house, leaving her standing there in the doorway to which she was far more of an alien than he was himself.

There was a fog before dawn that night, and in the fog the she-seals came wailing near Nick's house, and if they did their crying was half in his dreams for he dreamt that he opened his door to a woman and it was no woman but a little seal with Miss Parker's voice and she said, " Lady Bird has turned me into a seal for getting drunk and neglecting my duties." And Nick was responsible. A terrible tangled weight like a net full of stones was on him ; but what could he do for a seal or a governess? The one was as remote from him as the other.

XVIII

THIS was the Big Day. Eliza woke to the knowledge, admitting it with the flattened soured feeling one had when young on other people's birthdays.

This was Olivia's Thursday. The day of the garden fête. To-day should prove Olivia a more popular, resourceful, original woman, and a better gardener than that ambitious neighbour. Eliza was sure that Olivia had bounced in and out of bed already a dozen times to look at the weather and back again to ask Julian what he thought about it.

Eliza, burying her face in her pillow, pretended to herself that it was raining. She could see rain spearing the sea (waspish knitting needles of rain) and clouds sullenly obscuring the mountains. That was the sort of day that Olivia deserved for the way she had tormented everybody yesterday, and no doubt the social martyrdom would continue to-day. Eliza opened her eyes at last and beheld a revoltingly newly washed morning. A cloudless sky, an impossibly glittering sea, and out of her bathroom window on the other side of the house she would see a faint haze for heat on the mountains and a weighty air overburdening the may trees on the lawn, a weighty air between them and the grass.

Presently the sun would shine on bright groups of

three deck chairs dotted here and dotted there with
an apparent carelessness that did not in the least
conceal Olivia's unrelaxing determination that the
garden should be viewed from its most becoming
angles. And it will shine on those dreadful Pink
Pearl rhododendrons, enravishing the Beady Bonnets
of the town with their horrid splendour. The white
thorns (their whiteness now as near grey as makes no
matter in the morning) would be bridal and horrible
and the pink thorns almost as vulgar as their praisers
are. What a shocking afternoon it is going to be,
Eliza thought, and what a dreadful morning of
preparation is before us all. There will be more
labels to write saying, TEA ; saying, ICES ; saying,
TO THE SHELL HOUSE ; saying, MOTOR DRIVES 1/- ;
saying, GAMES ! (this with a girlish mark of
exclamation calculated to excite any but the
steadiest Beady Bonnet). There will be still more and
more dreary little bunches of rock plants to fasten
up and label this and that—whereas Eliza felt
pretty certain each bundle contained very little
beyond a hank of Aubretia at 1/3 a bundle. Olivia
was really robbing people.

The morning was like that, only worse. There
was an awful busy gloom about it. Olivia kept on
finding jobs for everybody, and when they had
done them to the best of their ability she came and
undid them and then gave them to somebody else
to do again. It really was horrifying. Like this :

" I wonder if it wouldn't be best to have the ices
in the Shell House ? Then people would go and look

at the Shell House and eat an ice as a matter of course."

" I should think they'd want a drink as a matter of course."

" You don't admire the Shell House. I always think it's just wonderful and shows what you can do with shells."

" My dear, I adore the Shell House now and then. But it's so exhausting. That industry ! "

" Well, darling, they love paying threepence to see the Shell House, so if you and Sheena would carry three or four chairs and the plates for the ices and some Woolworth spoons and arrange them there, I'm convinced there'd be big money in it."

When this was all accomplished and they had toiled up and down to the Shell House carrying chairs and tables and plates and spoons and arranged them in the draughts that always blew shrilly in this shady place which smelt darkly of cats and nettles and damp stone, they encountered Olivia— very brisk and not at all ashamed of herself—saying, " After all, I think *not* the Shell House for ices. I've arranged to have them under the horse chestnut where people can look at Pink Pearl. And darling, do you think you could print another notice, something like STOP ME AND BUY ONE, or, WHAT ABOUT AN ICE ? Just ICES looks so uninviting, don't you think so ? One wants something jollier, don't you agree ? " Then she would dash off into the house and move all the flower vases one inch to the left or right and dash out again to tell John he had marked out the Clock Golf Course in the wrong place, and didn't he think himself it would be better to have it in the Yew Square.

" I thought the band was to be in the Yew Square. Johnson has carried all their chairs there."

" No. I've put the band near the ices so that people can sit and listen."

" God help Sheena and Eliza." John moved himself and his whitening brush and his piece of string and his sticks to the Yew Square, rather comforted by the thought of other people's greater misfortunes. When he met Eliza, looking about as sour as he had ever seen her look, John said gloomily, " Wherever I go to-day I smell dead mice. And I keep on thinking it's Monday."

Eliza answered, " This is the longest week I ever remember. I thought it was Sunday on Wednesday, and to-day I thought it was Sunday, and I thought yesterday was Sunday too."

" Oh, Eliza, what shall we do for comfort ? "

" There's no comfort to-day. This evening we might escape."

Escape. Escape with Eliza to some quiet place where one could talk endlessly about oneself. How lovely that would be. John put down his whitening brush and for a moment he was lost from the busy burnished morning and from his horrid thoughts of the afternoon. But only for a moment. Then he caught sight of Olivia hurrying from nowhere to back again and saw her suspicious eye upon them. If they were not very careful another little job would be found for one of them to do without the other. Eliza saw this too. She started doing things with string and sticks and John leant down again beside her.

" Is this being awfully cowardly ? It's not, is it ? "

" No, it's only self-protection. If people behave like Olivia one must deceive them."

" Will it ever be luncheon time ? Don't you envy Markie at his lessons ? "

" He's not at his lessons. Olivia has found a good stiff job for Miss Parker. I saw her just now, carrying a stone as big as herself round and round the rock garden. Olivia made her shift it three times before she got it as she liked. I'd have gone and helped her for tuppence."

" I suppose nobody actually produced tuppence."

" No ; so I couldn't. I always keep my own bargains with myself."

Markie came to them at the gallop. He had seen them from far away and came at his best speed to them. No effort was too great for him. He had to spend himself somehow. He ran to them but flung himself on the ground beside them, a flinging sinking movement, and he lay there the only one in accord with the earth and the day. His bolt was shot now. For a moment he could be still.

Eliza felt a little excited as she always did when she saw Markie suddenly. So much that was beautiful. So much that could not endure, that passed as one dwelt on it. Too dear for any possessing. Unless one made jokes with Markie one was lost and one bored him. One must withhold oneself from him or be lost.

John had had much of this quality too, but now, since he had been forced to defend himself from life, much of this was gone from him. A great tenderness for John rose in Eliza as she lay there in the hot Yew Square, for she had laid herself down on the ground abandoning all pretences of work when Olivia passed. He was so sweet, working away there with his whitewash brush and full of answers to Markie's questions. He was too like Markie to have been hurt so much. What does he need ? she considered. What does he most need ? If I had it I would give it to him. But I have nothing that John needs—an old tired quag like myself. She hid her old fairy's face in her hands and wondered how near she was to tears. Now at twelve o'clock on a June morning. No. Not a tear.

John had completed his circle in whitewash. He looked all about him for Olivia, and as he could see her nowhere he sat down beside Eliza and together they sat there in the sun and made some fine jokes for Markie. They were both very good at this kind of gently balanced play-acting. Presently Markie fought with them on the grass. His eyes were wild and a wild and lovely colour was burning through him. He was in a storm of excitement. These short rapturous minutes were not enough. He must hurt somebody really before they were over. He must strike a blow that he might remember. But they were too cunning for him and the

moment passed. They had tired and would fight
no more, while the Little Boy was still screaming
with excitement. But this left him too, and he lay
on the grass beside them pointing sticks with John's
penknife in a quiet languor. Something within him
was spent. He felt better without it.

"You must finish making your clock," Eliza
said, "or shall I? I draw so much better than you
and so much faster."

"Yes, you do it for me, Eliza." He watched her
marking the strong quick figures round his uncertain
circle, spacing them with great sureness and skill,
he thought. Then, when she had finished, and he
thought for the next twenty minutes she would
sit and talk to him she went away leaving him
alone. She, the only creature with whom he was at
peace left him. Since she was gone even Markie lost
a part of his rare importance. This was because she
gave things so much by her knowing love for them.

Olivia's afternoon from her own point of view was
a complete riot. Everybody came. Not only the
faithful Beady Bonnets turned up—bringing their
Brownies with them to photograph Pink Pearl and
groups of their friends at the Shell House, and
wearing their new shoes, agonised but determined
to do honour to the party—but many other people
besides. Tennis players, and keen clock golfers, and
those who really paid a shilling for a row out to the
Bird Islands, and those who paid cheerfully for
motor drives to the mountains, for ICES and TEA and
STRAWBERRIES and conducted tours of the house—

where Lady Bird's bathroom was the special draw,
much exceeding in popularity pictures by the late
Mr. Raeburn or Mr. Lawrence. The bundles of rock
plants sold well too. Indeed their disposal provided
Olivia with one of her big moments of the afternoon,
for she discovered a Most Dishonest Person (whose
name she only revealed in whispers to the trusted
of the Beadies) going from bundle to bundle picking
horticultural treasures from Aubretia in the slyest
possible way. Perhaps this gave Olivia more
pleasure than any other happening in the day,
for there was nothing she enjoyed so much as dealing
with a ticklish situation in which somebody else was
hopelessly in the wrong. One thing perhaps she
did enjoy more—talking about it afterwards.
" What did you say to her, Olivia ? " they asked her
afterwards.

" I just asked her if she thought she was quite
playing the game."

" As one Gunner to another. And did she say,
' God rot it. Just my luck.' "

" I don't know what you mean, Julian."

" No. I'm glad you don't, darling. It's a very
thin form of wit to laugh at Gunners. But did you
really say that about Playing the Game ? I believe
you did. Oh, Olivia, you'll be the death of
me. . . ."

Julian had had a busy time all day too. He had
worked almost as hard as Miss Parker. But at least
he was able to talk about it and make everybody
pity him and have a nice drink, whereas Miss

Parker just went to bed feeling lousy. They thought she had had a very nice day for herself.

Sheena had spent such a day as never before she thought could come in her life. Things had happened to her—unforeseen, terrible and completely natural, and falling somehow so within the pattern of possibility as they happened to her that disaster seemed the only reasonable thing on earth or in her life.

At three o'clock Sheena walked out of the house and across the lawn to Pink Pearl with the prospect of selling ices for the afternoon affecting her as about the worst fate that could befall her for some time to come. Pretty hard, but there it was. One had to face it. Before she reached Pink Pearl the first car of the afternoon came round the turn of the grass and stopped at the front door. It was Silene's car and Silene was alone in it. This surprised Sheena so much that she stopped and turned back. Silene got out of her car and came across to meet her. She was wearing a pink dress and a pink hat, and looking like an enormous and consequential strawberry iceberg.

" I'm a bit early, aren't I ? No, I don't think I am."

" Yes, you are. You're the first person to arrive. It's extraordinary."

" I'm always surprising people. No. I think I'm most unsteady, really."

" It's lovely you've come."

" Oh, I love coming."

" Are the others coming ? "

" Rupert and Kirsty? No, I don't know. I think, doubtful."

" My dear, I must go and do things about these ices." Sheena looked shockingly bereft. She was too vulnerable. It was not quite decent. It left her too exposed—a wind blew between her and Silene dividing her from Silene because she was too young and meant what she said.

" I want to talk to you first. D'you mind ? I've got something almost impossible to say. It's been worrying me so much."

" We can't talk here, can we ? Olivia will come out and separate us."

" Yes. It's hopeless here. Let's go and stand on the gravel."

They stood on the gravel (though God knew why it was more private than the grass), and the wind dropped and the sun beat down on them, on Sheena's blonde head and painted face and on the cook's white overall. She looked so like a choir boy who had gone wrong (very wrong) that it was touching indeed to see her with that fat, hardy old tart Silene, talking sense to her there in the sunlight, with cars arriving all round them and they paying no attention to any but each other. Sheena listening and nodding her head in due acceptance of all Silene said. And Silene talked and talked, growing kinder and kinder and more indulgent the less Sheena answered her.

" You see it's been pretty desperate for me to

have to tell you all this. But what can one do?
It sounds a pretty stupid thing to say, but I love
Rupert. No, I don't suppose you understand. I'm
hurting him so much talking to you like this,
Sheena?"

"Silene, my dear—Sheena, will you go and help
Eliza with these ices. She's doing a screaming trade.
And tell Miss Parker I want her. Silene, don't you
think it was clever of me to get the swing boats to
come here? Such a draw. Shall we go up? Ever
so whoopsie, darling. Or dare we?" Lady Bird
gave one of her best girlish and party screams, and
catching Silene by the hand went jostling along
towards the swing-boats, endeavouring as she went
to infect a few Beadies with some of her own
enthusiasm.

"I'm not going up," Silene said sulkily. "I've
had enough dirty carriage accidents to last my time.
Let me go, Olivia, I want to play tennis before Mrs.
Critchley comes and spoils my afternoon."

A girl who was not Sheena at all was helping
Eliza with the ices. A creature who felt as sick as a
dog and as cold as a strawberry ice smiled and
nodded, and said, "Sixpence, please," again and
again to women in blue gabardine and lockets and
new shoes and hats trimmed with flowers and fruit.
The same creature laughed like hell when the Bishop
begged her to keep the change out of half a crown.
It was a truly episcopal way of buying a sixpenny
ice in aid of charity. And a fine episcopal joke
besides. One ought to laugh. Almost years seemed

to pass in this kind of way. And then Rupert arrived with Miss Parker.

"Miss Parker is going to help with the ices, Eliza," he said. "Do forgive me for once. But I must have Sheena."

"Not a bit, dear. As often as you like."

They went away together into the afternoon. They went for a country walk. Where they went affected them though they could not have put this into usable words. You think or speak about a thing too much and it becomes an untruth and lost. But the influence of a place and its presence was known to them both. It was not without intention that they left the sea behind them and walked up a small road made round the edge of the lake and leading into the mountains and nowhere else. The lake was on their left hand. The mountains on their right hand and before them. And the sea at their backs.

The sun was gone. The lake was the colour of a grey boat and the colour of the last primroses and the colour of moonlight. And the sky was grey. There was no bright sun to make the water dance and glitter offensively. But whenever they lifted their eyes to the mountains those heights were changed a little, for the light was not dead. There were winged spaces of light on the mountains as on a different country. Leaf green. The colour of bracken. Water green. Teal are cosy sweet birds flying two together close over the water, and tern are more lonely, flying high with dropped wings like knives to fly with. Their nests are on the lake islands. There were flowers by this road. Pale wandering crowns of honeysuckle. Foxgloves on every level, with them and above them. Fuchsia trained in a fence and fuchsia growing free, starved fronds on the rocks. Bell heather, turning the scabious to a true icy blue. And hazel nuts as sour as green apples. They went past a deep narrow well, dark as a bell, tented in stones with a worn stone like a chin before it. And a cold little stream deep beneath the roots of heather went down from the well to the lake, another element to that still water. The little road wound round a headland and there in the enclosed bay were many lilies laid upon the water, wax images on a sheet of lead, as still as that, as unconnected with any hoping or sadness.

They had come round a corner so they had a good enough reason for stopping now. Rupert said : " Has Silene been talking to you ? " He had been waiting to say this for the last twenty minutes and now it sounded more like an accusation than an inquiry.

" Yes, she has. She says——"

" I know exactly what she said, Sheena. She said your great-grandfather was as mad as a hatter and my grandfather jumped into the Rhine, and John has been a bit unsteady lately, and if you're at all fond of me you won't marry me. Isn't that more or less what she said ? "

" Yes, more or less what she said."

" And did she tell us anything we didn't know ?
Well, did she ? Tell me."

" No. I've known all about it just as much as
you have."

" Well, then ? "

" And always I've been just—that much—afraid."

" You're not to be afraid."

" Ah, but don't kiss me now. It's not fair for I
must tell you——"

" Tell me what you're afraid of then. No, I won't
touch you if you say not. Not for a minute, I
promise."

" It's all Silene says. It's true, I know, all she
says. About Bad Blood and Insanity, and if we
have a child the chances are it's born mad. Not just
unsteady for a moment like poor John was. I'm
unsteady enough myself."

" I'm not arguing with you, sweet, because there's
no betting about this. You are marrying me. But
look—I give you all you say about our poor little
mad child, but need we have a child in any case ?
Aren't we all right. Do you want one so badly ? "

" Oh, now you aren't being real at all. You're
laughing at me."

" I never laugh at you."

" No. Listen to me. You think I'm just being
girlish and making scenes and you'll give great love
out of yourself and everything will be grand."

" I don't think you're girlish. I think you're—
perhaps you're a tiny bit—I think you're
womanly."

" Oh, darling, how unkind you're being. Not listening."

" Well, now, what are you trying to tell me? Speak quite slowly."

Sheena spoke quite slowly in a detached and empty way, but beyond her detachment there was a thing fixed in her, an idea beyond speech or action, only Rupert could not hear it in her voice. He was nearly aware that she was being tiresome over all this.

" The thing is—I can't marry you. I don't intend to. I don't ever intend to. I tell you—I'm frightened. You needn't believe me unless you want to."

Rupert depended on his own power too much. He was not particularly vain but it did not occur to him that he could lose Sheena like this, or ever. He kissed her, and because she responded defence-lessly with virginal ardour he thought all argument was over. There were no words or reasons left against such love as this. This was not an older love such as understands itself, keeping its rules and knowing its own brief limitations, knowing how purely incidental its kisses are, knowing how time changes love and asking no imperative question of the future hour. Such love as they had was not schooled at all by accepted experience. They knew of no great lovers but themselves. Love was theirs alone for they had found it and the very meaning of these embracings lay in their belief that such happiness can be changeless.

A wind blew across the lake, wrinkling the water where the lilies were, bringing a cold smell of water and lake shore, blowing up as sharp as a knife into the mountains. Cold wind and wild birds, water and mountains never wholly known, their love was sharp and tender here. They were shelter and warmth only for one another. They had joy only of one another. There was no one else but Rupert and Sheena. The cold June evening, the wild birds flying to their surely known places, the smoke from a house they could not see, for all these things that shared their wild tenderness they had a gratitude and an acceptance. They were aware of them because they knew they ought to be there.

" Listen, Sheena, will you do something ? "

" Oh, it depends."

" Sheena, you've got to do this. I can't have people coming at you and upsetting you again."

" Well, what is it ? "

" You'll say I'm mad. But I know at this moment I'm right."

" Always right. It must be a grand feeling."

" Then, look, my sweet, will you do this ? Will you meet me to-night at the end of the Sea Avenue and we'll catch the Mail and be married in London to-morrow. Will you? Please, marry me. Just this once to please me."

" What time ? "

" Nine o'clock. Darling. Sheena."

" But it'll be dinner-time." Sheena wasn't going with him. No. She was back on earth now. Her

wild dreaming over and back in her mind all the
things Silene had said to her. She must defend
herself from Rupert for Rupert's sake. Now she
knew she could not love him more. But beyond
this love and this needing she had for him there was
a wilder sense of protection. Sheena knew things
Rupert did not know. She knew what it had been
like with John. She had a true feeling of what
John was suffering now. She had achieved in a
way to a hardness that comes of knowing, a decisive-
ness in accepting sorrow touching in one so young.
There were so many things Silene had said. About
Owenstown being left to her own child, not to
Rupert, and Rupert loved Owenstown so much.
All his soldiering years he would be thinking of the
time coming when he should live there. If Uncle
Jack had an object in life in which he was un-
reasonably bound up it was this thing of right
breeding. No difficult children or chances of
incipient insanity would get past him. This may
have been why he never bred a child himself, being
over anxious, but he was pretty particular about his
heirs for all that. . . . A year, Silene had said, so
reasonably, wait a year, my dear, and give yourself
time to think. . . . And time to change and time
to escape from this lovely happiness. Sheena knew
it all. She was young. She knew of no half-measures.
She gave or she took away. She didn't play at giving
or at taking, but where she found the blindness and
the courage to refuse was the strange thing. Sometimes the young have it before Life has shown them

how half-measures are best for tiding over the most cruel times. And how lies may be told and forgiven. And faith broken and mended stronger between two for its breaking. They are ignorant of this indeterminate hoping which they may learn. They have only their own harsh convictions and this courage to act up to them. Sheena was not going away with Rupert to-night nor any other night. Nothing could help her. She must deny herself for them both.

" No, my darling one, my sweet one. Not to-night."

" When ? "

" Not ever."

" But, child, you're unsteady. You're not talking sense. ' Never,' what do you mean ? ' Never ? ' "

" I'll write you a letter and tell you."

" Oh, don't be absurd. What good is that going to do anybody ? I'll write you a letter myself, and then I'll come and read it to you myself."

" It's no good. Laughing at me is no good."

" I can't get sense out of you. For God's sake now, be reasonable."

" And listen to you."

" And don't interrupt me. Listen. Silene doesn't want you to marry me, does she ? "

" Yes, she does."

" No, she bloody doesn't. You take that in. She doesn't like you, and Kirsty doesn't, either. They have a horrible woman they want me to marry. Rich as hell and a great girl friend of theirs."

" That has nothing to say to it, I don't think."

" All right, it hasn't. Well, then, she tells you a
lot you've always known about your grandfather
and a lot you mayn't have known about mine.
And then talks to you so kindly and tactfully about
dear John."

" All the same, it's true. It's all true. It's everything she says. It's Bad Blood. It's Insanity. It's
the Wrong Cross."

" Oh, my dear, but I've told you I don't want
a child."

" And what about Owenstown? You don't want
Owenstown either, I suppose? "

" Did she tell you that? She is a bitch."

He turned round to her.

" That's nothing to me, Sheena. Absolutely
nothing. Please, you must believe me. I've been
rather taken by surprise by all this, but I truly only
want you. I promise you. What good are houses and
children without you? "

And indeed it was true. Sheena sitting there
sullen and determined with the cold lake water
behind her, and the cold evening turning her face
pale under its paint. Was it the cold of the evening?
There never was a woman more loved. There never
was a girl so foolish. So entirely and exasperatingly
determined to hurt herself.

" Do you believe me? "

" Now you think so."

" Will you meet me where I said to-night? "

" No."

" You don't mean that. I'm going to be there."

" No, you mustn't come."

" What are you going to do then ? "

" Oh, I don't know." She was lost. " I think I want you to kiss me."

" Oh, you're so wonderful. Sheena, you know you must go on with this. You can't hurt me so much, can you ? "

Sheena did not speak.

" Well, can you ? "

" No. I can't."

" You'll be there to-night ? "

" No. I won't."

" If I say I won't make you come away to-night ? "

" You'll persuade me."

" I won't say one word to you. Will you be there ? "

" Oh, please, don't ask me."

" I'll be there. All by myself."

" No, don't. No, don't. You must not."

" But I will be."

" Do you know we've been here much more than an hour ? "

" Does that matter much ? "

" I suppose not. But we must go back some time."

" You're not going to do what I say ? "

" No."

" Do you mean that ? You can't mean it."

" Why ? "

" Because I'll be there—waiting for you."

" You're in a most tormenting mood."

" I swear I never felt more serious. I mean all this. I know it matters. I can't understand you."

" You're being a bit unlike yourself, yourself, aren't you ? "

" Because people are trying to mess us about and play hell to us."

" Now, can't you steady yourself, darling."

" I won't steady myself. I'm perfectly steady."

" Oh, you're not. And I love you so much. My sweet, I know I'm only a silly little virgin, but I love you so much."

" So am I a virgin. Isn't it awful ? You won't mind ? Ought I to discuss this with you ? "

" I don't mind. I'd sleep with you, you know. I'd enjoy to. But I won't marry you."

" I'll never sleep with you unless I marry you. I only want you to be my wife. You know I honour you. It's absurd, but I honour you so much."

" Ah, darling—so grand and so dignified. I've confessed to you I'm a virgin, but I know it's silly to go on like that. Not doing this. Not doing that. I know we're wrong."

" No. You can't convince me. I want to marry you."

" Perhaps you think I'm over-sexed. But I'm only thinking about you." Sheena really meant this.

" I don't think anything like that about you." Rupert was in his soul the faintest degree shocked. The discussion had got just a little off his own plane. Just a little way beyond him. Not difficult. It was lovely, really, to talk like this to Sheena. But ought he to do it. Perhaps it was her sudden girlish defence, "I'm only doing this for you," that had made the break in this confidence which mattered so much. He hurried back to his awkward and honourable plans. And so expensive too.

"You will meet me to-night."

"Oh, do please, kiss me again and stop talking about to-night."

"I'll be there——"

"You must stop saying that. You are to. Do you hear me?"

"I don't think I'll kiss you again."

"Just a tiny kiss. . . ."

But it got one nowhere, nowhere at all. No further in one's plans. Only in one's wishing and needing. . . . I'll marry you. No, I won't, I can't, but I'll sleep with you. No, I won't. Not unless you marry me. . . . It was all too difficult. Too absurd. And too tragic. It brought them nowhere. They left the cold lake at last and walked back down the stony wet road towards home speechless with too much love of a sort. The fuchsias wept for them and the wild birds cried more sadly and flew the farther and the higher from this human madness. The whole evening, having done its best to let them know and failed, was sullen as all good intentioned people are at their constant failures.

They came back to the end of the party by obviously different routes, and Rupert went into the house and wrote a letter still saying : *I will be there*, and left it on Sheena's dressing-table at great personal inconvenience, for Lady Bird was here and there too, and drove away without saying good-bye or good-night. So that she might gauge from that how confidently he expected to see her again that evening.

Sheena returned to the ICES in a sad state of emotional pain, and was distressed to find that they had all been sold. It was awful to have no employment to fill these minutes that hurt so much. How much they hurt and how futile all her determination seemed now that Rupert had gone and she was resolved not to meet him again to-night. She could find none but the best reasons to overcome her conviction, and distrusted these so much—to take what one wants often seems to the young so unreasonable that they must find some good reason to martyrise themselves before they dare to take.

Markie met her. He was wild with excitement, for he had just undressed the Aunt Sally and stuffed her body down a badger's earth.

" What was she like, darling ? "

" Like any other woman, I suppose."

" Wait till Olivia finds out."

" She won't know who did it. *I* did it."

" You're a horrible child. Where is Miss Parker ? "

" She's gone to the Bird Islands."

" Oh, darling, are you sure ? You know she hates going on the sea."

" Mummy said she was to. I got seven ices and three strawberries and cream, and this chocolate a woman gave me, and I won a whistle at a game, and I stole a knife."

" Oh, Markie, lists of things are so boring. I suppose you kissed your low friends from the village and changed hats with them. You'll have lice and ringworm too, I dare say. Disgusting little boy."

" I did not. I did not. Sheena, I'll kill you."

" I wish you would." Sheena spoke truthfully. She had been unkind even to the little boy.

"Ah, no. Kind Sheena. Tender Sheena. I wouldn't kill Sheena. Would I, Mrs. Mouse? But I'd kill you. You're a lousy bitch. Lousy bitch. You played with the village curs. I saw you. Let's kill her, Sheena."

" Ah ! No."

" Oh, do you remember when we threw her in the lake ? Wasn't it lovely ? "

" Down she went like a stone."

" My God, yes. Down she went like a stone."

" No my godding, you know."

" No, my God. Olivia'll come at me, will she ? "

" M'm."

" Will, she, Sheena ? "

" She will. Yes."

Markie was no help. That broad, romantic brow and angelic eyes, that cruel and sweet mouth, all the savagery of unpitying childhood kept him apart from Sheena now. Sometimes, where he understood pain, he could be gentle, restraining himself with a strange steadfastness. But now he belonged entirely to himself and to a state of things in which Sheena had trusted until to-day. Now she was left at the end of the land she knew. She could not see her way before her at all and to look back was more sadness than she was able to bear.

Markie was no help. Could she go to John, she wondered. To him, as to herself, things had been done that were outside himself. Far more than her he must know this feeling of terror for himself, helpless in a fate made by dead hands. Everything touched and weakened by the knowledge that one must not quite trust oneself, that one was set apart, the seed of danger sleeping in one.

Sheena did not say as much to herself. She felt wild and shaken. Tears were so near that she feared she would never reach the house to lock herself in some lavatory—if even there she might escape from the loyal and curious Beadies who still sat about with their bundles of rock plants and melting cream cheeses and agonising feet, and smiled at Markie and offered him sweets, all of which he delayed to accept. And in and out of the house they trooped steadily, like bees in and out of a hive. They could neither be avoided nor ignored, and if she had to speak these terrible tears would be shed here in the open knowing no shame.

" I'll race you to the house—sixpence," she said to Markie, ruling her voice with dreadful carefulness even to say this, and she ran across the grass and the gravel and past the groups of garden-viewers and applauding Beadies. She ran so fast that Markie was hopelessly outclassed—the form had never had such an upset before in a race with Sheena—which shamed him very much, so that he too, stopped and wept for shame, and for the loss of sixpence that he had thought so certainly within his grasp.

As for Sheena, she fled upstairs to find a belated party of the faithful in charge of the contemptuous Dora, peering one by one into her favourite lavatory, murmuring curiosity and appreciation. Wildly pretending that she was still racing with Markie, Sheena ran past them and through the baize doors that bounded housemaid's closets and stairs to the attics. Here among the water-tanks and the cobwebs and in the stored, unmoving heat she might be alone. And here she lay on the floor with old trunks and old boots, shivering and dizzy from running, but shedding not one tear. Things were not so easy as that.

XIX

Downstairs Olivia had ordained that Julian should show people the pictures while Byrne did his well-known conjuring turn in the tea tent. Admission sixpence.

"Come and see him, you really must." Olivia beamed on her Beadies. "And bring your husbands, they'll love him. You'll be amazed the tricks they'll learn."

"Ah, they're past learning anything new, Lady Bird," sighed the Beadies. Nevertheless, they obediently came and parted with their sixpences to watch Byrne do some rather obvious and dreary tricks with a couple of balls.

Julian went fitfully from picture to picture and invented nonsensical acts which he said his ancestors had done, telling absurd anecdotes about them. The pursuing Beadies thought they must have been very unsteady but politely refrained from comment.

"And who is this?" asked one of a more inquiring turn of mind than her sisters, pausing opposite that portrait of a lady to which Eliza had taken such exception a few nights before. "Hasn't she a great resemblance to Miss Sheena? The very two eyes of her, now, isn't it?"

"That is her great-aunt, Miss Sheena Curran,"

Julian said. He did not add any ridiculous story to this information. He looked at the portrait for a moment in a peculiar, hesitating sort of way before he led his Beadies on.

Out on the lined, hyacinth sea, as quiet as an old maid's tea-time, Miss Parker sat in Nick's boat, a rustling mackintosh over her sprigged muslin gown. She had been sent to tend a rather important Beadie who had felt squeamish at the thought of the sea and was at the same time girlishly anxious to pay her shilling and see the Puffins at their sexual play. It was called " seeing the sea pinks " and the Beadies told each other, and Olivia told them all, that they really should not miss it. But there it was.

Now they were returning and Miss Parker was being invited to supper and the pictures by the Beadie, who had taken quite a fancy to her. But the strange thing was that Miss Parker was able to refuse without a regret, explaining that she did not like bicycling at night. Such parties, which a week ago would have filled her with pleasure and satisfaction, seemed less important now. She felt excited and uneasy and far from herself. She did not know the reason why, but the reason was that she was waiting for the moment when Nick would help her out of the boat.

The party was nearly over. The garden which had been so obligingly at its best all day was cold now, with an air of unwelcome upon it ; a cold and a quietness nobody could disallow. Even Pink Pearl became a trifle remote and vinagrous. The night would soon be here ; the night in which a garden may be alone for a little and free from comment, adulation and criticism. Lady Bird was at last almost satiated with walking between her flowers, saying to the reverent : " I feel *so* like Ruth Draper, but I can't help wishing you'd all been here last week. . . ." Now she sat in one of the chairs near Pink Pearl, bracing herself to several smiles and aching for a cocktail. Prompted by John—who could play it on a comb—the band was halting through a version of " Good-night." Hesitant, incorrect, but romantic. Such of the guests as recognised the tune gathered themselves for a final leave-taking and the heads of the various entertainment departments (bearing heavy bags of money in their hands) clustered round Olivia. Weary but triumphant they counted the takings and found that they had exceeded by £3-11½*d.* their best previous record.

Olivia was so braced that she rose up and made a speech to the guests not already dispersed by the strains of " Good-night."

" Ladies and gentlemen," she said, motioning the band to stop. " Ladies and gentlemen, I want to really thank you all so much for coming here to support our garden to-day. I want to tell you we've made much more money than we did last year. And we all think it's for a very good cause. Don't we ? Where was I—— A very good cause, don't we ? And I want to really thank you all so much again for rallying round in the splendid way you

have. I think it's splendid of you. And with *other*
attractions too," finished Olivia, perhaps a little
on a weak note but determined not to sit down
without some public reference to that rival garden.

Markie got in before anybody in calling for three
cheers for Lady Bird. Exhilaration having passed he
was now feeling a little guilty and apprehensive
about the Aunt Sally and was in rather a blustering
mood in consequence.

Olivia looked lovely standing there in her pink hat
with her back to Pink Pearl. It appeared as though
she loved them all separately, anybody who was
there, she was so gay with them, saying good-
night and laughing and holding Markie by the
hand. And he was meek for once, leaning upon
her for he was tired, his blustering over, and a little
fearful about the Aunt Sally. And behind this last
group, beyond the trodden grass of the lawn, the
garden slowly recovered its isolation. Cold hands
were stretched out towards this group. A circle
closing even round Olivia's inspired good-nights
and Pink Pearl's vulgar excellence.

XX

It was Julian who broke the news very gently to Olivia after dinner, dimming for a time a little her sensation of supreme success. He said : " My dear, a note came this afternoon from the Rival Gardener. She sent you ten shillings."

" My dear, I wish I'd thought of doing that," said Olivia with immediate regret.

" Yes, it would have been a fine gesture of neighbourly contempt and good feeling. As a matter of fact, you can make it next Thursday if you still feel inclined to."

" What do you mean, Julian ? "

" Well, darling, it's all a mistake. She never thought of opening her garden till next week. You must have got the dates muddled up somehow. She hopes you'll manage to come next week as the azaleas are *past words*."

Olivia said faintly : " And I made such an effort."

" In any case, you'd have won with stones in hand," Julian said tenderly.

" Do you think I would ? "

" Yes. I always think so."

XXI

When at last the party had passed, but before dinner was within sight, Eliza and Julian met in the library for one of their cosy gossips over a glass of sherry. The room was full of the saddest sea light, and Eliza and Julian were both completely exhausted by the horridly successful day. Perhaps this was the reason why their talk was not informed by that inspired warmth which they both looked for in it. This sport of conversing on matters near to them was a favourite pastime of Julian's. For Eliza it was a different thing. There was always present with her the urgent necessity to make this one thing she had with Julian a sharp and real success. Even such a rare creature as Eliza can try too hard when she minds too much. Usually she was more amusing when she talked with John, and lighter and wiser. She was like that with Julian often when this loving did not unbalance her. She was the same, full of tender malice and new jokes, not striving to give more than she had, and giving herself time to wait and take.

But to-night was one of the wrong times. Julian seemed bored, tired and disturbed. He took very little notice of Eliza as though, having brought her there himself, he wished God would take her away. Nothing she said came out right or meant anything. All importance was lost. She talked about the

203

dreadful day and he said he had enjoyed it. " If Olivia's garden had been a failure I could have cried with vexation," he said. " But it wasn't, and I enjoyed every moment of it."

" You weren't selling ices," Eliza reminded him with rather childish venom.

" Poor Eliza, we do treat you roughly. You selling ices from three till six."

" Oh, I didn't mind." Well, such a thing to say. Suddenly she felt so emotional that she could have cried. Her hands and feet seemed to start up into enormous proportions. Only equalled by the unkindness of the world and of Julian—particularly Julian—with his pleasure in Olivia's success and his affectation of having enjoyed the day. Her anger towards him surprised her and gave her strength. It was so unreasonable.

" How lucky for you that you enjoy this sort of thing. I wonder you don't do it oftener. It must be nice if you enjoy that kind of vulgar feudalism. Breathless interest in bathrooms. Last words in modern sanitation. Seen at Silverue. Sir Julian and Lady Bird love their garden. One of Sir Julian's favourite hobbies——"

" My dear, what a very cheap, journalistic outlook you have. Perhaps you're tired this evening ? "

" Yes, I am rather tired," Eliza said. Something terrible would happen in a moment. Sheena had not been nearer tears. But Eliza was so old. She could put a name to emotion and that is half the battle in stilling unreasonable passions.

Half the battle obviously is not all the contest. Eliza drank up her sherry and sulked for a few minutes, because she knew sulking was safer for her than talking. Then she said she thought perhaps a bath would be a good thing and Julian let her go without one gentle word for he knew too, how near she had been to tears, and although he would coast dangerously near these moments with Eliza, he would not see her tears nor allow to himself that he had shaken her. It happened so rarely, at such long and dear intervals, that for long periods he would forget all the things he knew and then when the mood was on him he must prove to himself by unkindness his certain power. Prove to himself, but she must not know he knew. It was not entirely a malignant game on Julian's part. It was in a way a kind of defence he put up for the preposterous behaviour of Olivia whom he loved. He would prove, even for a moment, to Eliza that all her fine balance, her accurate perception, her acid comment, her successful pose at living were nothing. He would force from her an admission that she had not much. That she had nothing, indeed. Less to take and less to give than his silly Olivia for whose early faithlessness and perpetual stupidity she must not dare to pity him. If he chose to show her sometimes that he suffered, he honoured her. But if she let him know by any act or word that she knew he suffered, she dishonoured him. Then he must hurt her. To-night he had been exhausted and exasperated after the dreadful day Olivia had inflicted on them

all and because of this he had wildly defended
himself, Olivia's day, and Olivia before Eliza could
begin to be sympathetic or derisive or amusing about
any of the three. He did not feel very happy over
Eliza now, although he would hardly admit to
himself how much it was in his power to wound
the silly dove in her.

Eliza's silly dove was in a tiresome mood this
evening. After she had bathed she took her for a
little walk up the birch wood to see if that could
cool her ardour and her pain a little. The virgin
austerity of the birches had rather the same effect
upon Eliza as Markie's distance and beauty had
had on poor Sheena. They were too much apart to
be the least use or to assuage or in any way comfort
her. They were sadder than Markie and less distracting, so perhaps they helped and failed about
equally.

Eliza was wearing a long silver evening-gown and
a green tweed coat. She went toiling up the path
through the woods as though she were a tree herself
walking. Now the evening was more silver than it
was grey, and when the birches thinned and scattered
there were rocks among the scabious and the bell
heather where you could sit and see an angle of the
house which was like a dream of a place that you
will see and have known before you see it. Not a
very pleasant or comfortable dream. This was
where Eliza was going.

" The trouble is, of course, that I'm in love with
Julian," she thought as she walked toiling in her

lovely way between the birch trees. " I do know this—I'm always putting it on a plate and explaining it to myself—screeching old baggery that I am. Why do things look so much more awful on a plate ? I don't think accurate consciousness is the least help to an emotional woman like myself. I had better go back to London and recover my balance. I must be feeling very strong and right to survive Silverue for long."

A pause took place in her sad thoughts when she sat herself down up there by herself in the heather ; one of those queer mental rests when one thinks of absurd things like the first bicycles or the cost of a ciné-camera, and for a moment one's desolation becomes of less importance. Eliza sat on picking with a thumbnail at little pieces of lichen on her rock and thinking, not of Julian, nor of Silverue and its sad children, but of her London flat and of how much money she was prepared to spend on a new bathroom there.

Behind her on the mountains there was an even pale light. The heather and fern near her were clumsily brown and green, but farther away were those spaces of water-green light on the young fern, like countries marked in a map, but phantom and changing. Far below her was the sea like a cup half-full of water, one could see so little of it, and what one could see was only a repetition of the young birch leaves' colour ; an ice, green, still sea, as unallied to the grey skies as the far fern. For a moment, and by chance only, thus. In the hollow between the sea and the garden and the wood of birches Eliza saw the roof and the higher windows of Silverue, and one corner of the house only to the ground. There was a benignant air about this flattened view of roofs—a great wandering spread as of wings to shelter—which might have deceived a person who did not know Silverue well. Silverue of narrow steep beauty and unkind, inward-looking eyes. Silverue that had not even one ghost, only perpetual presences of things past and done. Looking down, Eliza shivered, afraid for the first time of Silverue as a place, and thinking she would be better away from it and knowing the place disregarded her really, and knew how anxious and helpless she was about those who lived there and whom she, a stranger, loved. There Eliza sat, picking still at the moss and lichen on her rock, and knowing for the first time an animosity between herself and this place she loved. It was as bitter to her as if she had suddenly found that Julian whom she loved too had turned on her.

It was then that John came walking down from the hills to her. Perhaps it was too dramatic a moment for him to arrive, but that was how it happened exactly. He had not been very far, he had spent an hour in a near plantation snipping double leaders off the young trees to save his soul from the effects of Olivia's party, and now he was coming back to dinner.

The sight of Eliza sitting there alone took John very much by surprise and when he could see her grieved and tender face he was quite shaken. Eliza to look like this—Eliza so safe and divine a shelter to the grief of others. Could she look like this ? More desolate, more in need of comfort than himself. John was very moved. He kissed the cold rim of her cheek and asked her : " What is the matter, my darling ? Tell me, my dear Sweet, dearest Eliza." He was carried away by his own foolish, loving words, and when she did not answer he took her in his arms, kissing her eyes and her cold cheeks, and then he kissed her.

As for Eliza, she always found love most natural and comforting, and she was entirely balanced and aware in her acceptance of this young creature's sudden lust ; for love it could not be. Nor does pity manifest itself in this way. She was a little puzzled for she could not decide what John thought he had found. Romance ? Love ? A creature to cherish ? Or whether he knew what he had found. Perhaps he did know. She felt very restored, very gentle and affectionate in herself. She found a new side-road open to her from Julian, from Julian who loved John, in this love that she could give to John now. This love that he had so fortunately discovered he needed.

" Eliza, look at me. Darling, you're so wonderful. Why didn't I know before you cared about me ? Darling, tell me. Don't be so obstinate. Oh, my God, I love you so much. I think I do, don't I ? "

Eliza leaned back from him to look at him. She did not think she could laugh with him yet at this

love. And she must not laugh alone. Then she did
not want to laugh at all for when she looked she saw
John as he had been before all this had happened
to him, with that renewed in him which she loved
so much in Markie—a deep life, a beauty, a cruelty.
That thing which had died in John was alive again
and she would shelter its living with all the power she
had in her. At that moment she would have made
any gesture of extravagance to keep this spark alive.
She would have put her two bare hands under
John's feet. She would have broken a bone in her
body. But no extravagance would be required.
Only that he should still think she needed him for
a little while. This thing would not endure for very
long. But for a little while it should be between them.

There is a month in the autumn which has the
same rare and passing quality as this love which
Eliza knew she could give to John. Beautiful, untrusting, and tolerant in loving. And aware. Aware
of the present and the future (put aside). Through
a past, through infinite experience both gay and sad,
Eliza was made kind and given a power to take much
more to her purpose than the giving and giving of
youth. She said :

"How can I tell if you love me, sweet one ? I
only know about myself."

"What do you know about yourself ? Tell me."

The sea below them had changed and the house
and the woods were alien and malign. Young and
cold, the summer evening had turned from them.
Eliza did not give *that* for the ignorant prudery of

the evening. She was now quite violently attracted by John.

"Are you ever embarrassed, John?"

"No. Or only with very young girls."

"How terrifying they must be."

"Poor sweets."

"Poor sweets."

"You haven't told me?"

"Well, I'll whisper it to you—I'm so afraid of echoes. Listen. I'm whispering now. Do you want to sleep with me, or are you indifferent?"

John said: "If I can't sleep with you now I'll die. But do you mean this?"

Eliza said: "My darling, I do. I do want it. . . . Look, John." She laughed. "I'm frightened to say this. But, it's past dinner-time. I think it must be."

"Well, it's just dinner-time. Do we have to go?"

Eliza stood up. John thought when he saw her standing there in her silver gown with the back of her sweet head to the birches and the sea that he would never again want any woman so much. And never he thought would he find one who needed his loving more.

They walked down together through the birches and John kissed her again before they left the shelter of those pale radiant limbs. How charming John looked, Eliza thought, so ardent in this grove of virgin birches. No doubt one day he would make such a maiden his wife and she would turn with chill incomprehension from the thought of Eliza.

Need she ever know about Eliza? There was no reason why any person should ever know.

"Darling, you must stop playing at Heavy Saturns and come in to dinner."

"Don't you mind that I won't be alone with you for hours? It's worse than starving. I suppose you don't mind."

"I do mind."

"I don't want you ever to be away from me. I don't want anybody else to speak to you. You must talk to me all the time, Eliza."

"No doubt we'll exchange a few words now and then."

"Oh, Eliza, you will be sweet to me? It's like losing you seeing you with all these people again. I think I've lost you already. You're so cold and gay."

"No, you haven't lost me yet."

They crossed the cold lawns so lately trampled by loyal and painful feet The table for ICES was still there and the clock-golf circle in the Yew Square. It seemed to John about seven days since he had made this with dreary carefulness in the morning. and had thought how pleasant it would be to escape with Eliza and talk about himself. Eliza remembered too. But she was more accustomed than John to these sexual surprises that life so often holds in store for the most determinedly platonic friends.

XXII

OLIVIA was in gay order at dinner-time, for this was before Julian had been obliged to halve her triumph over the garden's success. She was full of her jokes and laughed at them heartily, and when John came in rather late she repeated them all for him.

" I think I must be getting a bit old for Olivia," John said to Eliza at the first moderately discreet opportunity. " The more matey and contemporary she is the older I feel. I feel my bones positively creak at times. And I quite shudder at some of her dirty cracks."

Eliza had strengthened herself with a glass and a half of wine before John came in. She gave him a slow, provoking look, and said : " You're very grown up to-night in some ways—aren't you ? "

She had watched for him to come in and had seen about him (perceiving it with the exaggerated truth in which wine can illuminate a happening) that insincere air of oblivion which she had observed in Sheena on the first night of her visit. He seemed to have gathered himself out of all his defence and defiance for this thing he had found he wanted. He was the slightly grand, very complete creature he had been before madness had overtaken him. Even this rude little speech about Olivia was made with more tolerance than spite.

Sheena was not there for dinner. Her chair and her place were set between Julian and Olivia. " A tiny headache, poor girl," Olivia explained in a sisterly way. Eliza decided that she would go up and see the child after dinner. But when she did it was to find a dark and chilly room and a voice of repelling coldness and dignity which said : " I'm quite all right, thank you. . . . I thought perhaps I might go to sleep." . . . Well, if that was the way of it, Eliza thought, she might just as well be left till to-morrow. She shut the door and did not hear a dreadful changed small voice calling : " Eliza, Eliza, come back to me."

Passionately obstinate and of as single a mind as only the young can be and suffering as only the young can when they discover first that such a thing is, Sheena lay in her dark room, filled with the ignored sound of the sea, and with her grave acceptance of sorrow, and with the bitterness and strength of her refusal.

It was not in nature that she should have refrained from writing to Rupert when she had discovered the *I will be there* note on her dressing-table. She had written an answer which caused the tears to start to her eyes now when she thought of it. Had she been sufficiently tender? Had she been firm enough? Would he understand that everything was finished? No more love, " but I hope I will always be your best friend," with the extravagant belief in the impossible that the young have (along with their touching ability to write such things to their lovers in all faith), Sheena had written this, and added : " Perhaps we'd better meet somewhere and discuss this reasonably." And added to that : " Darling, promise to forgive me for not coming to-night." It was a wild, tangled, determined letter and entirely represented Sheena's state of mind. There was only one thing not set down quite clearly in it and that was her determination not to go away with Rupert to-night or any other night. Silene had said things to her with hysterical candour and brutality against which Sheena had no argument or defence to produce. There was no argument against a truth so presented when one knew as Sheena did that all Silene told and all that she foretold came well within the bounds of the possible.

So Sheena had written this touching letter of despair and renunciation and undying love and sent it by the hand of Miss Parker (a strange but willing messenger for Love), and now she lay in more grief and loneliness than she would ever in her life have imagined possible or ever, probably, know again. Such pain seemed not to be a part of life at all. And yet it concerned her whole life. It was her life now. She saw it clearly as her life for the first time, and with this moment of complete consciousness there came to her a savage refusal to accept so much pain. If such pain was to endure only for a little while she could face it, but she looked on with the conviction of simplicity and saw it living as long as she should live. And now to face this desolation was beyond her power. She was too young for that mercy of seeing things tempered, through a glass darkly, and so this sudden total awareness of desolation broke her resolution. It was more, much more than she could bear. . . . And she need not bear it. She had taken this upon herself and if there was need for it she knew a wilder need. All this she had done was wrong and mad—to refuse joy, to grasp such pain as she knew about now was not sane. And to hurt a creature so dear to her, whose every word and movement caused her such sweet disturbance, this was the cruelty of a poor mad girl. Sheena flung herself out of bed with a wild and single determination to see Rupert her love.

She looked at that extravagant timepiece he had given her and saw that there was twenty minutes still before he would be there, twenty minutes to get out of the house and down the avenue. It was possible if one wasted no time. Sheena seized a coat from her cupboard, gave her face a hasty dash of powder and lipstick, and went stealthily down the passage, her mind blank but for this one thing, this resolve to see her love. She escaped from the house without interference and started to run across the lawn stumbling in her vulgar, pink, bedroom boots— boots heavily plumed with ostrich feather, their sharp heels sank neatly into the turf and the wind whipped through their trimming and wound the tail of her nightgown into a flying wisp behind her. She was over the lawn and running down the avenue now, the trees over her, and her feet running on and on through the cage-like pattern of branches. She held her coat round her with her hands (for she had no time to fasten it) and cursed her pink boots (holding on to them with her toes as she hurried along), telling herself that she had oceans of time. But as she ran fear beset her that she would be late and the poor girl took off her pink boots and ran upon the beech nuts and gravel on her bare feet. And then, far off at the end of this cruelly long avenue, Sheena heard his car arrive and stop. And she ran on the faster, crying : " Wait for me ; oh, wait for me," like a lost child. And then she heard the car turned round and driven away. Now, although she should have understood the finality and hopelessness of her case, Sheena hurried on sobbing towards the road. " Why couldn't he wait for me ? Why couldn't he wait a minute ? " Then she heard Miss Parker coming briskly towards her, and she fled in among the trees, standing in the glossy shelter of an ilex like a poor white-breasted deer, holding herself as perfectly still. And when Miss Parker had passed by she leaned upon the tree shuddering and crying, and put on her pink boots again and went, crying as she went, back to her bed.

Miss Parker did not go back to bed so quickly. Since Sheena had promised to keep an eye on Markie for the evening, Miss Parker was determined to make the most of her stroll. She had not much enjoyed delivering Sheena's note to Rupert, for, although it was comforting to her to meddle herself once more

in the drama of current life (as she had done with
so much tact when Mrs. Little went to the pictures
with the insurance agent), this affair of Sheena's
had no note of cosy intrigue about it. There were no
confidences and private moments between Sheena
and Miss Parker. Sheena had come to her because
she was the handiest person to send with such a
message. . . . " Miss Parker, would you mind giving
this note to Rupert? He'll be at the sea-avenue
gate at half-past nine. Thank you very much. I'll
keep an eye on Markie while you're out." That
was all Sheena had said to her. No word of caution
about Lady Bird. No explanation as to why she
didn't go herself to meet Rupert. Miss Parker
recalled Sheena's prolonged absence from the ICES
this afternoon. She had been away so long that
either much love or much quarrelling could have
taken place. Indeed, there had been time enough
for both, Miss Parker had considered, as she served
ices to the insatiable Beadies and their still greedier
descendants. And this was the outcome of it all, Miss
Parker trotting down the avenue with Cheerio (to
whom a rather ineffective purge had been ad-
ministered to-day) on the end of a string—an
excellent reason for a walk should Lady Bird chance
to encounter her and question her nocturnal
expedition.

She had waited for some time in the dark embrace
of the gateway before Rupert arrived. It had a
disheartening effect upon her, this lovely gateway,
for it was sad as many gateways are. The curves of its

walls were melancholy and the perpetual damp of the climate had greened each separate fluting of the four cut-stone pillars. There were three gates. A central one of nice and just proportions and two high, narrow gateways for pedestrians, one on either side like two demure sad nieces. The sea-avenue was hardly ever used, except by Sheena and Rupert, and these pretty gates had a most neglected air in consequence. Evergreens crowded in upon them from the avenue side and on the grand sweep beyond there was faint light-green slime, in character partly fungoid and partly seaweed. There was an air of undisturbance over the whole place which was curiously depressing.

Miss Parker found herself thinking of Sheena's face when she had handed over the note. Sad. That was what it was. Oh, ever so sad. Miss Parker clicked her tongue ruefully, leaning her shoulders against one of the sad niece gates. Miss Parker began to realise acutely the extreme sadness of Sheena's face as she leant there against the gates, waiting for Sheena's lover. She said, " Ever so sad," but in her heart she saw Sheena in this dim forsaken place, a doomed nymph—set apart for sorrow. A feeling of panic overcame Miss Parker as she waited by the lonely gates. There was a cold dwelling of sorrow here from which she was set apart, but knew its presence. It was like an old truth made new to her, this unhappiness in Silverue. She had a sudden overpowering sense that those who belonged to such a place could not escape from sharing in its sorrow, and she thought with grief of her gay pupil, Markie.

Such wild thoughts are only true to those who hold them for the shortest moments. Miss Parker was distracted from them by the arrival of Rupert's car. She stepped out through a missish gate and handed over Sheena's note with a deprecating smile.

The gates and Miss Parker, like a little bearded gargoyle stepping forth from their embrasure, Rupert was staggered by this, for he had not thought that Sheena could fail him ; not in coming to meet him at any rate (though even he had cooled down a little over the dash for the Irish Mail), but this was too quelling. He looked at Miss Parker with hatred and surprise, then he recollected himself, thanked her politely, and drove away as quickly as he could.

Miss Parker walked sadly back down the avenue with Cheerio, still obdurately constipated, tugging her along. Sorrow and happiness—they were two states of being that Miss Parker had not before seriously considered. Now she saw that they were in places as well as in circumstance. She could not perceive this now with the same truthful brevity with which she had caught hold of the idea a few minutes ago, but all the same she felt it. Her mind questioned some matter not concerned with the efficacy of depilatories or the possible hazards concerning one man and sixteen girls. In fact she considered a matter which was strange to her and she recognised it as strange and as sad. When she came to where the avenue forked, turning either

back to the house or down to the sea, she chose
without much hesitation to pursue the turning that
led down to the sea.

She was glad when at last she came to the little
gate where all the encompassing jungle of greenery
ended and the clear emptiness of a field took its
place. After the heavy shelter of Escalonia, Fuchsia,
Ponticon rhododendron, and Portugal laurel, this
bare space of grass seemed as white as a bone that
the sea has washed and the sands have scoured.
Miss Parker stepped eagerly out of the dark
shrubbery and walked towards the sea. Her feeling
of sad presage left her here and one of sharp
expectancy took its place. She prepared a defence
to herself for herself as she went along. There is no
reason why I should not give Cheerio a run on the
beach before I go to bed . . . a very rational thing
to do. . . . A very good place to walk in the
evening. . . . The sea air makes one sleep. And
many other good reasons she gave herself for
walking along the hard sand towards the river
beyond which was Nick's house. It was a fairly cold
evening. There was no romantic weight of warmth
either on the sea or the mountains. The sand was
as white as paper near the cliffs and dark where
mean waves slid back from it into a stewing of
broken weed. It was not a propitious sort of evening
for Miss Parker to go looking for love. She had about
as much chance of finding it as had the two little
black cows that stood together in the clefted shelter
of a rock, perhaps dimly in hope that love might

come to them out of the sea as once it had come to
a lonely cow of their kind, and sea lion and Kerry
cow had bred the first Dexter. Cheerio barked
and scolded these incontinent little cows as he
passed by, but they only stirred about in their
shelter and settled themselves again to wait or to
rest.

Miss Parker walked on. She got as far as the
foot-bridge over the river, and there she stopped
to ask herself what she was doing. She answered
herself : I am taking Cheerio for a little walk ;
and she waited, leaning on the rail of the bridge and
looking now down at the dark outflowing water
beneath her, now out at the sea, so pale by contrast ;
and now across to Nick's white cottage. She felt
very timid and full of the best excuses for herself,
and she waited, thinking : He may come home
this way.

She waited for some time. Waited, indeed, until
she saw a light appear in the window of the house
she watched. The little white house which had
appeared so bright in the evening turned dim
because of the light that shone from its window.
At last, full of fear and shame Miss Parker tugged
at Cheerio's string and hurried back along the shore
(past the Kerry cows who had had no success
either) and through the cold unkind evening to the
big house where she lived, but in whose life she had
so little part.

XXIII

IT was a week later. The time was evening. Silene
and Kirsty were giving a dinner party at Owenstown
before proceeding to the fowl-and-damage-fund
dance which had now taken the place of Kirsty's
theatricals as a support for fox-hunting, and
possibly as a more reasonable way of enjoying an
evening and getting drunk in a good cause. Kirsty
and Archie were the only people who really minded.
But Cruise had managed to cool even Kirsty's
ardour for this rather Russian and forthright sort of
drama which she had copied out with such
commendable industry.

"It simply won't do, Kirsty," he had said. "It's
a grand piece and all that, but you know it made
me blush, any of it I could make sense of. The
District Nurse might enjoy it, but I don't think anybody else would particularly."

So the piece was abandoned and quite soon
Kirsty recovered from her ill-humour and joined in
the game of quoting little bits from the Piece in
answer to almost any question anybody asked. It
was a joke which was very amusing to those who
understood it—if inconceivably dreary to those who
did not.

There was one person who could not see any fun

in it at all and that was the authoress of the Play.
Kirsty had invited her to come and produce and
had forgotten to write and mention that the idea
of acting her play was off. However, Aunt Louisa
told her that they were going to have a fine dance
instead and she must stay for it. She would be sure
to enjoy herself. Nobody else wanted her to stay,
least of all, Kirsty, who found her intelligent
friend's appearance offensively corduroy in the
country air and felt miserably self-conscious when
forced to go about with a woman whose hair was
like that, and who wore a signet ring and almost a
dinner jacket.

" Why did you ask her? " Silene said dully in
answer to Kirsty's complaints on the evening of the
party.

" I've told you, I forgot I had. And how can I
always remember how filthy some of my friends are."

" She's going to have a hideous evening," Silene
said with satisfaction.

" We must stop Cruise quoting those nice pieces
about Labour Pains and only Wind."

" No, I won't have him stopped. I think he's
marvellously funny." Silene went on painting up
her face for the party and smiling to herself. She
was quite looking forward to the evening.

Sheena was coming to the party, and John, and
Eliza was coming too, because John refused to go
without her. For the rest, besides Cruise, Archie
and Jane, a couple of dim young men had been
bidden too.

Neither Kirsty nor Silene had really wanted to ask the Silverue party, but it seemed rather stupid and drastic not to do so, and Sheena had accepted only because it seemed equally stupid and drastic to refuse. For so long she had been asked because Rupert would not go dancing without her.

Silene said now, " I'm not worrying about Rupert and Sheena any more. It was a marvellous plan having it all out with her."

" Why are you so positive it's O.K. ? "

" O.K. Oh, darling, how I hate O.K. Must you ? Must you ? "

" Yes, because it's swell. But why are you so positive ? "

" Well, I just told her the dreary facts. And she saw. That's all."

" Poor sweet. But she'll recover. Rupert's been so impossible though. Have you noticed ? "

" Have I noticed ? My dear, he's insufferable. Poor sweet. But he'll recover."

" We were right ? "

" Oh, I think we were *so* right."

" How did you really put it to her ? "

" I just said it was up to her entirely. Rupert was never going to let her down. She must let him down. For his sake."

" I think we were right, you know."

" Oh, I think we were *so* right."

" It's not going to be difficult to-night, I suppose ? "

" Except for you and your corduroy girl friend.

I don't think it's going to be difficult for anybody else."

" Oh, my God, Silene ! Do you think she has another dinner jacket besides the ones we've seen ? "

" You ought to know, my dear. You saw a lot of each other in London."

" But you must help me, Silene. The shame of it all. And you know how distressingly normal I am. Anything like that terrifies me."

" Does it ? Yes, of course. Oh, look. Who's here ? Here's Cruise. Don't yodel, darling. I've such a headache. Do you want a drink ? There's some in the window. Do go away, Kirsty. I think I want love."

" No, don't go away, Kirsty, dear. I don't want love. Silene's so insatiable, and anyhow I don't mind you. How's your outdoor friend ? You look weary. Have a cordial, my dearie. What has she been doing to you ? "

" Oh, do I look weary ? I must dash myself up a bit. No, Silene, I'm *not* going away. Cruise says he doesn't want love. Didn't you hear him say so. That's the way to lose a man, dear. I'm only saving you from yourself. Isn't that right, Cruise ? Doesn't that sound fair to you ? "

" That sounds fair to me."

" I wish you'd both get to Hell out of here and let me dress myself." Silene was suddenly furious. She had run black into her right eye and the pain was intense. Soon she would be in tears. " Oh, it's not *fair*—you know I've a filthy headache, and I

feel awful. I haven't been right since that stinking
horse of Cruise's threw himself down and rolled on
me. My head's not right and my back's not right,
and I can't enjoy things like I used to do. But none
of you understand——" Silene flung her head
down on her dressing-table, her viper's curls a perfect
riot over her enormous blacksmith's arms.

"Now, now, Silene. Steady. My dear, steady,
now. You're a lovely girl."

"Oh, get out."

"You'll ruin your face going on like that."

"Yes, won't she. Shut up, Silene. You're so
boring and terrible, my dear. Oh, Kirsty, let's look
at her potions she has here. Let's read about them.
Isn't it bloody marvellous what these things do ? "

Cruise had a nice read at the labels on Silene's
bottles and sniffed away happily at their contents,
chatting to Kirsty while Silene recovered herself,
wiped her face clean, and started off again busily
dashing things upon it. Presently she drank up
Cruise's drink and felt more reasonable. It was not
perhaps a very happy start to the party, but then
plenty of Silene's best parties had begun like this
and gone on surprisingly well. They were all used to
her temperaments and took as little notice of them as
possible. She was a grand girl, lovely and generous.
She stood as sullen and dignified as a child being
dressed for a dancing class while they fastened her
pink dress upon her to-night. She was not very good
at dressing herself and never cross with the people
who did it for her. She put on her real pearls and

her false pearls and her rings and stood asking for approval without any dreary provocativeness.

"You look grand. You look swell," they told her approvingly. "Don't get over-excited at dinner and throw food down your dress."

"No, I won't."

"Now we ought to go and torment Kirsty's woman."

"Oh, don't let's speak to her any of us and then perhaps she'll know we don't want her to come to the dance."

"I do. I want her, Kirsty. I think I'll get drunk with her, to-night, myself."

"Nobody must get drunk," said Silene grandly. "I won't have anything like that in my party. I do hate drunkenness. There's something so very horrible about a drunken woman."

"You're so right, darling. You keep off it and so will I keep off it."

In spite of their resolves everybody became a little drunk and tiresome, without being particularly gay. As a party it was a failure for most people. But there are almost no parties that everybody enjoys, that would be nearly impossible. Still, there are some parties that almost everybody enjoys, and some that almost nobody enjoys, and some that about two people enjoy but everybody else hates. This party belonged more or less to the last named sort.

John and Eliza enjoyed themselves extremely. John was delighted with himself and enchanted

with Eliza. And, for her part, Eliza was for the
moment a little in love with John. Fond, indulgent
and quiet she felt, and she wondered for how long
this happy change in John would endure. She had
been entranced by this sudden deep happiness
and life which John had had from her. His quietness
and his gaiety now were lovely to her. She had
given herself an unexpected delight in this which
she cherished with the interest and surprise that are
only elements of the unexpected, and can only
endure into something of value if encouraged with
moderate intelligence. No doubt it had been bound
to be one thing or another. She was bound to be
either considerably more interested or considerably
more bored by John and all this youthful enthusiasm. She was determined, however it had turned
out for herself, to do this for John. He should know
the value of loving her at this time when he most
needed an emotional outlet of some kind. And
presently he would know the value of forgetting
about Eliza, an experience put behind him. Forgetting makes one feel so grand and independent
at John's age. But for a little while yet Eliza was
curiously eager to be John's loved woman. To-night
she knew she might have fallen far short of her wise,
gracious ideal of how an older woman should give
up, had John been inclined to show that abstraction
about herself and that quick unsatisfied interest
in somebody else, some young birch tree virgin,
as one day she knew it would happen. But not
this evening.

They were dancing in a queer empty house with high rooms and lovely ceilings. No one had lived here for ten years at least, and there was almost no furniture. It was an abandoned house, and yet for one night here was music and dancing and wine and rare food again. And love too. Eliza wondered if it was not a type of her years of barren loving for Julian, this house empty as a box and full of still air, for one night changed to a false happiness. Not false, but unshaped and unbecoming to its hollowness. Empty room after empty room, and sour nettles and elder saplings growing up beside the flight of granite steps leading to a forsaken garden. The night was hot, soft and still. Eliza and John° walked out into the night hand in hand, and down that long forsaken garden. It was a long time since lovers had been there making their unreasonable vows.

The rest of the party was not going quite so well. The evening was well advanced now and yet they were in that dismal state when the more they drank the sadder they grew. All of them. They were in bad form.

Cruise had found some quite absurd girl and Silene was in agonies of jealousy. It really was awful to see her in her pretty pink dress shrieking with laughter and dancing away with all the shocking and frightful men she could find. Kirsty spent a diligent night sometimes being asked to dance and often compelling men to dance with her, and compelling them to dance with her again after that.

She was quite determined not to sit near her girl friend for one moment or even speak to her because of the bitter and malicious things people might say.

Sheena danced with Rupert only now and then. She had not really seen him since that dreadful night of woe now nearly a week ago. She did not know how she stood with him, and she did not know where she was, so she danced with everybody she could find and was inclined to be wildly gay and girlish all round her. Poor Sheena, in a very grown-up black dress, which Olivia had not bought for her, full of her jokes and screaming away like Silene. But there was a kind of wild aptness about Sheena's nonsense which all Silene's noise could never approach. It was near despair, but it was near the true spirit of gaiety too. She was a Nymph Bacchanal laughing and leaping in a cat's skin, but Silene was a bacchanalian old trollop and a girlish cow-elephant.

Rupert did not see this difference at all. He considered that Sheena was behaving with pre-posterous foolishness, lack of reserve and absurdity. He felt furiously and confusedly insulted by her behaviour to-night. He drank a good deal and danced very little. When he did it was with rather old women. Perhaps he thought they lent dignity to his sulking. He cut a dance with Sheena and saw her dividing it in four parts and making the rudest promises to the fifth man who besought her favour. He come up to say that it was his dance but she was off. There was no way he could keep her.

It had all begun at dinner time. At dinner time
he had said (by way of opening the subject well)
" Aren't you rather ashamed of yourself about
Thursday night ? I hope you are."

And Sheena had stared at him in that blind way
she had, inward and unseeing. The anguish of
Thursday night had marked her. She was suffering
still from the shock of what she had done to herself.
She was strained and terribly aware of nothing at
all, of a tone of voice, of anything not meant. When
she was by herself all that she would say to Rupert
was plain to her. She was calm on a strange plane
of acceptance. But now she was with him and not
alone with him, and this light hostility with which
he spoke to her left her defenceless and angry.
It was such an unexpected attitude in him. And it
roused all the opposition that was in Sheena.

Poor Rupert, who had spent a dreadful five days,
hurt and puzzled, longing to see Sheena, but keeping
away from her with some vague determination
about leaving her alone. Nervous and cross as a
cat and wild with excitement at seeing her again—
he was almost bound to say and do the worst possible
things under the circumstances. She had not
answered his question about Thursday night. She
had stared at him, through him, and beyond him,
and turned away. How could Rupert guess the
sadness and disorder of her thoughts ? Or how near
she was to tears ? He could not possibly be aware of
how she felt. He was too excited and unhappy
himself. People are messing us about and playing

hell with us, he had truly said to Sheena. Indeed, they had. The need and trust and divine content they had been in together only a week ago was shattered and broken. Old jokes had lost their importance. They could not speak to each other in the words they knew. They were unhappy and at a loss and blamed each other most bitterly because they had no words to tell how things were with them now. Their happiness was broken between them. Rupert said Sheena had done this thing to him, while Sheena in her obstinate and greater loving had nothing but a blind resolve to guide her. And now she was hurt. Hurt to tears again. Her noble and unselfish attitude taken from under her by a few silly words. Sheena, who jumped off garden walls for faith and rode over the country with the bravest heart (but often with the greatest stupidity), went on because she was afraid. Because her whole life so far as she could see it was shaken and she was most pitifully afraid.

To-night she offended Rupert deeply. He could not put a name to this wild insensitiveness in her. It hurt him and upset him unspeakably to see and hear Sheena, his love, screaming and playing the fool, the wild motley of the evening. Her laughter echoed a little insanely in the empty rooms of this empty house. Hide-and-seek they were playing now. Presently she would be back to dance with somebody. She was the most lovely dancer in the world and all bands adored her. Even this band—not so far removed from Johnson and his melodeon—

played to her, halting romantically for her dancing.

Rupert found her late in the evening, in the bar. She had every right to be there, for she looked exhausted and as if she really badly needed a drink. She had had several, but so far felt as though she had drunk so much water, and kept on saying : Yes, please, to the amusement of her partners. " Sheena, you can't drink any more, darling," they said to her, and Sheena smiled at them wearily, rather proud of herself. She looked dreadful in the wicked unshaded light of the bar, a storm-driven eucalyptus tree, exhausted in resistance. But that was not what she suggested to Rupert. He had harsher names to call her by. For she was his own and she had offended most grossly. She must hear presently what he thought of her. And he thought her pretty cheap. And in all the world most dear.

The atmosphere in a bar is not so good really ; the lights, the leaning faces, the laughter, the exhaustion ; the endless important talk that doesn't count. But it does count for the moment. It is all wildly important. It has a present weight beyond its due. Only for the time true. Lives change in bars sometimes. But more often than not they remain exactly the same.

Rupert took Sheena out of the bar. He was very sore and angry with her, but he said the right word. That often happens in a bar. " I do want you, Sheena," he said, and she put down her last drink on the counter and went with him, absolutely defeated. She forgot in an instant all her harmful deeds. There was no bitterness she could think bitter now. Now that he had said this and she was with him again. A deep joy overcame her.

" I must talk to you, Sheena."

" Where shall we go ? "

" Out in the garden ? "

" But it's raining like hell."

" Upstairs ? Try to walk straight. Give me your hand."

" Are you saying I'm drunk ? I'm not. My head is wonderful."

" It must be a lot better than your feet."

" How sour you are ! I don't think I'm dancing this dance with you, am I ? I wish I wasn't. I wish I could be left alone sometimes. Not tormented."

They arrived at last in a room like an enormous faded schoolroom. There was not one single piece of furniture in it and a huge mushroom grew up through the boards in one corner. The dawn light, a fish belly light, was creeping over the garden outside and a very little penetrated into the empty room. You could not see how dirty the room was, but the feeling of pallid damp was through it—a damp that smelt coldly of mortification and bats and mice. There was a key in the tall white door and this Rupert turned in its lock.

" This is a fine place you've found," Sheena said. " Where shall we sit ? On the mantelpiece, I suppose. That will be so cosy." Sheena's voice sounded nervous and affable.

" Oh, Sheena, do stop being a jolly girl. I don't know what's come over you."

It might all have gone better if there had been somewhere to sit down in that room. But there was nowhere except the floor. With all this hostility there was no reason for them to be near each other. The dim cold light in the room seemed no more than breast high. They could hardly see each other's faces. Only their voices, hostile and weary, went on repeating things which had almost nothing to say to the matter in hand.

" The party'd have been splendid if we all behaved like you. You've been most gay and amusing all night."

" Stop talking like this. God didn't mean you to be witty. He forgot about that."

" Nor he didn't mean you to shut me up in here and torment me. Let me out."

" I won't let you out ! "

Sheena turned her back on Rupert and went over to the window and opened it. She stood there not speaking, looking down on the unhealthy dark garden. The rain came in through the window like branches of cold thorns on her bare arms. Rupert came over and shut the window. It was all too silly. Catching cold and getting wet on top of everything else. It was all a part of this unreasonable departure from Rupert and from common sense into a place where he was shut out and unable to explain himself. And very badly she'd behaved too. He intended to speak to her about that. So :

"I hate to see you making a little ass of yourself," he said. "It's not a bit amusing to go on like you've been doing to-night. People play up to you, I know, but really they think it's a bit cheap."

"*Oh*——" Sheena could scarcely speak with rage and grief. How could he pretend to need her and then speak to her in this pompous awful way. Nobody had ever spoken to her like this before. It seemed so much worse because she knew she was a little drunk and found it difficult to answer. Finding words were such a trouble, although everything she wanted to say was most distinct in her mind. She laughed, "Oh, really. Oh, thanks so much, Rupert. Would you like to tell me more? Don't stop, I mean. Get it over."

"I've said what I want to say now."

"Just that I'm pretty cheap and—and nasty?" She started this speech coldly but ended on a sort of sob.

"I never said that. I don't know what I said. Forget about what I said. I'm unsteady, I think. But I think it's your fault. Oh, Sheena, my dear sweet one, come here to me. Don't keep away from me any more."

Sheena thought perhaps she had never loved Rupert before she kissed him here in the sad dusk of the morning. She was always thinking this about these exhausting and frantic kisses. Her love was strengthened and left then in despair. In a minute she travelled a journey away from all her misery and fear. All such times were false and this moment only true.

" Well ? "

" Well ? to you."

" It's hopeless. You must see you can't ever leave me."

" I never wanted to leave you. I know it's impossible."

" I thought last week was the longest week in my whole life."

" I don't know what I thought. I thought I'd die."

" I knew I wouldn't die."

" No, hearts don't break, do they ? " Sheena laid her hands on her breast to see.

" How is it going ? "

" Oh, it's going great. But do you know there were times last week when it would have broken for tuppence."

" You must never give it tuppence when it feels like that."

" Ah, I knew it would be all right. Only threats. Like when I have a row with Olivia and walk out, saying, ' *All right*, I'll *go*. I'll leave this house and never come back.' Having not the smallest intentions of going."

" Your heart couldn't have felt a bit like that."

" I promise you that's how it felt."

" Let's stop talking about your heart. Tell me, do you often make threats you don't intend to keep ? "

" Like what ? "

" Like saying, ' I'm going out of this house for ever.' Like saying, ' I'll never never marry you, Rupert. Our children will be mad and Owenstown will be left to your Nephew, James.' "

Even in this light, which was no light worth speaking of, Rupert could see a sort of change come on Sheena's face. He knew the argument was going to be opened up again. He knew she was going to refuse again. He was defeated by the strength of his own need. This dead look of resolve defeated him. He feared she would not trust or believe anything that he could say. And even his love for her seemed to lessen in this anguish and strength that could find no words.

" Tell me, Sheena," he said, whispering, " It was like what you say to Olivia ? Tell me. Wasn't it ? "

Sheena's lips moved. She was saying, " No. Not like that." She could not tell him about Thursday night, nor how she had run down the avenue to him, all her resolution gone out of her. She could tell him nothing. Everything she said weakened her meaning, and left her with so little that was reasonable to say. She moved nearer still to him, whispering, " I'll do what I said on Thursday."

He did not hear her and bent down. " What ? " he said.

" What ? " is so very upsetting under the circumstances. " What " would have upset an older and hardier girl than Sheena. People should listen and not say, " What ? " when an earnest and lovely young girl offers them her body. Sheena gathered herself with an effort and tried again.

" Darling, I can't marry you——"

" You won't marry me, you mean——"

" I can't. I can't." Her voice was truly despairing, " I've told you why I can't. But I'll sleep with you, my darling, any time you like."

" No, Sheena."

" Please, yes."

How could she be so proud and sweet about it ? She didn't understand. She didn't know. And neither, indeed, did he. He was full of false conceits and importances on the subject. Perhaps he was right. For himself he may have been and in his idea of Sheena. But Sheena was a wilder, truer creature than he could know.

" Sheena, you don't know what you're saying. You hurt me so much saying things like this. And I love you so much, I can't bear it."

" Why ? Why does it hurt you ? "

" Oh, Christ——"

" Now—now, my darling. You must be steady."

" Shut up," said Rupert, suddenly blazingly enraged. " You're—you're to have everything your own way. I'm not to come first. Well, if I don't come first I don't want to be anywhere. D'you understand ? " He thought he was being most reasonable, as people in tempers usually do. " Tell me if you quite understand."

" I don't understand. Why are you so angry ? "

" I'm angry because it's awful for me. It's awful

to hear you talking like a tart. Like Silene. Like
that bitch, Kirsty. I want you for my wife. I don't
want you like that. Tarts. Bitches. You were
different. You were mine. And now you're trying
to be just like the lot of them. You've failed me.
And you've played bloody hell to me. And for
Christ's sake go away now. . . ." Rupert turned
from her and stared out into that dreadful garden
where the dawn light was a dirty pallid wash above
the green. " Please, do go away," he said in a
dreadful small voice, for strong men do not cry
any more than they go to bed with eager virgins.

Sheena hesitated and left him then. Tears fell
on her hands as she struggled with the key he had
turned in the lock of the door. She could not see.
She was defeated and he had made her feel
ashamed. Rupert had made her ashamed by the
dreadful things he had said to her when she had laid
down all her own defences. How could he have
said them ? How was he able to be so unkind ?
Sheena was not proof against such unkindness.

What should she do now ? Where should she go ?
The dusty weight of her black dress dragging behind
her, Sheena climbed up another flight of stairs.
Her head was bent. Her tears were falling still.
One must do something to one's face, she supposed.
It was the sort of act that must be done if one was
to die within the hour.

Through the open door of the cloak-room she saw
Silene and Kirsty and Kirsty's woman putting on
their coats. They looked very tired and cross. It

was quite impossible to face the idea of saying Thank-you or Good-night to Silene, so Sheena opened a door on her left hand and found herself in a large bathroom panelled (bath and all) in sombre brown wood, and practically veiled in cobwebs. Vast cobwebs were spun from tap to tap of the bath and deep fine black dust lay thickly everywhere. It was much darker than the room Sheena and Rupert had been in, for its window was made of ground glass and was as dusty as the rest of the room.

Sheena did not lock the door. She was in a panic about locking doors in this house since the last had been so difficult to open. She shut it and went gently through the dust to the edge of the bath where she sat down and shook all over. Now that she was by herself again she was only aware of feeling shamefully and terribly sick, and cold—as the saying is—as death. Her hands clung round the edges of the bath making ghostly marks in the dust, and the idea that from all this anguish she might die struck poor Sheena as only reasonable. She felt frozen up. No more tears. Only this unendurable sickness and this loss in love which she could not face. There are some griefs that are too much for the young, they cannot be resolved. They only destroy.

In about an hour's time Eliza found Sheena here. It was lighter now and she could see her face quite plainly, and what she saw gave her a brief but very real sense of terror. Sheena's face seemed sharpened and tightened up to half its own size. She was sitting bent together like a little old monkey, and when Eliza spoke to her she only whispered in answer.

" Stay where you are, **my** darling," Eliza said. " I'll get you your coat."

" I must do my face, Eliza," Sheena was whispering insistently.

" All right. I'll get you a glass."

After that Sheena spent a long time fumbling at her face. The result, when she had done with it, was pretty ghastly, but perhaps it was a help to her to gather herself up sufficiently to do it. The dance was definitely over when they came downstairs. The empty house seemed to hurry them away, its emptiness and squalor closing behind them down the long passages. A side door was open near them, as they turned the corner of the uncarpeted stairs they could see a pillar of green morning light lying across the narrow floor. It was more than time for them to go. John and Eliza packed Sheena into the car between them, and John drove back to Silverue as fast as he could.

Eliza felt completely exhausted. She, who liked to attend dances in the mincing and important manner—arriving at twelve perhaps, drinking a few nice glasses of wine, dancing now and then with a chosen partner, eating her supper, enjoying the pleasures of conversation and returning to her bed not later than three o'clock—to-night she had spent an evening of strong emotion and severe exercise.

For John loved dancing and was, mercifully, an exquisite dancer. At moments she had been blindly and absurdly happy and deeply ashamed that she could not detect in herself any of the right sort of light amusement and detachment from all this transient depth of feeling. At moments she felt quite earnest. Poor Eliza, she thought, you must be even a step older than we imagined. But when the time came that she and John, the last survivors of the dance, searched for Sheena up and down this empty house she felt almost hysterical at the improbability of her evening. At long last Sheena had been found. Looking at her now, as she lapped her in rugs and tender caresses, Eliza felt very much as though this were Sheena's corpse which she had dragged out of a pond. Nothing could be more unlike Sheena than this sad bedragged creature. What, Eliza wondered, had happened to her? What, indeed?

XXIV

It was far on in the afternoon following before she saw Sheena again. Eliza had slept late, as she felt herself entitled to do after such a night. In fact, she slept longer than she really felt inclined to do because she felt it was her right. Sleep she would. So she had kept her eyes obstinately closed on the successive visits of John, Olivia, and Markie. She very nearly kept them shut now, but she realised just in time that it might be Sheena and so she opened them and sat up to talk.

"Well, my love? How awful I feel. I wonder what I look like? Hand me my powder like a kind girl. And a dash of raddle for the lips. Thank you, sweet."

Sheena did not look much more natural to-day, Eliza thought, surveying her sharply as she tidied up her own face. Her eyes were still looking appalled, as though she could not quite take in what had happened to her. The unknowing look she always had was as though turned inward, knowing about pain. Such pain as Eliza had forgotten could not really be allowed to continue unassuaged.

"You must tell me, my little one, my precious, what happened to you last night."

"Yes, I must tell you, Eliza. Because I want to

245

ask you something. I want you to take me away
somewhere. Couldn't we go somewhere together ? "

" Yes, we'll go anywhere in the world you want
to go." Eliza made her large promise to one of
Julian's children, sweeping all difficulties to one
side as non-existent. What one did for these unhappy
children. " But tell me, what made you so unhappy
last night ? because I just might be able to help you
without dashing you away to the ends of the earth."

" Oh, indeed, my dear, it's not the ends of the
earth I want. It's just anywhere away from
Silverue."

" This is all because of Rupert. I've known for
the last week you were in a muddle about him.
Tell me all, I do beseech you, Sheena. It's so much
the best thing to do."

Sheena told all her story, told it in a quiet drowned
voice as she sat there in the afternoon sun on Eliza's
bed with Eliza's brown eiderdown drawn up to her
chin for warmth. The hot level afternoon sunlight
outside did not seem to reach her at all. She seemed
the coldest creature imaginable and the most
hopeless, she who had been so very happy.

Eliza was at first relieved and then beyond
anything saddened by the tale that Sheena told her
in a carefully composed and sensible voice. Sheena,
trying to be sensible, Sheena—whose only eloquence
was in her silences. Those radiant silences of
Sheena's. Eliza felt that Sheena had lost something
which she would never recover or pick up again.
She was set a little aside from what she had been.

What could be done about it? The matter as she
stated it seemed quite impossible. What could one
do but encourage her to pursue the agonising course
she had chosen? What else could one do?

"Darling, I think you're right. It might be a
little better if you came away with me. We could
go—we could go to Brittany again. We'd bring a
car. John might come, do you think? I wonder if
that would be a good plan? You could bathe and
go fishing. I might get the same little house. Darling,
I'll speak to Olivia this evening about it."

"Oh, you wouldn't have her, would you?"

"Oh, no, indeed not. And perhaps not John. I
don't really know about that."

"Yes, we'd let John come. John loves to be with
you."

"Yes, he's very quiet with me."

"I feel like that with you too, Eliza. Quiet. I
can't bear to be by myself. It's not right I should be,
is it?" Sheena asked this with the faint pomp of
young sorrow.

"No, darling. You won't be alone. Are we to
tell Julian about this?"

"If he could be any help?" Sheena's eyes
suddenly filled with tears. "Nobody's any help,
Eliza," she whispered. "Do you think, Eliza, I
must go on with this? What do you think?"

The appalling unscrupulousness of the young in
putting their problems up to other people. Eliza
must fail Sheena a little here.

"You can come away with me and give yourself

time. A little time helps so much. We can think together. You can write what you decide. Don't tell him definitely yet."

Eliza was ashamed of her temporising when she had said this. She saw a look which meant to her complete integrity come over Sheena's face. A withdrawal from Eliza and her half-measures. Eliza was conscious of values she had long forgotten about. Hopelessly impracticable values, but once as real as saying your prayers to God when you were young and afraid. She saw quite clearly in a moment what this meant to Sheena—this unkissing of the oath between her and Rupert. "Unkiss the oath between them," that was something like what had happened ; a severing and cruel wounding, not to be lightly met by the half-measures of the old and wise. This was real. Fantastic as reality is.

"But I have told him," Sheena said. "I don't know why I asked you that. It's over now. Only, Eliza, it's so awful. This pain. Is it despair or what is it ? I suppose it would be only what one would expect ? " She asked these things as she might have asked about an operation. She had not suffered before.

Eliza felt herself quite at a loss. This truthfulness and sorrow were beyond her. Sheena was in a different place from her. She could hardly help at all. Or only by her loving. All her life's experience was valueless here.

"I don't like being at Silverue when I'm unhappy," Sheena went on. "Do you really think we could go away? I'd love it for John to come. But we can't let him guess about this. We must keep it from John," said Sheena again with that slight importance.

" I suppose so. Under the circumstances. But he mayn't want to come."

" Oh, he will. Oh, here's somebody coming to see you—— Oh, it's John. Look, John—Eliza and I are going to Brittany to her house. Will you come ? "

" Yes, I'll come," said John inattentively. He wondered how Sheena was to be sent away so that he could talk to Eliza by himself.

" ' Yes, I'll come.' Why do you say it like that ? You might as well say Paris is the capital of France. Don't you want to come ? " Sheena thought his inattentiveness was rather rude to Eliza.

" What did you ask me ? " John did not mind being abused by Sheena, but he wished she would go away.

Eliza said, " John. Sheena and I are going to my little house in Brittany. We were asking you if you'd like to come too for a week or ten days."

" I'd like to come more than anything in the world. But I'd like to come for six weeks or ten months."

" You may stay till you're bored."

" We'd never be bored. Would we, John ? "

" I don't know about you."

XXV

ELIZA told Julian that evening, saying, "The children think they want to come to Brittany with me for a week or ten days. Do you think it would be a good plan?"

"When is it to happen?"

"Almost now."

"Oh, but this is too depressing. You haven't been here two minutes."

"Three weeks on Tuesday."

"Two minutes it seems like to me. Must you go? And why are you going? And why does Sheena want to go? Away from her love? I understand about John. You are superb with him. But Sheena? Only tell me what you like, of course."

He sat listening without interruption while Eliza told him.

"It all seems to me very hysterical."

The inadequacy of his comment left her speechless and for the moment without an idea or a line of conduct left her. She could not gasp, "Julian," although that was exactly what she felt like doing. She could only stare at him owlishly and then sip sherry to give herself time.

"Of course, you're so sympathetic," Julian said. In the way he said it it was like an insult. Then he

said, " Eliza, you must forgive me. All this is getting
beyond me. It was sad enough about John. However, she'll recover, won't she ? "

" She'll recover everything except what she's lost
for her life," Eliza said quite clearly and without
sentimentality. " I know what is lost the first time
one is really hurt. It doesn't matter, I suppose.
People are much more reasonable without it."

" Oh—reasonable ? What's the good of that ?
What has the child lost ? "

" I can't tell you. What Markie has. What
John had."

"——And is finding again—Don't you see it ?
I do. It's—it's too marvellous to me to see the young
recover. To see John minding less each day. I'm
surprised you haven't seen that."

" Oh, I have." By what strange cross currents is
gratitude sometimes borne. Eliza was wildly glad
now because this was apparent to Julian in some
form, the change in John was a real thing. It was
not there only for her because she wished to see
it. Julian accepted it and looked for no reason
for it.

" Well," Julian said, " but must you take John
away ? Isn't he all right where he is ? "

" It would be more fun for Sheena to have John
there. If you think it would be a bad plan, say so."

" No. I was only thinking of Olivia. She will hate
him going away so soon, won't she ? "

Eliza said, " Yes. Poor Olivia." It was the best
she could manage. It was odd how the tragedy of

Sheena seemed to be lessening through Julian's strange lack of life or grief about it.

Olivia came in and sat down with her back to the light window. She asked Julian in a furious voice for a glass of sherry. He looked only faintly surprised as he poured it out for he guessed what had happened, and when she turned round to Eliza, saying (only just not in the tone of voice in which she had asked for the sherry), " I hear you're taking the children to France for six weeks," it was only what he expected.

" Well, I'm going to France myself for two months," Eliza said in her clear precise way. " I should be enchanted if they would stay six weeks, but to tell you the truth I hardly expected them for quite so long."

Of course, no one had told Olivia six weeks. That was all rage and hyperbole on her part. Eliza did not like Olivia when she was in one of her tempers, but she was well able for her.

Julian, who hated scenes in which Olivia made a fool of herself and got the worst of it, fidgeted unamiably.

" I don't mind Sheena going to you. It might do her good and improve her French. But don't you think it's just a bit unnecessary to upset John again ? Now that I've got the child settled down, and so touchingly happy to be with me again, he'll rather hate going, won't he ? "

Eliza looked to Julian for a word of help, and when he did not speak she realised how little she could

depend on him in any matter that involved Olivia's
wish or happiness. She had always known this, but
under the circumstances it seemed to her almost
unbelievable that he should not do all in his power
to help poor Sheena.

" Only the other day I said to him how wonderful
it was for us to be together again." Olivia was going
on in a voice charged with unquenchable reminis-
cence, " and he said, ' Yes, Mum. Pretty wonderful
for me too.' Just like that. ' Yes, Mum. Pretty
wonderful for me too.' "

Eliza accepted this nauseating statement with
reservations and took a firmer hold on herself. She
must not let herself go and allow this to become a
distressing scene. And she must not give herself
and John away. No shaft of light must glimmer even
for a moment in Julian's understanding. Olivia was
all right. It would take flood lighting before anything near the truth dawned upon her. But Julian
was here, looking bored and impatient.

She said, " Look here, Olivia, my dear. You've
got to be very understanding and unselfish. It's
nothing to do with John, really, it's all on account
of Sheena. I hate hurting you so much, but I'd
better tell you the whole situation, hadn't I?
And then we'll do exactly as you say. I haven't seen
you since this dance, you see, have I? Well, listen,
then——"

Eliza did not see Julian's eyes telling her to stop.
Not to speak. Not to involve Olivia too deeply in
this. Changing to an appeal to keep this between

Julian and Eliza only. A demand that she should. Changing to a furious impatience at her lack of understanding. Eliza, who should have known. You're failing me, said Julian's eyes. But Eliza did not see. She was telling Sheena's story again, and she was telling it to Julian again as much as to Olivia. He must see that it was so, and it was so, that here was truth and here was a sorrow that they who were old must help and cherish through its travailing because such bitter suffering was new to Sheena and there seemed no escape could be found for the poor girl. So Eliza told the story to Julian again through Olivia. But it did not reach him. It seemed to reach no farther than Olivia who sat there listening, her eyes fastened on Eliza, and under Eliza's eyes her face seemed to change and become its true age in the flesh, though spiritually her sadness seemed no older than Sheena's.

When Eliza had finished, she did not speak at all. All her silly words were quenched within her as though perished away. Her attention seemed fixed still on Eliza as if she wondered what more she had to say, what there was still for her to hear. And her lovely face seemed more old and uncertain every moment.

After a silence she said, " Of course, John must go."

Eliza had never seen any person look so bereft of all her self. So shaken out of her own values. She only seemed like Sheena when Eliza had found her in the early morning by herself in that empty, dirty house.

"Of course, John must go," she said. "He'd be a comfort to her, I know." Her eyes escaped from Eliza. She was looking to Julian for help. He got up and moved towards her. And waited for Eliza to go.

XXVI

How long, thought Eliza, since I have walked in a garden in the evening? She looked through the deeply set iron gate, so narrow and so dark in the hollow of the garden wall, and wondered whether or not she would lift its latch and walk in among Olivia's carefully grown flowers. Since that glimpse she had seen to-day of something touching and quite unsafe about Olivia's serenity, she discovered a tolerance even for her successful garden. She opened the gate and walked in.

Down the long paths Eliza walked, where Olivia's delphiniums bore themselves with a pallor and reticence in the night—their blue quenched of its burning. The evening was so still and hot that all colour had soaked into the air except where a point of land, far out to sea, was the daytime blue of a pale delphinium ; absurd as a picture of a desert and as silly as it was lovely in the night. Droves of iris were grey winged, lost in the evening ; pæonies were white shells round crowns as dark as moss now, only in the daytime golden, and their scent past sweetness. Not a flower scent, but beyond that. A dark scent. A tree of lilac, a broody and exotic white hen, plumed and perfumed, Eliza passed and the nearly sulphurous depths of scent where lupins grew. All colour was lost, soaked into the darkness, breathed out in scent, given to the night, given to Eliza as she walked along, her mind held in an animal delight both sharp and languorous. I'd like to sleep here, she thought. If I had the courage of my romantic convictions, I would. But I'm too cowardly and besides it's too much trouble. Though, indeed, I see no reason why my ardent young lover should not carry a bed out here for me to sleep in. A large and heavy bed, piece by piece, and re-assembled close by a strong-smelling syringa, that would be nice exercise and employment for him, I do think. That would quieten his ardour, I imagine.

On Olivia's stone seat at the top of the garden she sat herself down, and from here she saw Olivia coming through the iron gate—a distressingly Burne Jones figure in a long white coat—and she asked herself whether she would wait where she was or make her escape now. She had plenty of time to escape and plenty of reason, for Olivia would most certainly and utterly destroy this hour's pleasures.

It was something unfamiliar in Olivia's way of walking down the garden that made Eliza stay where she was and wait for what should happen. Olivia's usual way of walking through her garden was to pause at every second step and poke or praise, blame, despair, or exult, and demand endless sympathy and praise. Even the darkest night would not have stopped her in this established procedure. She knew too well where wilted failure and where success wore flowers for a time. But this evening she came straight down the centre of the path looking neither to right nor to left, and there was a kind of hurried despair in her walking that was different from her usual complacent and studied movement. Down through her flowers Olivia came hurrying in this unknowing way. It appeared to Eliza that she was escaping from something and that there was no escape for her, or not here in the garden she had made.

Eliza got up from the seat and went towards her. She admitted to herself that she felt exceedingly curious and unsatisfied about Olivia. And to feel either curiosity or sadness towards this creature was a new sensation to Eliza.

" Oh, Eliza," Olivia seemed to be arrested and turned back in to herself again. Whatever thought it was that had so possessed her as she came hurrying through the garden was obviously lost now in this meeting with Eliza. She was herself, but Eliza still wondered at that change she had truly seen in her.

" My dear, no coat ? Won't you be hideously cold ? "

" Oh, it's as warm as milk, Olivia, here in your garden."

" I didn't know you were here."

" You haven't a cigarette, have you ? "

" Yes, I have." Olivia would certainly carry a bag covered in jewels and full of such necessaries of her life as paints and powders and cigarettes. How fortunate that she always did.

" How wonderful of you. Shall we sit down ? Or are you doing something useful ? "

" Oh, let's sit. I always feel this is such a wonderful time in a garden. You know—' a garden is a lovesome thing '—I'm not a bit literary, but that little poem always *means* something to me. I'd like to have it carved on a stone and let into the wall, wouldn't you ? "

" No, I wouldn't. But then I think it's a perfectly disgusting little poem."

" Do you, Eliza ? But you're not very fond of gardens, are you ? "

" Perhaps not." Eliza then reminded herself that Olivia it was who had made and created all this for her delight. She also reminded herself of her recent brief curiosity about Olivia. She must gather herself up and try not to be tiresome and precious. " But I thought to-night," she said, " that this was the most beautiful and exciting garden I have ever known. And you made it."

Olivia changed again. Eliza had never seen her touched and made vulnerable by praise before. Perhaps this was because she had so seldom praised her. Olivia turned to her with tears in her voice, in the evening Eliza could not see them in her eyes.

" Yes, I know," she said. " And what good is it to me now that I'm so unhappy ? "

" About Sheena, darling ? " Why was she so much more deeply stirred about Sheena than she had been about John ? " But you knew this was quite likely to happen. You discussed it with me."

" Oh, but I didn't think it would happen, not like this. And she looks so miserable, the poor lamb."

" It was worse about John."

" It was different. I wasn't hurting him so much."

" You hurting them ? "

" Oh, I know really I'm not much use to them. But I needn't hurt them."

" I don't understand you, my poor sweet. Tell me what you really mean."

" I can't tell you. Julian knows. Julian understands about me, doesn't he ? "

" Yes."

" You don't know, Eliza, how I feel about Julian. I'm so grateful to him for minding about me. It keeps me going. It's so lovely that some one minds about my still being beautiful. I mean somebody besides myself."

What had come over Olivia that she was talking like this ? Olivia, to whom her own beauty was the most important factor in her relationships with everybody she knew. Her friends and her children and her enemies. And now she spoke as though Julian was the only person left who knew and valued her beauty.

" I will keep it for him," she said, " because he does value it so." They had got a long way from Sheena and her unhappiness about Sheena. " Julian is the only person who doesn't mind my being so stupid. You know, Eliza, I'm not a brainy person, but he never makes me feel a fool in front of other people like the children do. And he's forgiven me all the things I've done wrong ever since I married him. Hasn't he ? "

" Yes."

" You know, Eliza," said Olivia, and she spoke now as one who has discovered a rare truth—that is, with honest sententiousness and without a trace of humour, " there comes a time in every woman's life when her Home and Children are more to her than any man."

" Yes, dear." Eliza accepted this too. It was not unconnected with the attitude about Julian. He was part of the Home and Children, no doubt. After all he had done his share in the production of both. . . .

" And so I ought to do what Julian says now, shouldn't I ? If you were me, Eliza, would you put what Julian says first ? "

Yes, he was certainly part of it. But Olivia was being tiresomely indefinite. " I don't think I understand what you mean."

" Never mind. I can't tell you. But do advise me, wouldn't you follow what Julian said if you were me ? "

" Yes, if I were you I would most certainly."

" Yes, I will. But, you know, Eliza, even so, even doing as Julian says, doesn't seem much real help. What would you do if you were me ? "

" My dear, how can I help you if you won't really tell me what is saddening you so much. Can't you tell me ? "

" No, I can't."

" Why not ? "

" Because Julian said—— No. Just I can't tell you."

Eliza felt a sudden queer coldness overcome her, and after it a hurried rush of knowing. There was something Julian had warned Olivia not to tell her. Not to tell Eliza whom he had trusted and loved for so long. She felt lessened in her own estimation of herself and most bitterly grieved. As sad as we only feel if we discover those we love trust us a little less than we thought. Nothing is more wounding or destructive of sympathy.

" Don't tell me, then," Eliza said. " Probably it's better not." She threw away the end of her cigarette and stood up. She looked away from Olivia and out to sea where the light on a floating buoy was changing in the night, swinging in like a great flower. Going out. Stilled, and burning again. And in the mountains fires were burning too, inconstant and romantic fires. Eliza turned back again to Olivia.

" You do think it would be a good plan for me to take the children away for a little ? You do want it ? " She wondered why she was asking Olivia this so earnestly. She really did not mind what Olivia felt about it. But in this consulting of Olivia she felt that she was taking a step away from Julian, and that was what she most needed at the moment.

XXVII

MARKIE's summer holidays were over and Miss Parker had just returned to Silverue. Markie was rather cold in his welcome. While Parker was away he had done so much that he really felt too grand to tell her about it all immediately. Therefore, he was cold and unconfiding and swaggering and distressingly independent in his manner. Miss Parker understood about this in her own way, which meant that she was rather hearty and jolly with him and asked him none of the questions about his doings which he was longing to boast of in a guarded way. Parker should have asked :

And how many fish did you catch?

And what on?

And how many rabbits has John shot?

And how many did you kill?

And how many strokes can you swim now?

And which runs the fastest now, you or Johnny Byrne?

And what sort of crop of nuts have we?

And have you been on the mountain with John and Nick?

But she did not ask any of these questions. She asked about Mummy Mouse and the other dogs, and Sheena and John and when they were coming back, and the weather. Markie was sulky and unresponsive, feeling quite constipated by the grandeur of keeping everything to himself.

This was at tea-time in the schoolroom. If a picture had been drawn of Miss Parker's last tea-time at Silverue it would this afternoon have been most faithfully reproduced on the schoolroom table. The same bread-and-butter, the same little buns, the same last half of a chocolate cake, the same strawberry jam. It was really an incomparably nicer and better tea than any which Miss Parker had eaten throughout her holidays at Skegness, but somehow coming back to it depressed her very much. So did the renewal of that eternal argument with Markie about finishing his milk. Miss Parker was not going to allow these feelings to get the better of her. She gave herself a brisk mental shake and had just reminded herself that she must go and unpack her suitcases when Dora came in with a piece of paper in her hand (not on a tray, Miss Parker could not help observing).

" Her Ladyship said I was to give you this, Miss."
" Thank you, Dora. When is her Ladyship expected back ? "

" I couldn't say. To-morrow I think." Dora had read the list of duties on that piece of paper and she saw no reason why Miss Parker should not be mildly goaded on towards their completion.

" She told me Thursday, and so did Byrne tell me Thursday," Markie said suddenly   He was aware of something he was entirely at a loss to understand in the air between Miss Parker and Dora. " Please, can I go ? "

" May I, darling, not can I. Yes. Where are you going ? "

" To Nick."

" All right. You'll be back at seven."

Miss Parker was reading Lady Bird's list. It said :

Markie's new Laxative. I tea sp : *last thing*.

Worm doses. Cheerio. Chuggy. Mouse *Watch Mouse*.

Dress Chuggy's ear. Canker.

Cheerio—Excema dressing.

Try new purge (in rod-room) on Mouse. *Watch effect*.

Pick dahlias and Michaelmas daisies Wed. Evn.

Please wash vases.

Plant 1,000 crocus in Yew Square. Plant " Windy Morrow " daffodils in Cedar tree bed.

Please weed rock garden in spare time.

Please *watch Mouse*.

Miss Parker looked a little nervously about her for Mouse. These repeated warnings were so very cryptic. She was more than half afraid of what she might see. Then she read the list again and stuck it in the mirror on the schoolroom mantelshelf. She felt suddenly and sickeningly overwhelmed but, as she reminded herself, she had been an idle little creature for some time, and it was always more or less of a struggle coming back to work again. However.

Mustn't Grumble. Life is mostly Froth and Bubble.
Two things stand like stone. *Kindness* in another's
trouble. *Courage* in your own. This excellent little
rhyme often met Miss Parker's eyes for it hung,
neatly framed, on the schoolroom wall between
the photograph of Lady Bird in her court feathers,
and Sir Julian in his hunting cap. She was quite in
agreement with its sentiment which she felt to be a
great truth neatly expressed. And so Helpful.
Although in wild moments it sometimes seemed to
Miss Parker that fighting the constipation of her
dogs and the weeds in her rock garden were the
heaviest troubles that Lady Bird would ever be
called upon to face. Still. Mustn't Grumble. Might
have been worse. There's a Silver Lining——
Miss Parker trotted out to the Yew Square where,
before seven o'clock, she had planted 300 crocus
bulbs. She then shut up Chuggy and Cheerio
for their twelve hours' starvation and went down
the fuchsia path towards the sea to look for Markie.

Then it was that the hollow sadness and excitement
of the Autumn day caught hold of her, so that she
felt her own loneliness and lack of anything as a
matter beyond her endurance. In this separate air
apart between Autumn and Summer there is a wide
space for joy or for despair, and Miss Parker, at the
end of all her briskness, felt herself not so far off
despair. Oh, she thought as she walked past the long
front of Silverue with its many dark windows and
its empty curving niches for statues, if I had something to call my own in the Autumn, something

to make safe for the Winter, how wildly happy I should be. She walked on past the cold house that did not live for her, and past a lovely blazing slope of Tritomas where last year she had dug and delved and dug under Lady Bird's able direction. They had such brave life about them, a bugle blast of colour, these Red Hot Pokers, they did give her a childish satisfaction for a moment. She went on comforted down the narrow path, red with the fallen flowers of the fuchsias, and red walls of blossom closing in perspective towards the sea. Markie came up the path from the sea and joined her.

She watched him coming along with a sudden knowledge of disappointment within herself. She had intended (not telling herself her purpose) to meet Markie at the river and hale him back to bed. I would have liked the walk, she said to herself, and now she stood looking down the long path to the sea with a furious enmity in her for all the silly jobs Lady Bird had set her to do, and a rage against her own ineffective obedience. What had she lost? She felt nearly panic-stricken for a moment before she knew as clearly as ever that she had lost nothing.

Markie came running along the path to her. Behind him the sea was as bright and thick a blue as the coat he was wearing. His beauty seemed beyond truth to-night. As beauty sometimes will it caught a surprising moment and was God-like. He bent his head as he ran and the wind of his running blew his dark hair in a speed line backwards. The colour in his cheeks and his eyes was exotic, of a southern depth and tenderness. What might be subdued in flesh? You might think of carnations, you might think of different ambers. You might think: Thus in his cheek the map of days outworn, when beauty lived and died as flowers do now——

You might think almost anything and be no nearer to this rare child or to any memory of him.

He stopped beside Miss Parker.

" I think I showed speed, did I ? "

" Great speed. I was surprised. And aren't you early ? "

" No. Nick sent me."

" We have to shut up Mrs. Mouse. She is to have a dose in the morning."

" Oh, and I want her to-morrow."

" Well, Mummy said she was to have this dose."

" Must she ? " Markie came closer to Miss Parker. He seemed to be more tender and more gentle than he had been earlier. Only because he was tired and he too needed some outside warmth of kindness on this more cold and lonely evening. And he wanted Mrs. Mouse for some reason of his own to-morrow. Usually he liked to see her well purged, pretending to exult in her discomfort.

" Please, must she ? I want her."

The necessity for Mrs. Mouse's immediate physicking became of less importance to Miss Parker. What after all did it matter whether she was purged to-day or to-morrow or ever again? It really did not matter. Lady Bird might show temper at the delay, but otherwise it made no vital difference. Miss Parker decided that Markie should have his Mouse to-morrow if he wanted her. This decision gave her a curiously complete sensation of independence. They walked back to the house together quite amiably and went in the back way so that Mrs. Mouse might be shown the other patients starving miserably in the rod-room.

There followed an interval in the evening which was Markie's bed-time. At last it was over and Miss Parker, with the steam of Markie's bath taking a little of the horrid life out of her newly waved hair, was completing the unpacking of her suitcases. . . . Really she must put a stop to the ladder in that stocking—Yes, perhaps this very evening. They had been a disappointing buy. This green jumper wool was nice, she still thought. Rather a lovely shade. Would she ever find time to run up the sprigged Celanese? The ghost voices of 700 crocus told her, No. At last everything was tidied away and Miss Parker's bedroom looked as like itself as to-day's schoolroom tea had looked like its predecessor of July 29th. Feeling rather exhausted, she washed her hands, cleaned up her face and powdered her nose. Then she wiped the powder out of her beard (where it produced an unbelievably ageing effect: the snows of many winters) and went into the schoolroom, her neat writing-case in her hand, for she intended to write a letter to her still less fortunate sister, telling her of her comfortable journey and safe return.

As she walked along the passage from her bedroom to the schoolroom, Miss Parker's intentions for the disposal of the evening hours did not go one step beyond these things : to write to her sister. To eat her supper. To mend her stocking (if she found the energy). To read the paper and to go to bed. How should she guess or know what it was in her to do on this strange evening ?

Now she shut the schoolroom door and walked over to look out of the window at the evening. Not a very safe thing to do if one is inclined towards vague despairs. Again to-night that separate air of Autumn filled the evening as a bowl is filled. There was heaviness and sharpness in the air, a watching and a change. Beyond the smoke of fires it was there. Beyond the fact of stiff, fleshly autumn flowers. Beyond the first lightening of the summer green ; if all these things had not been, this fatal interval, this thrilling interval, would still have been.

Miss Parker took a deep breath to steady herself, but before she had drawn it, it was altered into a sort of sob. But this she disregarded and walked away from the window denying to herself in an obstinate puppet-like way all such emotion. On the mantel-piece to which she turned, Lady Bird's list confronted her. Miss Parker read it through again, and as she read it the sense of not being to others a person filled her for the first time with anger. This confused and arbitrary employment of all her time, this expense of the power and energy that might (or might not) be in her was unfair. Who had the right to expect so much of another? And yet it was only by this and by that (by watching Mouse, by planting Windy Morrow daffodils) that she kept at all in touch with Life, that she had any happy matter in common with the people she lived with and worked for. Of herself and by herself she still had nothing. Her holidays told her that plainly enough, for she found in them neither excitement nor adventure, nor any friend less dreary than herself.

Miss Parker stuck Lady Bird's list back in the mirror's edge. She accepted it and all that it meant, but in her conscious acceptance there was a cold and bitter discouragement of spirit. She felt impelled to show herself some mark of assertion. She even thought she would like to show some kindness to herself for whom nobody cared. So when Dora came in with her supper she asked her to light the schoolroom fire.

Dora looked at her with hard pleased eyes. " Her Ladyship gave orders that fire was not to be lit until the chimney is swept."

This answer which she guessed to be a lie, filled Miss Parker with real rage. Horrible disgusting Dora. Her anger against Dora made her feel nearly sick. And she was helpless to contradict her. She was now, as usual, a person for Dora to despise, and whenever possible to neglect. If Miss Parker loathed anybody in her life she loathed Dora, and

the strength of this gave her power for fierce
rebellion now. Was she after all so helpless to assert
herself?

" Nonsense," she said with trembling briskness,
" that chimney was swept during the first week of
the holidays. Her ladyship wrote and told me so
herself. Please light the fire at once."

Dora stood and gobbled weakly at Miss Parker.
She was too taken aback for argument. And she
was well aware, as Miss Parker too was aware, that
Lady Bird never grudged anything in the shape
of animal comforts to the schoolroom. On this
occasion Miss Parker undoubtedly held most of the
cards, and for once she managed to play them.
Dora flounced out of the room muttering vindictively
to herself, but reappeared in a remarkably short
space of time, a box of matches in her hand, and lit
the fire. Before she again departed Miss Parker
with a most creditable air of superb carelessness took
a cigarette out of a rather battered packet, and said,
" Give me a match, please, Dora, I've left mine
in my bedroom."

Smoking. And in the middle of her supper. Dora
had only seen the most London of her Ladyship's
friends smoke between courses at dinner-time. And
Sir Julian always looked faintly sour when this
occurred. What then had come over Miss Parker?
Dora wildly surmised that she had found on her
holidays a rich young man who was fond of fur.
What else could give her such supreme confidence?
She handed over the matches in quite a respectful

way and left the room without as much as a flounce.

As soon as she had gone Miss Parker threw her cigarette in the fire. She hated smoking really, and only did it to give herself confidence in the lounges of boarding houses and other such places in the Great World. Miss Parker felt excited by her victory. She ate her supper in its glow. She was absurdly warmed and triumphing. Matters became possible to her which before had filled her only with a shadowy sense of defeat. She was alive now. A true person. It was extraordinary that such a small thing could have given a turn like this to her whole self. It was a transient change, no doubt, but for the moment it was real. She was gathered out of her diligent and subservient life, and to-night she thought she was able to take for herself what she chose.

She did not turn on the light after her supper, although now it was nearly dark. She went to the window again and from it she saw one high star. She breathed deeply for she was desperately excited.

One high star. She thought of a summer night when stars had been so many, when the night had been a steep arch, and fires had burned between the mountains and the sea. She remembered that night as the only time she had been fully glad, and the many reasons she had shown herself since then for her gladness she laughed at now. She really laughed, for she was as theatrical as only the completely innocent and desirous are. As only they can be, thinking they have found a thing for the first and only time.

Besides, Miss Parker had a right to a certain share of drama, for she intended now to do a dangerously dramatic act. She intended to walk down to Nick's cottage and see him, which was the same thing as asking plainly for Love. To-night two things had met in her—two forces. Her almost unbelievable loneliness and timidity and that sudden power she had found in herself to worst her enemy. A ridiculous combat. A still more absurd enemy. But not so absurd a victory for Miss Parker, timid, bearded, passionate, ineffective little governess as she was. It was enough to give her this moment's madness, this strength of madness, to carry out her present intention. For it was one thing to stand looking towards reality through a schoolroom window and it was quite another thing to put on a coat and go out into the night to seek it, perhaps to find only failure and the terrible shame of failure.

Miss Parker might never have found the blind unknowing will to carry out her project but for an accident. This was what happened. Fixed in her mind was the notion that to take one of the dogs with her was reason enough for a walk in any direction, and such a reason was a help to her too in the event of an encounter with Byrne or Dora or any other curious person. The shortest way to the rod-room was through the dining-room and down the kitchen passages.

Miss Parker put on her coat and took a look at Markie (who slept in the deepest and most obliging way). She went through the doors that divided the schoolroom wing from the rest of the house and she ran down the lovely flowing staircase, with that alien sense—of which this part of the house made her so fully conscious—strong in her. The thick sand-coloured carpets and the Eastern vases and the sweet strong smell of flowers or scent, or anything that was far apart from furniture polish and soap and schoolrooms, affected Miss Parker oddly so that she felt shy and resentful as she often did when she came in contact with any of Lady Bird's uncaring friends. Suddenly there came to her as she went through the hall and passed two great flowered jars (not much shorter and not much stouter than she was herself) the consciousness that she was looking for something of her own now, something that had no connection with any of these people that she served. Something of her own she was looking for and, if she never found it, then the desperate nature of her effort would give her a standing and a dignity with herself. Yes, even if she failed. Poor Miss Parker, she went bundling along out of the dim hall and down the passage to the dining-room, and here it was that the happy accident befell her which has been already mentioned. As she was about to turn the handle of the farther door which would let her into the pantry and kitchen passages she observed upon a table beside her a square, squat, rich-looking brown

bottle, with a red seal and a loosened cork. Miss
Parker paused a moment longer. An abandoned but
most sensible resolve had seized upon her mind.
She would have a nice drink for herself before she
went any further in this matter. She took the cork
out of the bottle and sniffed, and as she sniffed a
delicious and curious fragrance caught her in the
back of her throat. Miss Parker had never before
smelt or tasted Cointreau. She poured herself out
a generous port glass full of it and looked insolently
round the room. Catching Mad Harry's malignant
eyes upon her, she lifted her glass to him before
she drank. It was for her a supreme gesture
of revolt. It was too, the second real and
perilous act she had accomplished within the hour.
Feeling wildly exhilarated she went on into the
night.

If Miss Parker felt a strange gaiety upon her as
she set down her glass and nodded impudently to
the Bird ancestors and to the shade of Byrne's
presence, it was nothing to the melting and fiery
sensation that possessed her as she strolled with
new and glorious confidence down the fuchsia
path to the river. She was a separate creature now
from the Miss Parker who washed Markie's ears and
troubled his youth with insoluble problems, the Miss
Parker who dressed the dogs in sulphur and planted
bulbs and watched for the horrid results of worm
powders. She was a free woman. She was in love
and in wine, and she went grandly through the
night to find her lover. Down she went towards

the river and its bridge, through the depth of the fuchsias, their flowers dark above her now and dark under her feet as she walked. The sky arched pale and tremendous over the sea, and the headlands and the mountains were as dark in the evening as the red fuchsias. Miss Parker held her head high in the evening and walked on to the river, where a cold white fog was as high as the bridge. But no higher than her feet as she crossed it. Her whole being was in a different rejoicing air. She felt as though should the stars sing together she could match her voice against them. She knew that if a wave came impossibly ravening from the sea to engulf, she could give herself to drowning with ecstasy. In fact, she felt simply fine.

She felt like this until she was within a short distance of Nick's house and here some influence changed her mood a little from this high and drunken buoyancy. About Nick's house and trodden into the used careful path from the river to his house there was an extreme sense of civilisation and of rightful care for the decencies of life. There was a sense of ownership and well-being in the air of the place that was proud. Miss Parker, who had never owned anything that she valued truly, was aware of this. It humbled her. She was quietened and made grave by this which, without reason, she knew. She stopped at the low wall of stones behind which the great fuchsia hedge towered as high almost as the roof of Nick's house. The sea was on her right hand with its constant whispering. The sea was only just below her. Before her, through the narrow gate in the wall and the high darkness of an arch in the fuchsia hedge, she could see the little house, solid, dignified and sharply white in the autumn night. As she waited there her courage or her madness was shaken in her and she knew the wildness of her plan and felt the certainty of defeat. Let me go back now before it's too late, thought Miss Parker. Oh, whatever brought me here? A summer night when she had turned back from the bridge came to her mind and the cold misery of her return and the thankfulness next day that she had gone. To-night too, she must go. This unfinished adventure would be lost in this strange night. Soon she would forget how one night she had defied all custom and gone seeking Love.

While she hesitated and that courage died in her with which she would have outsung the stars, and the fatal mood for Love was passing into coldness and cowardice, the door of Nick's house was opened and a path of lamplight was ruled suddenly across the garden and upright against the hedge nearest to the sea. Trembling a great deal, Miss Parker walked towards the light and the dark man who stood in the light. A moment before she had been lost and dismayed. Now a confused sense of courage again possessed her.

Nick was more than taken aback by the unexpected appearance of Miss Parker. He did not understand it at all, and in his mind now there was no connection whatever between this arrival and that confused summer's dream of she-seals and Master Markie's governess.

Nick was in his own house. He approached any guest with dignity and charm of manner. He asked Miss Parker with gentle amiability whether she had come to fetch Markie's mackintosh which had been left in one of the boats, and when she said yes (surprised at this extraordinary stroke played by Fortune to the Proprieties), he asked her to come into his house and sit down for a minute while he fetched it for her.

" There's a change for winter these nights."

For a second they stood outside his house in the clear changing of the year and then Miss Parker turned blindly and confusedly into the light and the shelter of the small house.

Nick was very charming to her. Sheena's friends and Olivia's friends often came to see him and he entertained the Silverue governess as though she were one of these. That is to say with tales of fishing, and of Master Markie, and of the numbers of grouse shot and other matters regarding the countryside and those who lived in it. It would be wrong to say he tried to entertain her. He treated her for the moment as a companion, if not as an equal. And there was nowhere a man who could talk so sympathetically and with so faithful and poetic a turn of speech as Nick. In every word he spoke there was life and the gaiety of life, or its sorrow. Always the meaning of his thought was true and able.

Perhaps Miss Parker spent ten minutes in his

cottage listening to his talk. She sat very still, her
feet propped under her on the rung of her chair,
with Chuggy sitting as solid as a wooden dog
in her lap. Her dark little face was quite in shadow
and all the time she hardly spoke. Only her eyes
kept passing from one thing to another in the low
square room. She looked from the fire to the dark
panes of the window and then to the dresser with
its rows of delft and back again to the fire. It was
not because she was restless to go. It was some
other restlessness. She hardly spoke to Nick at all,
but kept looking round his house in this queer,
seeking way as though she did not know whether to
go or stay, speak or be silent. At last she said :

"I must go now. If you'd give me the mackintosh."

He gave her Markie's absurd little coat—a child's
clothes look so nonsensical when a child is not there
to wear them—and watched her go down the path
to his gate and heard her say, " Good-night, again "
from his gate. Nick shut the door of his house and
stood outside it looking down his garden and
through the gap in his hedge to the little port where
his boat and the Silverue boats were tied and
anchored.

XXVIII

ABOUT the third week in September Eliza came back to Silverue. She did not come because John demanded it, for as she knew, John needed her much less now, and although she was glad about this, knowing that she had not meant to hold him, knowing that she had done as she had with the purpose only of restoring to him his proper confidence and arrogance in life, yet the completeness of the restoration left her at times a little dismayed and almost at a loss.

Now as Eliza sat in a railway carriage within an hour of Silverue, she was surprised and not truly amused (try as she might to capture this most helpful attitude) to find herself short of confidence for her meeting with John. Not embarrassed, for she was not a person embarrassed by the simplicities, but without a line to follow, lost with this creature she had given back so wholly to himself. Weeks ago she knew that he had recovered. Weeks ago, before the end of his visit to her in Brittany. Not that he seemed less loving or to need her less, but there was a faint air of indulgence towards her about his loving which told Eliza how completely she had accomplished what she had set out to do. Success can leave one empty-handed. Eliza felt more truly alone than she often did at the ending of a love affair. Not that there had been any dramatic admission of conclusion in her parting from John. He had made frequent and eager plans for seeing her again, but it had not been hard for him to leave her. He had talked a great deal about Markie and Silverue and the hunting during the last week in Brittany. He was glad to be going back healed and self-established to Silverue, a very different return from his last. He was quite excited with the thought of seeing Markie again, he and Sheena would talk about the Little Boy very often. When he was secure, Markie and Silverue were the things John minded about. Eliza knew these signs. She was very careful to make no claim on him herself, and she was careful to assent to all his future plans ; while she knew there was no future and this was a changing if not an end. Not yet an end, perhaps.

Now it was Sheena and not John who had brought her back to Silverue. She must see for herself how far Sheena had recovered because she knew a strange thing now, a complete defence of Sheena's happiness, of which Julian and Olivia must have known. It was beyond Eliza's understanding that Julian should have known this and preserved his elaborate silence, but if she must she would betray his silence. If Sheena was still the queer stricken creature who had recovered so little in Brittany Eliza was ready to hold light even Julian, so that he did not weigh against Sheena's need in this.

And why, Eliza asked herself, as her train brought her nearer to Silverue, do I struggle against accident and fate, and against Julian himself whom I so love for these children of Julian's? What wild quality in them is it that excites me to such ridiculous lengths of sacrifice? And they are lost to me. Except in their unhappiness I have no real share of anything with them. We are quite apart. And why should I demand anything of them? How accursed and tiresome is that sympathy which indulges its lust for giving, binding itself about the object of its love and sending down parasitical roots into the life it cherishes. It is all quite hideous, Eliza thought, and all forms of sympathy are at times near to this form. The dangers of giving are so much beyond the dangers of taking.

The train was now very nearly in the station, and Eliza gathered herself out of the mood of spiritual isolation and questioning which so often overcame her in railway carriages, and prepared herself to meet her romantic friends the Birds. She felt clearer and more self-sufficient when she stepped out of the train into the windy day, and she looked so unlike her own fears and imaginings that it was really ludicrous. If she had known how Sheena felt when she kissed her it would have re-established all her sense of importance or vanity, or whatever it is that is most valuable to us in our human contacts.

For Sheena felt that sense of excitement and distance to be bridged of which all Eliza's friends were aware when they met her again even after

the shortest parting. Sheena did not feel that Eliza
had stood still where they had parted. She had
bought new clothes and heard amusing gossip and
real information. She had lived and experienced a
little more. She had changed a little. She was not
quite the same. That was what they all thought
when again she charmed them. But, alas, poor
Eliza, she knew that she was much the same in that
inner creature she so pitied—her gay and lonely self.

Now her little face that seemed a mile away
among the wind and the steel girders was stooped
for Sheena's kissing and lower still for Markie's. . . .
"Well, sweet villain——" But he did not kiss her.
He flung himself against her and left her to play
some horrid havoc of his own upon his enemy, the
stationmaster.

They went out to the car. It had rained in the
night and the day was full of wind. The sky was
very high and swept out to hollowness by the wind.
A village on a hill was a little shining city encircled
by a curious air. Its white-walled houses were as
important as towers. The heights and slopes of its
roofs had an excellent quality suggestive of quietness.

Sheena said : " It's so wonderful to see you.
Darling, why did you suddenly say you'd come ? "

" I wanted to see you, I suppose."

" You're looking marvellous. You've got a new
colour on your nails and a new colour on your face.
I do love changes. Such a gay coat and skirt. We
only got your wire last night or John would have
come with me to meet you."

" Yes, why didn't he ? How idle."

" Oh, it's a cub-hunting morning. He couldn't have escaped possibly. He's whipping in to Cruise this season. Did you know ? "

" Yes, he said something about it. No, I didn't know it was definite." She felt glad about this, and insanely sorry too. She knew how little John would need her now.

" And Julian is away till to-morrow."

" Oh, how sad."

" Where do you think that awful child has got to ?" Sheena asked. " Shall I sound the horn ? " She sounded it wildly.

Eliza looked out at the wet station walls and back again at Sheena. So Sheena was sick for Love still. It was evident to Eliza. She could hear it in her disconnected talking and see it in the restless, broken look which was not more in her eyes than in a sharpness that denied her even the dignity of melancholy. Beyond belief she was a creature dis-improved by unhappiness. Eliza could not fail to see this and the knowledge grieved her sadly.

Now she blew the horn again for Markie, angry and insistent, and when he still did not come she went off to find him, looking to Eliza not so unlike Olivia in a temper. When they came back together Markie was watching her like a tempersome little monkey who has offended and will again as soon as the opportunity arises. Eliza had never seen this guarded untrusting look in his face for Sheena before. It startled her considerably. Sheena who loved

Markie so greatly, how had she brought him to this state of defensiveness ? By what unkindness had she undone his absolute trust in that tender one, Sheena ? It was only for a moment that Eliza saw this change and she told herself that she exaggerated it beyond any truthful meaning, but the impression it made on her remained beyond a sensible view of the matter.

All the way back to Silverue Eliza was only three parts alive in the present. Half the life of her mind was before her and so the present lost its usual vivid accuracy. She was aware of Markie in the back of the car, eating chocolate with sloven greediness, and of Sheena beside her, still talking away of this and that and nothing at all. The drive back to Silverue, preciously exciting to Eliza, to-day seemed to have dropped in value. She saw the deep, low shining of lake and sea, and the shadows of the clouds moving as the shadows of wings flying and changing on the mountains. For a moment things would be real to her, as when they drove round a wide turning in the road and she saw a thatched yellow cottage standing in the embrace of the turn, plum-coloured mountains and a violent green field beyond it, and hanging over the stone wall an elder tree heavy in fruit. So heavy the berries had grown that their flat growth fell forwards and downwards showing their backs, a web behind their berries, like pigeons' red feet. But only by moments such as this was she entirely conscious. Otherwise she might have been on her way to some house she did not particularly mind about one way or another.

Olivia, in superb autumnal tweeds, was arranging dahlias in the drawing-room when they arrived. Cold water was shining on her cold ringed hands as she embraced Eliza and bestowed that kiss in which the claims of friendship and her own *maquillage* were balanced with such conscious nicety. " My darling, this is so lovely." As she kissed Eliza she seemed only suspended for a moment in her act of decoration. She turned back to the dark and narrow glass before which she was arranging flowers in their brief postures. How ably she created the perfect shape and attitude—there was a quality in Olivia's power to decorate for which Eliza could find nothing but envy.

Presently they went in to luncheon, where Eliza shook hands with Miss Parker. Was it the same governess? Yes, without a doubt it must be. Shadowy, befurred little creature. " How do you do, Miss Parker ? "

Olivia ate an immense meal, complaining a great deal as she did so about the way her cook cooked French beans, about the way her cook made curry, about the way her gardener grew lettuce, about the way her cook made cream cheese, biscuits, plum tarts and coffee.

Sheena said very little. She ate a great deal of lettuce and nothing else, and drank a quantity of black coffee. Eliza wondered a little whether she was not being slightly dramatic and tiresome. On the whole she feared it was all genuine.

" Well, now," said Olivia heartily towards the end

of the meal, " and what are Markie and Miss Parker going to do this afternoon ? "

" Going with Nick," Markie hastily dissevered himself from any possible partnership with Miss Parker.

" Very well, darling. And what about Miss Parker ? "

" What about the Gentians, Lady Bird ? "

" Yes. What about the Gentians ? Or shall we let them wait till to-morrow ? I do think *all* the dogs should have a good Pulvexing and a sharp walk. What do you think ? And then there are the library books to go back. Perhaps you could manage to walk the dogs as far as Kiljennet. And after tea would do for the Gentians—or perhaps the bonfire ? Of course if you got the bonfire going well you might leave it and finish the Gentians. That is if all the Muscarii are planted under the copper beech. I love to think of them in the spring—just a shining lake of blue, don't you ? It makes it all seem so terribly worth while, at least to me it does."

Eliza wondered for an idle moment how deeply Lady Bird's vision of the spring would assist Miss Parker in her autumn sowing. She doubted its efficacy herself, but one never knew. The little thing seemed quite eager and busy.

" What are you going to do, Sheena ? "

" How do I know, Olivia ? Anything."

" Reading a book in your bedroom, I suppose. I can't think why you didn't go out hunting to-day."

" Because I hadn't a horse."

" Nonsense."

" Because I wanted to meet Eliza. Because I
didn't want to go out hunting."

" Nonsense," said Olivia again in a large,
aggravating way.

Sheena turned quite pale with nervous anger.
She got up and went out of the room.

" What's the matter with her ? " said Olivia to
Eliza. " You see, she's always like this now. Do
you see how changed ? " Her voice was quite little
and tired. She was not really asking Eliza what the
matter was. She was telling her how things were.
Eliza felt that it would be reasonably easy to make
Olivia act as she wished her to do now. But she
must give a little time before she spoke. The afternoon would have that afternoon quality of bridges,
and she would walk across it first before she spoke.

John came back about half-past two. Eliza was
standing on the gravel in front of the house waiting
for Olivia when he came. The wind had dropped
entirely and here in the shelter of the house the
air was still. It could not have been morning
air nor summer heat. It was as gay as the morning
air, and as hot as the summer, yet without any
durability. No future promise, but an ending.

Eliza kissed John lightly in the sweet, sharp
afternoon. Already, she thought, he is entirely lost.
It's quite extraordinary how little I mind. The
work of restoration was indeed completed. She
wondered whether he was not in the faintest degree
amused at himself, he kissed her so lightly too, and so

happily. " Eliza, my dear sweet, how are you going?
How lovely to see you. Why did you come?"

" To see Olivia. To see Silverue."

" No. To see me?"

" To see John? Indeed no. I came to see Sheena
really."

" Olivia and Silverue and Sheena and Markie
and Julian and Miss Parker too, I suppose. Why not
John?"

How dear John was and how entirely uncaring.
Eliza put her arm in his as they walked back towards
the house. She did not mind much, either. Not
really.

" Was it a good morning?"

" Yes. Wicked struggling and striving through
the country. Fox-hunting really."

" How naughty."

" Ah, they slipped away on us. We couldn't help
ourselves. But it was lovely. It's lovely hunting with
Cruise. You must come out one morning, Eliza.
Have you ever hunted with him?"

" No."

" Oh, you must."

" Yes, I must come out one morning. But I hate
cub-hunting. Horses are so fresh and fat and
frightening. And I'm always being compelled to
leap some dreadful fence which isn't right so early
in the year."

John laughed inattentively. He was divided from
Eliza and all she was saying. The long morning
behind him : the trial and joy in which she had no

part : the weariness now in which she had no part.
All these things gave him a strength and a quietness
and a deep safety of his own in which he scarcely
knew how he had once needed all her help of words
and gentleness.

"Oh," he said, suddenly remembering a thing
that mattered. "Sheena's dog is in the car. Poor
Mrs. Cooney, she got a little nip. I put iodine on it,
but Sheena'll want to meddle it herself, won't she ? "
He went back to the car and fetched Mrs. Cooney,
carrying her in his arms into the house calling,
"Sheena, Sheena."

Olivia came out presently and Eliza and she
walked up to the garden as they planned to do. They
walked up the dark fuchsia path. The moss on it
was emerald—new life in the damp, changing year—
and the tree roots that crossed it were slippery and
knotted under their feet. High through the tree
stems, held apart by this great hedge, smoke was
blown from autumn fires. And dropped low beneath
the limbs of the trees and the hill a wedge of sea
was as blue as an enamel box.

All the way up to the garden Olivia discoursed of
her servants. "And as I said to Dora if you can't
make her do her work you aren't fit to be over her,
so don't let me hear any more complaints."

"Did you ? "

"But Dora said the thing was Byrne always
wanted her to help in the pantry, which simply is
ridiculous. And as Dora said, it's much more sport
for her than doing her own work upstairs."

" Yes. Of course."

" So I went down to the pantry and had it out with Byrne, and all Byrne would say was, ' Indeed, my lady, I'm feeling *very* unsettled myself,' and with that Dora came bouncing in and gave me a month's notice, and said she thought I ought to know the things that were going on in the house."

" No ? "

" But she wouldn't tell me what. So then I went to Mrs. Wiggin and said I didn't like this sort of thing and I must know, and she said it was all because Nora got off with Dora's young man at the last party they had in the servants' hall. Dora hadn't been the same since, she said, and full of complaints about the schoolroom, and of course she had it in for Nora and said the most unpleasant things about the length of time she spent in the pantry with Byrne."

" Disgusting."

" And you know I may be stupidly prejudiced, Eliza, but to my mind a butler ought to be simply like Cæsar's wife otherwise where are you I ask you ? "

" Yes, indeed."

" And I'm not a bit certain that Mrs. Wiggin hasn't got ideas about Byrne herself. It was astonishing how her cooking went off when he was laid up with shingles."

" Did it really ? "

" Yes, really." Olivia looked at Eliza with great disarming eyes, halving the boredom of this domestic disquisition. She endowed possibly the least dramatic aspects of life with a sort of excitement. Living in them herself day by day without boredom, she could not see how they could overcome another. Whence hast thou this becoming of things ill? Eliza might have asked her in a moment of extravagance; or Julian, in a moment of despairing forgiveness, might have cried: Oh, from what power hast thou this powerful might, with insufficiency my heart to sway? Neither would have asked her or cried to her in this way at all. The possibility only breathed in Eliza's mind for a moment and was gone. But it was a truth about Olivia all the same. She would always escape.

They ambled round the still, autumnal garden, with now and then a violent pretence of business as when Olivia gathered Michaelmas daisies, put out the gardener's bonfire, and conducted an exhaustive search for the last figs. Olivia talked endlessly of the glories and failures of the summer months in the live ordinary way in which she talked of her servants; rapid in abuse and praise, particular in retrospect, while Eliza listened or did not listen and thought again of what she had to say to Olivia to-night.

The thought of Olivia's summer garden came to her, its memory stronger than the actual and present garden she walked in, and on a different level entirely from Olivia's ceaseless recallings and vulgar prattle of success and disappointment. Here and now among the strong bright autumn flowers she was more truly aware of a dark night in June and the night time animal breath of flowers than she had been at the time itself. For a moment the chilly aromatic scent of autumn flowers was not there, and Eliza remembered the happiness of the past summer and its hours of grieving and of beauty so extreme as to have a sword-like wounding quality. She thought of Olivia who had sat here crying because of her child's unhappiness, truly grieved and despairing for her child, but unable to sacrifice herself entirely for any person's sake. No matter how she loved them she was actually powerless to hurt herself on their account. That night when they had sat together in the garden, she and Olivia, and Olivia had cried to Eliza about her poor child and about Julian, and her love for Julian, and her gratefulness, then she had known as well as Eliza knew now that she could set the matter right. It was within her power to do so and she would not, but sheltered herself behind tears and pretences and Julian's loving will. And neither child nor friend counted with Julian beside Olivia. Eliza had known that always, but never so clearly or with such imperishable certainty as now. Through all things Olivia was first. In lesser matters he might help and protect their children from the dreadful antics of her posturing, but beyond that, in any real issue, they were set aside and Olivia only counted with him. They were shadows and she the very substance of life. This could not be denied. Was it this power she had, this talent to delight, that was in her children too? Had they in reality much more from

her than they inherited from Julian? Julian, whom
so few people besides Eliza loved. Had Olivia, in her
vast unintention, given them more than she would
ever wrong them of? Their beauty and vitality
and unawareness, for they had that quality of hers,
an insensibility of their own power to disturb or to
wound or to be boring. How strange it was that they
should owe so much to Olivia, and how probable
that they would live and die without any faintest
knowledge or acknowledgment of their debt.

From these musings Eliza arrived at a state of
mind in which it seemed to her important that Olivia
should not be too much hurt by this which she was
going to tell her. It seemed to her to matter that
Olivia should hear this thing as easily as might
be. And when could she feel more truly at ease
than in this garden which she might be said to love?
The conviction grew upon Eliza that here she
would speak to Olivia. She would not wait till this
evening as she had meant to do. Now she would
subdue all her own feelings of cowardice in the
matter—those frail defences that one puts up rather
than pursue the appalling difficulties of such dis-
cussions with one's friends. It is easy enough to
pursue such discourse when Praise and not Blame
forms the keynote, then the more paralysingly
intimate their tone, the more like oil their flow, but
now——

Eliza said : " I didn't say much to you after
luncheon. But I was simply shocked by Sheena.
What do you think yourself about her? "

Olivia came out of her keen gardening mood at once. It was as though she fell from a height. Always this look of shock about her when Eliza spoke seriously of Sheena.

" I'm terrified about her," she said. " My dear, do you know what she's doing? I may as well tell you because I don't know what to do about it. And you are always such a help."

" What is she doing, Olivia? "

" She's drinking gin and drugging herself with *Câchets Faivre*."

" Oh, my dear, what nonsense ! "

" It's no use your saying nonsense in that nasty way. I know you think I'm a fool, but there you are; I mean, there it is."

" But how do you know? How do you know she's going on like this to any extent ? "

" I went to the chemist and had a look at her bill the other day."

Olivia would have done that.

" And about the gin ? "

" Empty bottles." Olivia dropped her voice in the most sinister way.

" But it's too absurd. It's not like Sheena. It's unbelievable."

" Yes, but it's not like Sheena to be unhappy. She's never been unhappy before now. It does change people, Eliza."

" Despair changes people ? "

" Yes, that's what I said to Julian——" Olivia caught herself up on a breath.

" Did you tell Julian about the gin ? "

" No, he's been away. He's been in Scotland since I found that out. Julian says she'll be all right."

Julian says she'll be all right. Eliza felt overcome by a pitying rage for Sheena's sake that Julian could have spoken with this tolerance about so great and so young a grief as Sheena's. It was not that he did not know. It was not that he could not see. But Olivia was his dear one and he put her before all else in life, it seemed. She was not to suffer any hurt however sadly Sheena might be changed or defeated. This elaborate protection of Olivia must go on.

" I suppose it never occurred to Julian that all this mess might be cleared up if Sheena was told that Julian wasn't her father at all ? If you told her that she was Rowland Weston's daughter it would alter things entirely, wouldn't it ? "

Eliza had seldom accomplished anything more difficult than the explosion of this Ouidaresque bombshell in an ordinary and conversational tone of voice.

Olivia said nothing. Nothing whatever. Quite a long pause followed, so long that in it Eliza was aware of one of those officiously brisk autumn robins singing away near them with cheerful persistence.

" Or has it ever occurred to you, Olivia ? "

" Oh, Eliza," said Olivia most pitifully, " I haven't thought of anything else for months. Not since I first realised that Sheena was badly hit by this. I haven't been able to put my mind to anything.

Not to my face, or the house, or the garden, or anything. My dear, I've put on four pounds weight—that shows you."

Curiously enough it did indeed.

" Did you think she'd come out of it? She'd recover ? "

" Yes, all the time she was with you, I thought then she would."

" And when she came back ? "

" Oh, I knew at once she hadn't. And it's got worse. She's trying to hold out till Rupert goes, you know. I think that's it. He's off to Egypt quite soon. Julian says she'll be all right then. He said if she wasn't I could take her for a nice cruise to the East Indies or the West Indies. But what I tell him is she won't want to go on a cruise with me."

It occurred to Eliza that Olivia was sometimes very brave about accepting her children's dislike. Were her affectations of the same gallantry ? No. There mercifully she could deceive herself.

" You're convinced all this messing at cruises and changes is hopeless then ? "

" Eliza, I can't bear it—to see her so unhappy."

" Then why not tell her."

" I must discuss it with Julian. It's not fair to him quite, is it ? "

" There have been times when you've been—less fair ? "

" Oh, *yes*. But they're over. We're through them, and we've got something left. I don't know what it is. I'm so stupid. It's Julian's dignity, I think.

I do belong to that. You can't understand. I can't
explain, I'm so stupid. . . . Of course you can't
understand. How can I let him down again for
Sheena? Sheena's not even his child. She hasn't
that much right. And he's so sweet to her——"

" And over this—— ? "

" If it had been over John or over Markie he'd
have done just the same. You know it's true. You
know he would."

They were silent again. The robin's singing
ravished the air piercingly, for the moment a
complete thing. The afternoon was growing late.
There was a darkening now as of rain but not for
rain. It was the day closing.

" I think you must tell her."

" Without asking Julian? Let's wait till he comes
back, Eliza. My one comfort is she's not a Bird.
She won't go mad like poor John. I don't mean
mad——"

" Darling, don't contradict yourself always when
you're talking sense."

" Must you be so unkind ? "

" I know I'm being unkind. I want you to look
at things as they are for a minute. At everything if
you can. Look—John's your child and he went mad.
You suffered hell. It was the purest form of agony.
He's recovered entirely. He's himself. He has more
strength and vitality and charm than ever he had
before. It's true, isn't it? But it was almost a
miracle. It was touch and go last June when he
came back here to Silverue. You knew that."

"Yes, I knew that. Thank God I was able to help him."

"Yes, thank God you were able to help him. Now here's Sheena. For John you weren't responsible. But you're putting Sheena through it properly. Well, aren't you?"

"But Julian says——"

"Julian—Julian doesn't think of anything beyond you. Not, really."

"That's why I must be loyal now. Can't you see? Ah, you can't, I know. Luke was killed so soon after you married him. You never knew what it was to depend on him in spite of not loving him. Oh, I can't explain at all. What we have, Julian and I, it's not because of me. It's Julian forgiving me and being blind often and often. It matters much more, what Julian's done for me, it has much more value than all the rotten things I've done to Julian."

"But, Olivia, compared to Sheena and John, our lives—yours and mine and Julian's—are over. They don't count."

"They're not over. Mine's not over. There comes a time in Every Woman's Life——"

"'When her home and children——' I know that bit, darling."

"You don't understand. You can't understand. You haven't got a home and children."

"No. You're quite right. And that was so cheap of me, and so sour. But I can't let you get away with this. You must be fair to Sheena. You must tell her."

" But Julian——"

" You must tell her."

" I can't, Eliza. I can't tell her."

Eliza was silent again for a minute. Almost quite a minute.

" I'll tell her," she said. " And you can tell Julian I told her."

" Oh, Eliza, would you? Would you, really? Of course it's nothing to you, I know, but it means so much to me. If Julian knew I'd done this it would be too awful for him. In any case, it's bad enough. But I can't stop you, can I? I'm not being disloyal to Julian? "

" No. I'm doing that part."

" But you're not his wife."

" Indeed no. The merest friend."

" I can't see that you're being disloyal, Eliza."

" Oh, well. Does it matter? " Eliza felt deathly tired. " After all does it matter so very much? "

" Compared to Sheena, you mean? "

" Compared to Sheena, if you like. Yes, compared to Sheena, I suppose was what I meant." To forget even the direct reason for sacrifice and to feel no excitement in the oblation, nothing but this sick exhaustion. Eliza felt cheated of all that mattered to her, a sentimental stupid woman. The stupidity of this suffering appalled her. She felt confused and disgusted.

They went back to the house. Out of the garden the evening seemed more definite. The air was clear and heavy, the weight of a summer's life seemed

present in the evening. The whole evening was
charged with it. Again Eliza felt the past summer
and knew about it much more truly now. It had
nothing to do with the changed trees nor the ripe
fruit nor the smoke of fires. The difference was all
in the air with its aggressive sense of division and
waiting.

On the way back to the house Olivia was obviously
trying to gather her determination to say something
more. She failed more than once. Finally, she said :

" Darling, you're being so wonderful and understanding about this. Do you agree with me that
we'd better tell Julian I did try to dissuade you from
telling Sheena ? He does so dislike Rupert's uncle,
and of course he'll have to know, I suppose, if it's
all to work."

" You'd better tell Julian, or I'd better tell him ? "

" Well, I will if you think it would be better."

" It might be more convincing. Yes, tell him
whatever you like."

Before dinner that evening Eliza went to look for
Sheena. She found her lying on her bed, still wearing
her shoes and an expensive fur coat. She did look
rather cold and she had neither a book nor a dog to
entertain her. There was an empty tooth-glass on
the table beside her bed, and she seemed only just
able to contain her exasperation when Eliza came in.

" So you've taken to gin," Eliza said without
much affability. " Do you find it a help ? You might
give me a tiddle, will you ? "

" In my cupboard," Sheena said. She refused to

be discomposed, but she looked, if anything, more hollow and distant. Eliza found the bottle in a corner where hunting boots lolled against the skirts of evening gowns. She poured herself out a nice drink and lit a cigarette.

" You're being very grand, aren't you," she said, " with your secret drinking ? "

" It's not secret, and it's not grand, and it's not your business."

" Oh, Sheena, I have begun badly."

" It doesn't matter, Eliza. Go on."

There was something gone in Sheena. Something sound and distant and remotely holy that had been in her. Something unbetrayed. Her trust and her bravery about life seemed vanquished, and this shaken creature all that was left. This sordid, flattened creature who had once been so mild and gentle. She would be all right, Julian had said. No doubt she would in a measure recover. But never entirely. What mattered most was very nearly lost. She would not recapture it all at once. Eliza, drinking gin out of the tooth-glass considered her with a desperate kind of pity. She must catch hold of herself in a minute and tell Sheena the truth. And the story must go all in Olivia's favour. It was difficult to put that unrestrained mother's case in an unreal romantic light. But she thought it would be better if she could do so. Sheena need not know that there had been any forcing of the maternal conscience. Yes, it would be best to tell it like this. It was a cue that Olivia would take up very quickly.

It would be easier all round. And having done this, Eliza would go away, because she had defeated Silverue twice now, and this time at the cost of Julian's trust. But then his trust in her existed no more than his love, Eliza remembered. He had not loved Eliza nor trusted her. She had created for herself a state of mental excitement in which she could half-believe in these things. She was losing nothing real, only a false and precious conceit which had failed her very often.

Sheena lay as quiet as a young mouse while Eliza told her that she was not Julian's daughter and, therefore, there was no reason why she should not marry Rupert in the morning if she chose to do so. Then it appeared to Eliza as if Life quickened in a creature that had perished. Sheena asked her no questions about how she knew or who would suffer for this telling. The thought of Sheena and Rupert only possessed her. It's not true, she kept saying, Promise me it's true, Eliza. She opened her window and leaned out into the evening. It was as though no house could contain this wild joy. Round her the air seemed changed. She was translated. She was once more that tender enraptured creature who dashed paint upon her face and flung herself immoderately ahead of time towards all assignments. Having no fear or vanity to delay her. Trusting because she knew herself loved and charmed from sorrow. Soon she had fled and gone. Gone into the evening, fled from Silverue. She must instantly find her love, Rupert, and tell him. Without restraint or any mistrust she took herself off at high speed into this first hour of the night.

Eliza went slowly down the lovely curving staircase. Step by step as she went her elation died in her and when she reached the library she felt quite stilled and cold with the thoughts of loss that overcame her. In the library she did not even look at that weak, silly copy of a picture by which Julian had elaborated and betrayed his defences. The original had not been a portrait of Miss Sheena Curran but of quite another forebear of Sheena's. It was unfortunate for Julian that the original should have been discovered so lately, and still more unlucky that Eliza had been principally concerned in the matter. Oh, she thought, unfolding the day's paper, I feel quite desperately disgusted with myself. No one loathes more than I do those people who become gods in machines to their friends, or else imagine that they have failed them. We ought to fail our friends at times or we find ourselves on too ridiculously exalted a plane. Thus they are lost to us indeed. Forever lost to us.

From another thing Eliza kept her eyes—the flowers Olivia had arranged in the morning. During the day this decoration had changed a little, the flowers altering their positions to that exact perfection towards which they had been directed.

XXIX

Two days Eliza had spent at Silverue and now on the third day she was going. Olivia and Markie were taking her to the station. She did not feel much more conscious than she had done on the morning when Sheena had driven her along this same road from the station. She was aware of things that had happened, of a change that had come into unpassing existence in her life. She was aware, but she was not yet conscious of what this meant, of what it ended, or of what it began. She could remember very precisely every event of this short visit to Silverue but she could not yet quite place each happening in its proper relevance to another.

There had been the evening after she had told Sheena. Sheena had not come back till very late and John had gone to bed very early because he was hunting again in the morning. So Eliza had sat for hours with Olivia after dinner and heard the tale of her long ago affair with poor Rowland Weston, and why Olivia had given him everything, my dear. Unfortunately for Eliza she could still recall every one of the romantic reasons for this bestowal of her favours, and the story lasted for an unbelievable length of time, each circumstance most particularly reviewed. Eliza looked away at her piece of *petit-point* and said very little. But afterwards she could remember precisely which of those sour and twisted green leaves she had worked on that evening. They had been a help to her. Later, when she went at last to bed and leaned from her cold window, the roses below it, pallid and frozen roses beneath the autumn moon, were truly a help to her too. Their tapestry quality of immobile reserve she thought a good pattern for a romantic woman's observance.

She had decisively refused to pursue the early semblance of the chase, so she did not see Rupert and Sheena take forth at dawn, or nearly. Later, when she walked out into the chill and russet air of the day she felt immeasurably apart from them, belonging to the day with its brief strength and its awareness of change and ending, not to them or to their extravagant happiness or to their renewed belief in living. Life will deceive them again, Eliza thought. She was ashamed of the faint solace she found in this thought, but she would have felt a deeper shame had she not admitted this resentment towards entire happiness. Her terror of unconsciousness was frequently a form of extreme self-torture with Eliza.

I must go away, Eliza decided; while I can still pretend to myself that I've made a success of all this I must go. It doesn't do to hurt oneself too much. If I could get away before Julian comes back it might be a good plan. She spent some of the morning making a bonfire with Markie, while Miss

Parker was sent on an errand to Kiljennet post office. The notion of asking the obliging Miss Parker to bring back a telegram demanding an instant departure crossed Eliza's mind, but she dismissed it as a little too fantastic. She must just be firm for once and say she was going to go. For the moment her unhappiness was pausing. She enjoyed Markie's terrific importance over his bonfire. It must be lovely for him, to have some person he could bully completely, as he was bullying Eliza this morning. He seemed extravagantly happy in a stern way ; ordering her about, muttering to himself over her ignorance and incompetence, and using all the tools he was forbidden to employ, from Olivia's garden scissors to a peculiarly aggressive looking bill-hook. Their fire was situated in a lonely part of the shrubbery where Markie wished to make a good clearing, he said, as it was time he had a new outdoor lavatory. He had wearied of all his old favourites. At about twelve o'clock they ate some milk chocolate which was very nice, and Eliza lit a cigarette for herself and tried to find enough re-solution to tell Markie it was time that he went in for his rest. The greenish air in the shrubbery was full of gnats and still and desolate when they walked away from their fire and back to the house again. As they went along Markie made a strict assignment with Eliza to meet him here again at three o'clock. But although she went there at the appointed time she did not find him, for he had embarked himself upon a more delightful afternoon's entertainment with Nick, ignoring, if he had ever remembered, their compact. Again as in the morning, she turned away from the quietness of that untended place and went back to the house restless and distressed.

At tea-time Olivia was superbly and aggressively herself. Eliza, her mind on Julian's return, excited and at the same time unbearably distressed by the sense of loss that his presence would make so much more real, found that Olivia could still astonish her. No doubt the spectacle of a creature completely true to one's own conception of its character and reactions is always a little surprising. Can one really have been so right?

Olivia was looking radiant and at least a better imitation of youth than Sheena who, exhausted by early rising and the renewed excitements of love, sat in a quietness from which none might rouse her. She was apart again as on that former night, her thoughts were for none of them. She was as much withdrawn from them in body as in spirit, a creature seen in water and at a distance. A creature unencumbered by gratitude or any sad retrospect. And John was there again, talking of his morning's hunting a little and thinking of it all the time, like Sheena for the time completed and set apart. To Eliza now an object out of reach, like some piece of work she had herself created, finding in its completion all power and passion towards it spent, all connection forever lost. She was able to see with detachment that the work done was good, but she would never be able to find a word to fit the piercing regret she knew for what had endured only so briefly. It did not matter, before the word was found she would have forgotten ; her regret too, would be brief for this.

Olivia told them that she had spent the day in a rubber suit and had lost nearly two pounds weight. She was delighted with herself and felt emboldened by her success to eat at least four pounds of chocolate cake. " What did you do to sweat ? Race Miss Parker to Kiljennet post office ? "

" No, I walked over to see Jessie Blow. My dear, how she has aged. You know she's no older than I am, but India has such a horrifying effect on most women. But, really, poor Jessie, she has got old."

" Did you tell her so ? "

" My dear. No. I told her she looked shockingly ill."

" What a lovely day you've had, Olivia. You took off two pounds weight and you found some one who looked twenty years older than yourself. Don't you feel grand ? Was her garden looking terrible ? "

" Yes, awful. I told her if she went for a good tramp with her dogs every day she'd feel a lot better. And if she bought a rubber suit and did something about her figure she wouldn't know herself. I promised to lend her my book about constipation. But it's not that, I said, I suppose, really, it's being Big Sister to my children that keeps *me* so young."

" She must have felt fine when you'd done with her, Big Sister."

" I just tried to cheer her up a bit Her life is

pretty drab, I expect. All that archæology she goes
in for—and always eating sandwiches. . . . My
dear, the time ! I must fly off and meet Julian.
When does that train get in ? Six-fifteen or six-
twenty five ? "

She had gone. Did she not, Eliza wondered, mind
at all, or know at all how deeply they must be
hurting Julian ? There are some betrayals that are
painful, betrayals of a truth, but to have one's
pretences betrayed, that is unendurable. And that
was their betrayal of Julian ; this elaborate pretence
about Sheena ended, and his defence, not of Sheena
but of Olivia, made a silly thing, a matter of vanity
and inefficient lying Poor Julian, who lied so
seldom and had so few pretences. Eliza knew whom
he would condemn for his undoing, it would not be
Olivia whom he had forgiven so often because of
his love for her, but Eliza who had never before
hurt him, or ever would again. No doubt he would
show a great restraint and forbearance towards her.
No doubt she would live beyond his return and her
departure to-morrow. All these things would be,
but all that mattered to Eliza seemed disastrously at
an end.

She was right about Julian's ability to restrain
himself. His manner to her was superbly and
ironically ordinary. There had been only one
moment when he had failed a little, and that was
over such an unnecessary thing. When he said :
" Shall we drink one of Olivia's cocktails ? I've
been finding sherry so boring lately." There was

really no need to stress this point, Eliza had no
further ambition towards those dead hours when
they had sat together drinking and conversing. This
was gone. On a summer night it had suffered a
change and now it was not any more.

Going in to dinner Olivia had hissed in her ear :
" I told him. He was wonderful. Has he said
anything to you ? "

" What did he say to you ? "

" When I told him your point of view he said he
entirely understood."

" Oh, indeed," said Eliza. An ineffective comment, she felt, but about all that she could manage.
At dinner-time she had made stupendous efforts,
talking herself sick and silly and getting faintly drunk.
Talking a little too much perhaps, just within
danger of being tiresome. One or twice she was
aware that only her reputation for being a bit of a
wit saved her from being a bit of a bore. I must
never do things like this again, she told herself,
I'm almost sparkling—it is terrifying. Only Julian
was listening to her with attention. An active and
sweet attention, such were his manners. And when
she stopped he helped her to the end with an
inquiry. He knew so many unfortunate things about
Eliza, perhaps he knew too about this moment of
complete pain.

Eliza went away at two o'clock on the day
following, leaving behind her the dim, complacent
house, the air of afternoon about it, this air of
autumn like water in a sea-shell, a thin and angular

shell and sharply transparent. Inviolable in the isolation of its afternoon she left Silverue behind her, saying good-bye to Julian and to John and to Sheena (who had scarcely taken in that Eliza was going). They stood on the shallow circling steps of Silverue and waved farewell to Eliza. Farewell indeed it was. . . . "Farewell, thou art too dear for my possessing . . ."

" I do think," Olivia said as they drove along, " it's time I got a new governess for Markie. I thought of a Swiss girl. Miss Parker is hopeless about Latin and cricket, and I believe these Swiss girls sew too marvellously. If you hear of any one likely, Eliza, you'll let me know. Or perhaps I'd better write to an agency. But it's such a bore writing letters. By the way, what did you think of the new notepaper?—My dear, I thought we'd hit that sheep, didn't you ? "

" Yes, I thought you had."

" I thought it was quite fun, I must say. It's very expensive, though. What a nice day for your journey. The lights and shades on the hills are wonderful. I can't help noticing things like that, do you ? "

" Now and then I do."

It was very cold in the station, and, on the hill above, the little town seemed sharp and forbidding, the shining, city-like air it had worn on the morning of Eliza's arrival was perished from it. She bought herself a ticket and begged Olivia not to wait for her train to come in. But Olivia wanted to wait.

She still had a great deal to say about the Swiss governess and underclothes for Sheena's trousseau, about a school for Markie and about her bulbs which had not yet arrived from Holland.

A shower of rain came down with sudden definite venom, as cold a rain as February's. Markie was screamed for and came at last, running through the rain from his shelter near the penny-in-the-slot machines. He was pretty wet. There was rain on his face, even his eyelashes seemed to hold the rain. Olivia scolded a great deal and made him put on his mackintosh although, as he did not fail to point out, he would be better now without it, however, it was buttoned on to him and his sou'wester hat tied under his wet chin.

Still Eliza's train did not come in.

Markie produced chocolate and match-boxes from his pockets. Eliza asked him for a match-box, but he said definitely, No. He had bought these for Julian. And the chocolate for himself. He was sullen and unkind. The scolding Olivia delivered was well deserved. In the middle of it, and before the matches had been delivered over, Eliza's train came in to the station. She kissed Olivia and ran through the rain. All the commotion of departure was in the little station. Not a moment was to be spared. The train was late. The great train of the day could not waste a minute in such a small place. It must instantly be off. Eliza's suit-cases were flung about, the door of her carriage was banged. Through the rainy glass of the window she saw a figure running frantically down the length of the train. It might have been a girl child, this figure in its long black coat and flapping hat. Wildly it ran, and wildly called : " Eliza ! Eliza ! " The rain beat in its face. Its hands were full of match-boxes and pieces of chocolate.

Struggling with her window, Eliza cried to him to be careful (that futile cry to Ardour). A porter caught him by the long skirts of his coat. Match-boxes and chocolate were scattered on the wet platform. The train moved out. Markie was late. He too, was defeated. Eliza leaning from her window could not tell whether rain or tears were on his face. He stood very still now, waving and waving to her. Eliza was glad she could not see Olivia recapture him. He was still standing there in the rain with a kind, indulgent porter picking up his match-boxes when the train bore her out of sight.

As she settled herself in a corner of her carriage it occurred to Eliza that, had this particular situation affected not themselves but two of their friends, how enjoyably she might have discussed and dissected it with Julian. She sighed. Yes, it was a situation she could have discussed with him most profitably had it concerned any of their friends.

THE END

AFTERWORD

Admirers of Molly Keane will be very grateful for Virago's republication of this early novel. "Sometimes I think that I should have broadened my canvas", she once said to me. She then hesitated. "But I'm not sure. Maybe writers should only write about a world that they really know." Her canvas may not have been broad but her palate has always been very rich.

In *Full House*, as in her later novels, the reader has the pleasure of being taken into a world which the writer really knows. There are no tricks, there are no deceptions.

Molly Keane "really knows" the shallow, sheltered world of Anglo-Irish gentry which has provided her with so much excellent material. She knows the facade of the beautiful romantic houses that her characters inhabit, and because she knows that facade so well she can make us see it. In *Full House* she gives us Silverue the lovely Irish mansion owned by one of her most monstrous and vivid creations, Lady Bird.

And now the house. It was dark and flat and just too high in the middle like some early Georgian houses are, but its wings were of such extreme grace and proportion that this steepness was a welcome and faintly acid contrast to their inevitable correctness. A correctness where line answered line and each curved statue niche owned its precise fellow. The face of the house was partly covered in ivy and partly in a fern-like growth of Good Neighbour. They were indeed mistaken who covered stone houses with creepers, but, although we may defend ourselves from committing their errors, in fact, we do not find these errors half so disagreeable as we may pretend.

The House is so "known" by the writer that it is there for the reader in a paragraph. And with the same dexterous economy Molly Keane is able to evoke its setting.

Between the hills and the sea, this house called Silverue had been built.
Groves of birch trees came chasing down the feet of the hills nearest the
sea. Chasing because birches are forever in flight, maidenly and unsteady
as maidens are. Springs burst up among them, wetting the rocks and
soaking the dark mosses. These groves were quiet and drenching and full
of the sea mists. A perfect buttress of a fuchsia hedge, almost, in parts
quite, a tunnel divided them from the climbing path. Polite and formal
distances of lawn held them farther apart from the house.

The Irish "Big House" has a great importance in Molly Keane's
fiction because the Anglo-Irish families that she writes about are
dominated by it. As English exiles and conquerors of a foreign land
it is their island fortress where they can carry on an upper-class
tradition of hunting, shooting, fishing, Englishness. They have no
real contact with the Irish who surround them. They see the Irish
as only fit to be gardeners and domestic servants.

For this marooned Anglo-Irish class the fields of their estates are
their only source of income. Their power to rule exists only while
they remain within the walls of their demesnes. Their beautiful
"Big Houses" are all they have to make them feel they have
importance. Once they leave the confines of their estates they lose
identity and become penurious, lost and pointless. They are not at
home in Ireland and they are not happy when they go to England.

Lady Bird's oldest son leaves and goes to England. He has a
nervous breakdown and he goes mad. He soon ends up in a mental
institution. He comes back to Silverue emotionally broken and his
family feel that he has made a full recovery only when he starts
fox-hunting, for they see his return to traditional Anglo-Irish
values as a sign of recovered sanity.

When whole families cling to the glory of the building in which
they were born, the mother who runs that building has an unusual
power. In *Full House* there is a portrait of a monster mother just as
brilliant as the portraits of other domineering, ruthless mothers
that appear in her later novels, such as *The Rising Tide*.

Lady Bird is a very silly woman. She is beautiful. She looks
"oppressively young" and sees herself as just as young as her

children. Vain and mindless, she does flower arrangements, she complains about her servants, and she bullies Miss Parker, the sad little bearded governess. But her idiocy does not make her harmless to her children. Her selfishness rules them. Their lives are warped by it. Lady Olivia Bird's children all dislike her but she is so interested in herself she doesn't really register how much they resent her. Despite their dislike for her, they find they cannot break away from her power and domination which is entwined with her rule over the "Big House". She ruins the life of her daughter Sheena. When Sheena challenges Lady Bird, the girl storms out of the room saying "All right I'll go. I'll leave this house and never come back." But Sheena admits that whenever she makes this threat, she has no intention of going.

Molly Keane once told me, "I think I may have been the child my mother loved the least." Maternal cruelty has been a recurring theme in all her novels. She has created some of the most frightening mothers in fiction. Running their "unkind houses" the "unkind" mothers of Molly Keane create emotional devastation.

In *The Rising Tide* Lady Charlotte and Lady Cynthia are appallingly cruel to their children but their cruelty takes different forms. They are both women dictators and they create very harsh regimes that appeal to their individual characters. Lady Olivia Bird is just as cruel and selfish as the mothers of *The Rising Tide* but her cruelty is of her own special brand. She does not resemble Lady Charlotte or Lady Cynthia. The regime she imposes is unique to herself, but it is just as oppressive.

The female dictatorships that are established by Molly Keane's mothers flourish unchallenged by the fathers. The fathers in her novels are recessive. They have a lazy and blind belief in their wives. They are the nominal heads of the "Big Household" but they abdicate from all responsibility. They allow their spouses to run everything. They admire the way that their wives handle the children and the servants. They choose to think that their wives are doing it all beautifully. Lacking any real occupation they lead a pottering and ineffectual existence. Their lives are spent in the pursuit of favourite hobbies.

Sir Julian, the husband of Lady Bird, likes shooting snipe, breeding Kerry cattle and heraldry. He is besotted by his narcissistic wife. His children do not really exist for him. They are "shadows". Lady Bird likes her husband because he is the only person who appreciates the agonising battle that she has to wage in order to retain her beauty. He admires her fear of having a late night so that she can preserve her youth. He knows how Lady Bird suffers to be beautiful. She goes in for cruel dieting, and crueller exercises. She spends endless time and energy on her skin-care. Only Sir Julian Bird thinks it's all worth it.

When Molly Keane takes her readers behind the imposing facades of her beautiful "Big Houses" in order to explore the pain and the frustrations of their inhabitants, she makes their unhappiness just as vivid as she makes their kitchen gardens. She explores the schoolroom of Silverue and examines the wretched, lonely life of Miss Parker, the governess, with her embarrassing beard that needs so many depilatories.

Keane gives us a memorable picture of the pointless existence of this little spinster who is trapped in an "unkind" house in which she has no real part by her love for another woman's child. Miss Parker teaches her charge, Mark, arithmetic lessons in the schoolroom and her days are passed in performing sublimely monotonous little tasks. She has to exercise Lady Bird's dogs and take them for boring walks down the drive. She also has to devote her attention to the bowels of these dogs and is given the unsavoury responsibility of deworming them. The barrenness and the dullness of Miss Parker's life is painful to read about. Molly Keane has always been adept at describing the agonies of humiliation and in her characterisation of this unfortunate governess she gives a chilling portrait of a human being whose whole experience is excruciatingly humiliating.

Full House can be enjoyed as a comedy of manners for it is very witty and entertaining. On another level it can be read as an exploration of human cruelty and the effects of cruelty on the victim. Silverue is "a house of sorrow" and Miss Parker has "a sudden overpowering sense that those who belonged to such a place could not escape from sharing in its sorrow".

At the very heart of Silverue the values that are worshipped are trivial. In an idle society individuals have to try constantly to amuse themselves. They are like children fighting boredom on a rainy afternoon. Days in the country can seem very long. Games have to be played to dispel the tedium. The games start to seem like urgent occupations. Lady Bird throws herself into the organisation of the local flower show. Her daughter hunts and she organises the local gymkhanas. The son goes out to fish for a Brownie. His father, Sir Julian, takes his gun and he tramps the woods in search of a snipe.

In the stagnant world of the remote country house love affairs can be used as games. They help break the monotony. Molly Keane observes the love affairs of her characters with shrewdness and compassion. She gives us every move the lovers make, every countermove. The games they play are sad and no one wins.

At one point Lady Bird asks her unhappy daughter why she hasn't gone hunting. What has she been doing—reading a book in her room? The question has contempt. The Anglo-Irish society that Molly Keane describes is profoundly philistine. It despises girls who like to read. It sees reading as a waste of time.

Molly Keane came from a background that had contempt for girls who liked books. Even today she becomes nervous and apologetic if she is questioned about her work. She seems to find her writing rather embarrassing. She hates to talk about it. For years she concealed it under the disguise of a pseudonym. In the world in which she was brought up girls were scorned if they read books and girls who wanted to write them were thought to be "going beyond the Pale". The "Pale" is an area that surrounds Dublin. Its geographical boundaries once separated the lands of the Establishment Anglo-Irish from what they considered the barbarian terraines of the peasant Irish. As a writer, Molly Keane went "beyond the Pale", and her many admirers will always applaud her.

Caroline Blackwood, London, 1986